HUNTER KILLER

A PETER BLACK THRILLER

DAVID ARCHER

VINCE VOGEL

RIGHTHOUSE

ISBN-13: 978-1-63696-330-3

ISBN-10: 1-63696-330-7

Cover design by: Damonza

Printed in the United States of America

www.righthouse.com

www.instagram.com/righthousebooks

www.facebook.com/righthousebooks

twitter.com/righthousebooks

PRAISE FOR THE PETER BLACK SERIES

PETER BLACK THRILLERS

Burden of the Assassin (Book 1)
The Man Without A Face (Book 2)
Unpunished Deeds (Book 3)
Hunter Killer (Book 4)
Silent Shadows (Book 5)
The Last Run (Book 6)
Dark Corners (Book 7)
Ghost Operative (Book 8)

ONE

"You need to run," he says into the phone. "Run right this second before they find out what you've got."

"I'll leave tonight," a man's voice replies.

It is a voice shaking with terror.

"Can't you leave any earlier?"

"Not without them suspecting something's up. Is the plan still the same?"

The best laid plans of mice and men, he thinks, quoting the poet.

Ben Knight is standing at an upstairs window of a cold, musty-smelling log cabin. Staring outside at the rows of pine that surround the place. It's a misty, moonlit night and the trees look like the silhouettes of tall, stick-thin men creeping closer and closer.

Downstairs, his wife and daughter prepare dinner, and he half listens to the sounds they make.

"No," he eventually says. "With me suspended like this, we can't trust anyone within the agency. You'll have to stay in Europe."

"They'll send everyone after me."

"I know. Give me a chance to figure something out. I might know somewhere you can hide that's off gird. Then I'll come meet you when the coast is clear."

"What about your family?"

"We're out in my folks' cabin. I've got someone coming here that'll be able to protect them. I'm waiting for her now, and once she's here, I can make my way to you. All you gotta..."

The words dry up in his throat and the blood turns to ice in his veins.

Four figures have just emerged from the trees. Four figures dressed in dark clothing. Wearing masks. Night-vision goggles. Holding battle weapons.

The power goes, the cabin thrown into darkness.

He hadn't expected them to come for him so quickly.

"Daddy?" his daughter calls upstairs.

"I'm gonna have to go," Knight whispers down the phone, his heart pounding in his chest like a jackhammer. "Bury yourself. I'll make contact as soon as I can."

"But Ben—"

Knight cancels the call. Swaps the phone for a SIG Sauer P320 he takes from the drop leg holster strapped to his right thigh.

"Sandy?" he calls out into the darkness.

"Ben?" his wife calls back.

"Take Hayley down into the basement. NOW!"

Sandy knows the tone, and it fills her with dread. She grabs her daughter from the bottom of the stairs and races away with her.

Opening the top drawer of a bedside cabinet, Knight picks up the PVS-7 night-vision goggles, the two spare magazines and the second P320 that rest inside. He'll have to duel wield for this. Four against one. Not good odds.

The sound of his wife bolting the basement hatch is quickly followed by the noise of someone busting in the front door with a sledgehammer.

Here goes.

Knight snaps the goggles down and moves quickly from the room. He has his work cut out to protect his family. But this isn't just about one man's family. This is potentially about millions of them. Because the CIA man has finally gotten substantial evidence on something he's been working at for years. Something that threatens to change the balance of power in the world.

And not in a good way.

No turning back, Ben Knight says to himself as he engages the first man from the top of the stairs.

And that's when all hell breaks loose.

TWO

IT IS AN APRIL MORNING AND THE TWO FORMER assassins are sitting on the veranda of their little pad in Sorrento. Surrounded by sunny clifftop villas and apartment blocks, the sparkling waters of the Tyrrhenian Sea spread out below. They sit there at peace, with few worries, no one trying to kill them, and it makes them absolutely—bored.

A year since Ukraine, they have their pile—enough for an easy life and plenty to have fun. But it doesn't appear to be enough to stave off the hopeless ennui that retirement brings. During these past twelve months Peter and Michael have hiked the Himalayas from Pakistan, through India and Nepal, to Bhutan. They've climbed the peaks of Clara-purna II, K2 and the sacred mountain of Kangchenjunga; avoiding, of course, the overcrowded tourist trap that is Everest (a mountain so overclimbed that the only qualifica-tion needed for surmounting it is, most importantly, money, a strong pair of lungs, and the ability to climb stairs).

As well as that, they've been through the Amazon. Crossed the Andes. Partied in Rio. Raved in Buenos Aires. And all of it left them feeling dispirited and slightly empty. For sure, the most interesting thing that happened to them in the whole of their travels took place in Ecuador. While canoeing the Amazon, the two were set upon by a group of armed bandits that had come across their camp. That was by far the best fun they had. Those poor bandidos never had a clue what they'd gotten themselves into.

Nevertheless, none of it quite stirred the sense of raw adventure that their former occupation had, and the travelers returned to southern Italy with a sense of having been unfulfilled. As for the amusements of their adopted home, they weren't any better, feeling as flat as a Coke left out in the sun.

It would seem that after you've lived the life they have, it's hard to return to a normal, quiet existence, and the lack of action has become overwhelming.

This morning, the two sit on the veranda drinking their espressos and watching their smartphones. Peter is checking some investments he's recently made. Michael reads the news.

It's full of the row in the Ukraine.

The US Secretary of State and Secretary of Defense are due to meet their European counterparts in a month at the NATO Summit, with Europe preparing for the conflict to spill over.

"Man, we should still be out there," Michael says.

Peter looks up from the laptop. "You say something?"

Michael is about to tell him when he stops himself.

Since Anya, Peter hasn't liked talking about the war. In fact, the other day they were at the deli when international news came on the radio. The second the newscaster mentioned the war, he turned on his heels and walked out, the shopkeeper calling after him as he held up the abandoned order of smoked ham.

"Nothing," Michael eventually says.

The kid moves on to the next news story. It's an eye-catcher.

"Wow. You see this?"

"What?"

Michael reads the headline. "Disgraced government agent on the run after family massacred."

"Does it name him?"

"Yeah. Ben Knight."

Peter is frowning. "Ben Knight?"

"You know him?"

"Yeah."

Peter logs into the New York Times under a fake name. Back in his CIA days he'd performed several missions with Knight. He'd always seen him as a standup guy. An agent with a moral compass. Something that is, in the agency at least, as rare as rocking horse shit. "White Knight" was what they used to call him at the agency. That was until a week ago.

The article states that Ben Knight was suspended after evidence came to light that suggested he was colluding with a foreign government. That the White Knight may not be so white. Under investigation, it appears that the story has taken a further twist.

"I don't believe it," Peter mutters under his breath as he reads on.

GOVERNMENT EMPLOYEE BEN KNIGHT, currently under investigation, is wanted by the FBI after his wife and thirteen-year-old daughter were found dead at their vacation home on Monday.

Police believe Knight, 50, shot his wife, Nancy, 43, and suffocated his daughter, Danielle, by placing a bag over her head, at their cabin at Lake Brittle in Bluemont, Virginia.

Detectives admit they are mystified as to the motive behind the killings. Nevertheless, speculation has been mounting as to whether this was a case of someone breaking under the strain of current legal woes.

A twenty-five-year veteran of the CIA, Knight had recently found himself under...

"IT MAKES NO SENSE," Peter says. "I always saw Knight as one of the good guys."

"It's the CIA, Peter," Michael retorts. "There are no good guys."

"Well at least one of the better guys, then."

———

ABOUT TWO O'CLOCK they go out, dine at a local café built into one of the tall cliff faces. Their table is on a little protruding balcony overlooking the crystal waters of the sea.

After their food, they pay a visit to the local movie

theater. The picture they choose is an American superhero farce that is badly dubbed in Italian, making it worse than it actually is. Neither Peter nor Michael enjoy the film, finding the whole experience as flat as everything else.

Pouring rain greets them on the streets outside. They run back to the Ferrari, then pick their way through the rain to their place.

"Aren't you bored?" Michael suddenly asks as he drives them home.

Peter doesn't have to think about it. He answers immediately. "Of course I am."

"It's been a year. Aren't you itching for a job?"

"We don't need one," Peter cuts back curtly.

"Not financially. But don't you feel a need for it inside?"

"We've had enough of it. Now is the time to be normal."

"Then we need a change of scenery."

Peter gazes through the windscreen at the blurred old stone villas pitting the hills and clifftops of Sorrento.

"Maybe," he says as they turn onto their road.

Their house is a three-story villa that pokes out from a jagged corner of the clifftops. Because of its protrusion it is the only house on the street that has a complete view of the entire area. A tall wall cuts it off from the narrow road, and a gate wide enough for a car is its only feature. Due to the building backing up against sheer cliffs, there is no other access.

The gate opens electronically. Peter parks the Ferrari inside and it closes up behind them. Apart from the two of them, only one other person has access. A little old wrinkled Italian lady named Bella who comes three times a week to clean up and do the men's laundry.

They run to the shelter of the porch, and it is as Peter goes to fit the key in the front door that he stops. "You smell that?"

Michael sniffs the air. There is a faint odor of cologne. A cologne that smells nothing like anything in their own collections.

The kid nods. Makes a couple of hand signals.

Peter checks the villa's cameras on his cell phone.

They're dead.

Michael gets up on his toes. The ceiling panel of the porch isn't attached. It lifts easily and he slides a hand into the cavity—brings down two fully loaded Sig Sauer 9mms. Hands one to his father.

Next come two suppressors.

Twisting his on the end of the pistol, Peter nods sideways. At the edge of the place is a set of stone steps sunk into the hillside that takes you up to the veranda. It is the only other entrance to the place once you're past the gate.

Michael ascends the steps carefully. As he reaches the top he notices a faint yellow glow reflecting off the rocks that tower over the back of the villa.

The light is on in the living room.

With his back to the stucco and the rain beating off his head, Michael edges around the corner and along the rear of the property. Comes to a stop beside the sliding door.

Peeks.

There is a man in their house. Sitting in the middle of the room, on their couch, playing nervously with his hands. He is side on to Michael, doesn't look armed, but there could be a weapon on the other side of him.

The intruder turns sharply when the door slides open on

its runners. His eyes widen at the sight of the pistol and he lifts his hands to shoulder height.

"I'm-I'm real sorry f-for this," he stutters.

"Keep your hands where I can see them," Michael snarls.

A shadow moves across the floor from the other side of the room. When it reaches his eyeline, the man twists that way and is faced by a second gun aimed at him as Peter moves silently into the room from the hallway.

"Stay perfectly still," Peter tells him.

"I couldn't just wait outside," the man says, turning from Michael to Peter, Peter to Michael. "I didn't know if they were still following me."

"Who's they?" Peter asks.

"I'm not really sure myself. Please. I can explain."

"Good," Michael says cheerily, "he can explain. How about you start by explaining how you overrode our state-of-the-art security system."

A flash of pride falls over the man's expression. "Well, actually, it's not so state-of-the-art. I mean, it is for two years ago. But trust me. Not anymore for people who know their way around such things."

"And you know your way around such things?"

The pride increases. He grows bigger. "Yes. I do."

He stands up. But not for long. Dropping quickly back down when both Peter and Michael move aggressively toward him and tell him to sit.

"S-sorry," he mutters.

"What's your name?" Peter asks.

"John. John Harker."

John Harker looks like he hasn't slept for days. He's scruffy, unkempt, and his stale body odor can be smelled under the cologne. He looks to be in his late twenties. Skinny and long. Clean shaven with hair that is a big brown curly frizz. Essentially resembling some Forbes "thirty under thirty" internet entrepreneur.

"And who is John Harker?" Peter asks.

"I'm a journalist," comes the reply. "Though some may call me a hacker. I work freelance, but most of my work turns up in online publications such as Bellingcat."

He is steadying his voice with an effort, and his held up hands tremble.

"And what are you doing here?" Peter asks.

Instead of answering, John Harker gazes at the open sliding door.

"Is it okay if we close the door and curtains?" he asks. "I only left them open so that you could see me and see I wasn't armed. I didn't want you to think I was waiting here to do you any harm."

Keeping the Sig Sauer on him all the time, Michael side-steps to the door and pulls it shut. He then tugs on the cord to bring the blinds across before twisting a little rod that closes them.

"Is the front door locked?" the intruder asks Peter feverishly.

Peter answers that it is.

"I'm so sorry," John Harker says humbly. "I know breaking into here was really dumb. But it is all I could do. I couldn't wait for you on the street."

"How do you know who we are?" Peter wants to know.

"I'm a hacker. My life is breaking into secrets. And you, Azrael, are a secret. I heard what you did in Ukraine." He twists around to face Michael. "What both of you did. It's all over Russian intelligence channels. The Ukrainian and American ones, too."

"How did you find us?"

"I followed the money. Mikhail Gutseriev, the man you were working for in Ukraine, he set you both up with a trust fund. It was easy, really, once you got through all the false company names and crisscrossing on the accounts. Eventually, I found the purchase of this place through one of your offshore companies."

"Great," Peter groans. "That's another safe house ruined."

"Oh no," Harker disagrees. "It's pretty safe. It took me days of work to find you, Azrael."

"And what makes you so desperate to find me?"

"Because you're the only one who can protect me." His eyes grow large, like a child begging for food.

"From who?"

He looks about to cry. "I really don't know," comes out in a whisper. "Or at least not yet, anyhow."

Michael is frowning. "So you want us to protect you, but you don't know who from?"

Harker nods.

Peter stares at him. Then he flicks the safety on the pistol and lowers it. "I tell you what, Mr. Harker. We'll let you tell your story, but all I can promise is that we'll listen."

Both assassins put their weapons away.

The couch sits in the middle of the room on a sprawling Persian rug. In front of it is a square-shaped glass coffee table. A bottle of Macallan thirty-year sherry oak single malt, from which the intruder has already filled himself a stiff glass, stands on top. As Peter and Michael take seats either side of him, Harker grabs hold of the glass and finishes it in four gulps. It makes a loud crack when he sets it down.

"Sorry," he says. "I'm a mess. You see, none of this should be happening. I should have made contact with you days ago, but somehow they found me."

"Why somehow?"

He looks up from the table, turns to Peter and says, "I'm going to tell you and your son everything I know. Because I need help worse than any man ever needed it before, and you, Azrael, are the only man who can give it."

"Get on with your story," Michael says, "and then we'll let you know if we can—give it."

Harker pours himself another whiskey. He looks like he's bracing himself for some huge effort as he drains it off. Then, he begins recounting one of the most off-the-wall conspiracies either assassin has ever heard. They have to stop and ask questions throughout, but here's the gist of what he tells them:

As they'd already guessed from his accent, John Harker is an American, from, as Peter picked up earlier, Pennsylvania. Philadelphia to be exact. His father was a computer science teacher, so from an early age he's been building and programming computers. He developed a love of hacking in his teenage years. At first it had been nothing but anarchy; the love of finding a way through a locked system like a safe-cracker. But the older he got, the more his moral compass began to develop. He got into journalism and combined the two to get intel on stories. Though he followed WikiLeaks he was never a contributor, explaining that the website has no editorial responsibility, and is essentially state sponsored by certain aggressive parties. He writes a lot about international matters, the United Nations, NATO, trade deals, the movement of money from one country to the next.

"Follow the money," he tells them, "and you'll find the true motive of it all."

Two years ago he began looking into the interconnection of politicians in different states. Looked at the way they say one thing to the voter and another entirely to their foreign backer. In essence, John Harker got a little deeper down the rabbit hole than he would have liked.

"There is a group," he says, "who live within the shadows, but who control it all on puppet strings."

Michael rolls his eyes. Sensing it, Harker turns on him.

"It's true," he says. "It's a group of families. A group that have been around for generations. Who have borne witness to every single catastrophe or turning point that has faced mankind. The War of Independence. The French Revolution. World War One. The march of Communism. The Great Depression. The rise of fascism. The Korean War. Vietnam. Iraq. Afghanistan. The Financial Crisis. At each point, they've bet on disaster and won."

"That's nothing new," Michael says. "People have been profiting from a failing market since the stock market has existed."

"But what if someone is forcing that market to fail? What if they are maneuvering in the shadows and starting these wars?"

Harker claims to have come across some huge conspiracy all by accident. At first, he wondered whether he should just let it go; stop picking at the thread. But it fascinated him, so he went further. And then it unraveled completely. He got caught.

Harker speaks quickly and nervously, constantly playing with his hands. Often his statements come crashing into one another. Several times the two lose the thread of what he's saying. They gather that this "group" consists of some of the wealthiest families in the world. He mentions Rothschilds and Agnellis; and for some reason claims that surviving members of the Romanovs are involved.

He tells them that apparently the latest conflict in Ukraine is all them. That they have spent the last ten years setting the two nations against one another. He also claims that they have been twisting the knife between China and Taiwan, as well as making sure that the Koreans are on as hostile terms as possible.

When Michael asks him why they wanted the world to fall into complete chaos, Harker's initial answer is blunt and four words long.

"A new world order," he says.

Michael cracks a smile. "Really? So what—9-11 was an inside job?"

"Yes," Harker responds with a straight face.

Michael once more rolls his eyes at the stranger.

"So what about this new world order?" Peter asks.

Harker turns back to him from the kid. "From the ashes of the chaos, a new world will arise. They will use their fortunes to buy up what is left after the crumble of civilization, when whole economies will be on their knees or no longer exist, and then, once and for all, they will own every man, woman and child."

Both Peter and Michael are frowning.

"But something is coming," Harker goes on. "They have all their ducks in a row. In one month they are going to play their ace."

He stares at Peter, who asks what the "ace" is.

Harker's eyes glaze over and he shakes his head. "I'm not sure."

"You're not sure?" Michael puts to him.

"No." Harker's gaze then floats to the archway that leads into the kitchen.

"I brought a bag with me."

He goes to get up from the couch, but Peter plants a firm hand on his chest and pushes him back down.

"I'll get it," Peter says. "Where is it?"

"In the kitchen. On the countertop."

The bag is like Harker: hipster. A vintage waxed canvas roll-top rucksack. It's light. Peter guesses from the feel and weight that it contains a laptop and a few other items.

He hands it over to Harker and the journalist unbuckles it.

"This," he says, pulling out a black portable hard drive no bigger than a wallet and laying it on the glass coffee table with another sharp crack, "contains all my work from the last two years. Everything I've found. But I haven't been able to decipher all of it yet." As he adds this last statement, a look of bitter disappointment fills his face.

"What have you deciphered?" Peter asks.

"You read the news?"

"Vaguely."

"You know who Anthony Eustace is?"

"United States Secretary of State."

"Right. Well, from what I've gathered from my research,

Eustace is a problem for them or at least a part of it all somehow. He may have discovered some scheme of theirs, or it could be something else."

"What scheme?"

"I don't know. But a lot rests on it, so they've marked Eustace's card."

"Is that what's going to happen in a month?" Michael asks. "They're going to do something with Anthony Eustace?"

"I think so. See, they can't do it in America. Way too risky. No, it'll be done in Europe. In one month, Anthony Eustace is leading a delegation to the annual NATO summit in Rome. It's why I faked my own death. I need to survive this month."

"What about the hard drive," Peter says, "why don't you hand it over to the FBI? Let them deal with it."

Harker frowns at him. "You have a lot of faith in law enforcement."

"But how else are you going to save this Eustace guy if you won't tell them?"

"Look, the group have been around since the Holy Roman Empire. They have access to all avenues of power. These men have every important world leader on speed dial."

"And this you've gotten from the encrypted files?"

"Some of it. Other stuff I've put together from scraps. For instance there's lots of mention of the 30th of May. The final day of the summit."

"One month's time," Peter says.

"Why don't you warn the Italians?" Michael chips in.

Harker swings around to him with a grimace, like what Michael said was the dumbest thing he ever heard.

"The Italians? Really? Have you seen the current Italian government? A far-right coalition. One that was sponsored and paid for by the group. That's why I'm begging you both to let me stay here for a month so I can finish decrypting those files and find out what they're going to do."

"And then what?" Peter puts to him. "Save the day? Be the hero?"

Harker's eyes glaze over and a gentle smile curls the corner of his mouth. "Why not?" he says.

Though Michael dismisses him offhand, Peter is actually beginning to like the guy. Despite the hipster look of surf T-shirt, cargo shorts and Crocs, there is a seriousness about him. A need to get to the truth. A fire that burns in his eyes, telling Peter that in spite of his fear, he really is ready for some future battle.

And, anyway, if this is all bullshit, like Michael suspects, then he is doing a pretty good job of acting it out.

"Where did you come across all of this?" Peter asks.

"Where does anyone ever find anything these days: the internet. One of my hobbies is breaking into the financial records of the elite. You know, expose where they hide all their money. How little in tax they actually contribute. How much they invest in countries or activities that are supposed to be banned. Where they get their money from. All that."

"And that led you to this group?"

"Yes. See, I started finding a lot of crossover from different entities. Foreign governments given access to the United States through elite businesspersons. That's when I intercepted the encrypted files. Started reading communications where Eustace was discussed, and the 30th of May. That night, an hour after I finished downloading those files, a car pulled up outside my house and two men got out. They didn't knock. They just came around the back and broke in. I took the hard drive and left through a window. Luckily, I've always been paranoid. Ready to run at any time. I've seven fake passports from different countries. Several hidden bank accounts in different names. A bunch of disguises hidden in different places. I'm wearing one now."

He tugs on the curly hair and shows that his head is shaved underneath.

"It's how I got here to you guys. By zigzagging across various locations, using a different passport each time. I flew into Paris as a Canadian. Rented a car as an Australian. Flew out of Copenhagen as a Brit. Arrived in Vienna an Irishman. And so on for the past week. I was beginning to think I might have escaped. That was until yesterday."

Harker appears to shudder at the recollection, and he gulps down the remains of his whiskey.

"I was holed up in Rome. Getting ready to come down here to Sorrento and approach you. That was when I looked out the window of the apartment I was renting and saw a man standing on the other side of the road. He was staring right up at my window. Like he was watching the place."

He sits there staring nervously at Peter. Whatever it is that he's found himself embroiled in, Peter has finished weighing him up, and though he's not sure he fully believes in some "group" pulling international strings, he believes enough of it to feel that Harker is in genuine trouble with some force that is far beyond his capability to deal with.

"And you're sure you haven't been followed here?" Peter asks.

"Yes," Harker replies confidently. "The moment I saw

the man in the street, I gathered my things and left the apartment. Went to the roof and climbed out of there by the fire escape. I had already hired a boat which I kept moored on the Tiber. I used the river to reach the sea and make my way here by that way. Avoiding roads and public transport."

Peter is nodding. "Good," he says. "I'm going to trust you, Mr. Harker."

Relief floods the journalist's face. "Oh thank you," he says, twisting to face Michael as well. "Thank you."

Peter's eyes then go dark and his voice becomes a growl. "But if you make me regret that trust, you won't have to worry about some group. You will have to worry about me."

Harker swallows down a lump and nods.

THREE

THEY MADE HIM UP A BED ON THE TOP FLOOR OF the villa; essentially an attic. It was small and more a cupboard than a room, but its windowless state was an advantage for hiding someone.

The next morning Peter awakens to the sound of Bella making a row as she enters the villa through the front door downstairs. The old Italian housekeeper has a habit of talking to herself, and often these talks turn bitter and she begins arguing. Today, it would seem, she is in a foul mood. Her husband, Giuseppe, is getting the brunt of it, and, as if he is here in person, she remonstrates with the absent spouse.

"Bella, Bella," Peter whispers as he meets her on the stairs. "I have a friend staying."

Her wrinkled brow folds like the bellows of an accordion. "You have a friend staying?"

In the year that she has cared for their home, Bella Tomasi has never known of anyone ever visiting Peter. The boy, yes. Girls mostly. But not the master of the house. And certainly no one staying the night.

Peter tells the old Italian a little tale about a friend of his coming to stay because he's had a breakdown and needs to get away from America.

"He needs plenty of rest and quiet," Peter explains to her. "So you must keep away from the attic."

"Sì, Signor Swartz," she says, and soon the housekeeper is preparing breakfast.

It is Michael who takes it up to their guest. He finds the door to the room not just locked but wedged with a chair under the knob.

Before knocking, the kid brings an ear to the wood. The guy is tapping away at his computer. Something he's been doing since they shut him in there ten hours ago.

Eventually rapping the door with a knuckle, Michael calls out that it's breakfast. Harker stops typing, gets up. Scraping the chair away, he opens the door a crack. He takes one look at the breakfast of sausage, eggs, toast, and grimaces.

"Have you got anything vegan?" he asks.

"You like grapefruit?"

"That would be nice."

And with that he closes the door on the kid and the breakfast.

The first two days he stays with them he doesn't come out of the room. All they see of him is what they get through the gap in the door that he pokes his head out of when he takes his meals. The only sound he makes is from his fingers tapping away on the laptop—like a scratching rat above their heads.

On the third night, he creeps out from his den, comes downstairs, asks them if they have a chessboard. They do, and so begins a nightly ritual of him beating the bejesus out of them both playing chess. It is during these games that John Harker gradually comes out of his shell. Isn't so nervous around them.

Indeed, as the days gather into a week, there starts to show a restlessness in him. The refrigerator has a calendar on it. He begins marking off the days until May 30th with big red marker pen Xs.

Excepting the nightly chess tournament, he spends all his hours inside the attic on his laptop, hard at work making notes or trying to decipher the files. At these times he becomes very despondent. When Peter or Michael bring him his food, they try to enter into conversation with him. His answers are vague and come in as few words as possible, his eyes glazed over, looking like he hardly hears a thing they are saying, his mind far away in some distant meditation.

On the eighth day he becomes really edgy. He doesn't touch his laptop all day and spends the time listening out for any external noise that stands out. Then, when Peter brings him his evening meal, he asks if Bella can be trusted.

"I trust her with my son's life," Peter tells him. "Her husband, too. I know good people, and they are good people."

Twice over the next days Harker actually leaves the room with all his belongings packed inside his roll-top rucksack, ready to bolt from their abode and get out of Sorrento altogether.

Each time, Peter convinces him to stay, and, eventually,

the computer hacker apologizes and gets back inside the room.

During the nightly chess battles, Harker speaks very little, but when he does, it is to voice worry. Not for the safety of his own skin, but to the possibility of him not lasting the month until the summit. Lately, he has been working on a way of getting himself physically close to Anthony Eustace while there.

"The thing is," he says while taking Michael's bishop, "I may need your help in it."

"Isn't babysitting you enough?" the kid quips. Upset that another piece has fallen to the journalist.

"Ha-ha," Harker replies dryly.

On the eleventh day, he begins talking about his time spying on the people he believes responsible for the conspiracy. He mentions a "cuckoo" and a giant of a man who he still sees in his nightmares. There is also a man with deep-set eyes ringed in black, who he is sure is at the bottom of it somehow, but who he'd never learned the name of.

Like a lot of what he rambles on about during his days as their guest, much of it is incoherent. No sooner does he begin speaking on one subject than he's onto the next. It is almost like he's not talking to Peter or Michael but to himself. At first, they ask questions, but soon they don't bother. Because he never really gives them a straight answer, just continues to go around in circles.

After a week of being hunkered down in that cramped attic, he begins speaking about death.

"I never knew my father," he tells them. "He died when I was only six months. A car accident. One minute he was on his way back from the grocery store with Pampers. The next he's being poleaxed by a forty-ton truck with a sleeping driver behind the wheel. He was the same age as me. Twenty-seven. Just like Kurt Cobain or Jim Morrison."

"Do you fear death?" Peter asks.

He thinks about it. Looks up from the chessboard. "I don't think so."

The next day Harker is actually upbeat. They find him in the kitchen cooking them breakfast. Afterwards, they have to leave to go to their boat, the Mother-Magda. Harker gets nervous. It is the first time that both of them have left him alone.

"Don't worry," Peter says. "You're perfectly safe here."

"But I got in."

"Dude," Michael says, already a little tired at their guest's antics, "listen. We have to go check on our boat and pay our marina fees. If we don't, they get shitty. We gotta do about half an hour's work on the boat and pay a visit to the office. We'll be back in less than an hour. Promise."

The two leave him, and are back fifty minutes later.

They are chatting as they push open the living-room door. The lights are off and the blinds closed. But they can sense that someone is in the room with them.

Michael snaps the lights on. At first, they see no one. Then they spot something in the far corner which sends a cold sweat charging from their pores.

John Harker is lying sprawled on his back. His face is twisted into a look of painful horror. Blood oozes from the corners of his mouth. His chest sinks in. Someone has stomped him to death.

FOUR

THE TWO OF THEM IMMEDIATELY DROP ONTO THE couch.

"I feel sick," Michael says.

They sit there in silence for about a minute, when Michael turns to the dead man and makes eye contact with his wide, desperate eyes. The kid gets up from the couch, goes over to the body, and turns the head so that it faces the other way, the body still warm, not stiff yet.

"That's brutal," the kid says when he sits back down. "They could have just killed him. A bullet, maybe. Even a knife would have been less cruel."

Peter shakes himself. Grabs his cell phone from his pocket and flicks the screen across; checks the security cameras. "Nothing went off," he mumbles. Turning to Michael, he adds, "Someone's overridden the system."

He shows him the phone. It is an image of the living room. It is supposed to show the two of them and the dead body. The time stamp is correct, but the image is of an empty room.

"That's it," Michael says. "The security system you got us is..."

Peter is looking at him with wide eyes. He makes a few hand signals. We need to check the place. An idea has seized him. With all the cameras out, they don't know whether the killer is still here.

Michael is already kneeling at the side of the couch, passing a hand underneath and unclipping the Beretta that is hidden there. Peter is taking a Colt King Cobra snub-nose revolver from inside a lampshade.

Armed, they search the three stories of the narrow villa. Each floor contains no more than four rooms. Two bedrooms, a hallway and a bathroom on the bottom floor. The living room, utility room and kitchen on the second. The attic and another bathroom on the top. The search doesn't take long. There is no one else in their home. The killer has left.

Nevertheless, there is something.

As they move from room to room, they discover that whoever was here has ransacked the place—the insides of books, bureaus, cupboards, boxes, all the drawers in the kitchen, even the pockets of their clothes in the wardrobe. They find no trace of Harker's laptop or the hard drive.

"They've obviously found it," Peter asserts at the end of their search.

"Well, that confirms it," Michael says.

"Confirms what?"

"That he wasn't bullshitting. Maybe this is the 'group.'"

"Maybe. But that's not what's worrying me."

"What is?"

"He was here for less than two weeks and his enemies found him. But that's not all. In their minds they must think that during that time he must have told us something of it."

"So what?"

"So what?! So we're next. We need to get out of here."

Michael is frowning. "And go where?"

"Into hiding. Vanish until May 30th."

Michael rolls his eyes. "You mean get involved in Harker's business?"

"We're involved as it is."

"Are we?"

"If something is coming, we need to warn the American government."

The kid is grimacing. "So, and correct me if I'm wrong, you're saying that you want to make contact with the American government?"

"Yes."

"The same American government who want you dead?"

"Yes."

"Be that the CIA—who would kill you on sight—or the FBI, who want your arrest—hopeful of getting the death penalty from your subsequent trial. That's who you want to make contact with?"

"Something's going on, Mikey. It could cost the lives of innocent people. Where's your sense of patriotism?"

"Patriotism? Peter, if you hadn't forgotten, they sent you to a farm in Alaska when you were just a child to be brutalized."

"Okay, then. What about this? If these people are now after us, doesn't logic tell you that if we can get to the bottom of their scheme, we can draw them close to us. Turn the killing on them. I just wish we had Harker's hard drive."

"And I wish I had listened to him more when he rambled," Michael confesses. "Half the time I just shut him out."

"Me too," Peter adds. "It's going to make it much harder to convince the American government if we have nothing."

"Then we need to stay alive for the next three weeks. See what we find out."

"It won't be easy," Peter says with some thought. "In my reckoning it won't just be the people who killed Harker that'll be after us. It'll be the police as well. I can bet you that's why the killer didn't stick around. He's probably tipped the Italian police off already."

"Shit," the kid mutters under his breath.

"The second they look into us, they're going to pin Harker's murder on us."

"Then I hope all this R&R hasn't slackened us up too much."

Their next thought is to search Harker's body to see if he has anything on him that could give them a clue. His face watches them with that distorted grimace of horror as they go through the pockets of his cargo shorts. They find nothing except a few loose coins, a pack of Camel menthols, a lighter, and a bishop chess piece. Peter pats him down to see if anything is hidden anywhere, but the body is clean. No sign of the hard drive. The killer must have it.

Michael stands there looking at the chess piece he holds.

"Why'd he have this on him?"

Peter turns to him from the body. Then both of their eyes light up. They rush to the chessboard. It's a big bulky thing carved from wood that they'd bought at a flea market in Naples. It has a solid frame which the board sits in. The border is decorated in carvings of chess pieces. They find it on the floor, discarded during the killer's search.

Peter pulls the board out of the frame, something that isn't immediately obvious, and there it is, wedged underneath.

The hard drive.

FIVE

PETER SPREADS A MAP ACROSS THE COFFEE TABLE.

"Your phone," he says to Michael, "leave it here. We're taking nothing electronic with us."

"So we're going old school?"

"Yes. This will be a walkabout with purpose. How much cash do you have on you?"

Michael checks. "About eighty euros."

"I've got about another two hundred in my room. It should see us through until we reach Switzerland."

"Switzerland?"

"Yeah. We'll need to go to Zurich. Pick up some cash from one of the accounts. Do it in person. Less traceable. That way we'll be able to move about Europe until the 30th."

"We could," Michael suggests, "just get some cash out here in Sorrento tonight."

"No. We leave the cards here. Just take what we need and what won't get us caught. Anyway, you can only get five hundred out the machine. We would still need to get to Zurich."

"We should take some props. Whigs. Maintenance uniforms. Disguises."

"You're right. We can't leave here looking like we do. I'm absolutely certain they're watching the place right now."

Michael can't help looking toward the window. Even with the blinds down, he feels like someone is watching them.

Peter leaps up from the couch and takes something from a chest of drawers. It is a train timetable, which he lays out over the map.

"We'll take the train," Peter says, a finger moving down the lines of information. "Ah, the next sleeper to Zurich leaves Rome in four hours. Perfect."

"A train?" Michael says with a frown.

"You wClara take the Ferrari?"

The kid tilts his head and grins. Peter dismisses him with a wave of the hand. "We need to be incognito."

He folds up the map and timetable and goes to stand from the couch when Michael lays a hand on his forearm.

"If they're watching us," the kid says, "then how are we gonna get out of here?"

"Already thought of it."

Peter gets his cell phone out and dials Bella. He asks if both she and Giuseppe can come over.

"Si, signor," she replies before asking if anything is the matter.

"No, nothing," Peter replies in Italian. "I have a job offer for the both of you."

The old woman is much relieved and promises to be there with her husband within half an hour.

"Right," Peter says. "Help me with the body."

They hide Harker upstairs in the attic.

As he prepares to leave the room, Michael turns to the corpse. "We'll do our best to get the people who did this, John. I promise you."

The two of them pack a few shirts, some props for disguise, several passports, field glasses, and guns. They'll need guns. A couple of Sig Sauer P365s and a couple of silencers. Both fitted with extended magazines.

Then comes the next part. The doorbell chimes. With the security system in the house jeopardized, they've switched it off from the mains. Michael has to check the window to see who it is rather than using the camera on the bell itself.

"Is it them?" Peter asks.

"Yeah."

"Is there anyone else in the street?"

"Nothing. No people or cars."

Peter swallows. "Then I hope this works."

He presses the button to release the locks on the gate, and soon the old couple are tramping up the stairs to the living room. The Tomasis are both quite tall and dressed conservatively. Giuseppe is about Peter's height and Bella roughly the same as Michael. Giuseppe wears a flat cap to cover his bald head and Bella has on a scarf to hold down her curly gray hair. It is a windy day and both are wearing thick coats with collars that hide most of their faces.

Perfect.

"I asked you here," Peter says in Italian, "because I have a huge favor to ask."

He explains. Essentially, he wants to trade clothes with them and for them to stay inside the villa until they get back. For this, he will pay them both a thousand euros on top of their wages.

At first, the couple are confused. Michael steps in at this point and explains that it is a bet between the two. That they are trying to trick the neighbors into believing they are someone else.

The vague explanation appears to do the trick. After all, they are Americanos. They have funny senses of humor that appear odd to a couple of old Neapolitans like themselves. So the exchange is done, Michael adding a gray wig to the long skirt and tights of Bella.

"Why have I got to be Bella?" the kid complains.

"I told you. You're more her height and build."

Peter sticks on Giuseppe's flat cap and bulky coat. Michael wraps the scarf around his bewigged head. It takes him several attempts and in the end it is Bella who helps him out, the couple giggling the whole time at the play of it. The assassins even empty out a large leather-handled canvas bag that the couple have brought with them and place their own two rucksacks inside.

"Right, now remember," Peter whispers to the Italians before they leave. "Don't go to the windows and stay inside until we're back."

They check their appearances in a mirror hanging on the wall of their hallway, and then, they are gone. With the collars of the coats up, they are the spitting image of the old couple. They even add a little stagecraft, the two of them bending their backs and shuffling out the door as though their bodies are old and stiff.

As luck would have it, it is raining. Therefore, it doesn't look odd when they exit through the gate and step onto the street with their heads down and coat collars up.

Using only their periphery vision, they discreetly scan their surroundings. The street is narrow and lined with the tall walls of two-story villas. At first they think there's no one around—that there has been no need for the ruse. But a hundred yards down they pass the doorway of a small apartment block and spot a man hiding within the alcove of the porch. He looks like any other middle-aged Italian male: leather jacket, gelled-back hair, a good-sized pudge of belly. But it isn't the general sight of the man that gets them worrying as they continue down the street. It is the crackling radio he is holding.

They next spot a man on the corner of the street smoking a cigarette underneath an umbrella, feeling his eyes burn into them as they pass. Thanking the heavens for the rain, they go on, and when they cross an intersection, they notice the police vehicles lined up down the road. A big black van with SWAT written across the back.

They want to hurry across the street. Want to run. But they have to fight the urge. Sure that their journey is being watched, they must imitate the old couple in every way. So they work their way across the road in stiff, old-people movements, never looking left.

Fifty yards on, they take a side street, then a left-hand turning that takes them up a set of stone steps that passes vacant ground. There they take cover in some old broken-down sheds and change out of the clothing.

They have barely got their coats off, however, when a tramp looking for somewhere dry to wait out the weather walks into the dilapidated shelter and stops dead the second he sees them.

Michael is still wearing the wig and the dress. Peter has his trousers around his ankles.

"Mi scusi," the tramp apologizes with an embarrassed look.

He backs out of the shed and, shaking his head the whole while, leaves the vacant land. A semi-practicing Roman Catholic, he even goes so far as to cross himself.

They finish quickly and dump the clothes.

"I feel bad," Michael says as he stuffs the rolled-up skirt and coat in a cavity between the back of the shed and a wall.

"Why?"

"It just feels a bit cruel to keep them sitting there all that time waiting for us."

"I'll make sure to repay them."

At the moment they pass a churchyard, the bell begins to toll for seven. The sun is almost down by the time they reach Sorrento Train Station. With luck, they find the train to Naples at the platform about to depart. The whistle goes right at the moment they jump on and the station clock shows fifteen minutes past seven as the train works its way out of Sorrento.

At Naples they have just enough time to buy the ticket for the sleeper and get on. They then work their way to their cabin and lock themselves in. As they sit themselves down, they breathe a huge sigh of relief.

"And to think," Michael says. "A week ago we were bored."

SIX

It is dark when Bella and Giuseppe Tomasi decide enough is enough. They try calling Peter and Michael's cell phones, and are further dismayed when they begin hearing both of them ringing somewhere inside the villa.

Bella asks her husband what they should do.

"Leave," is his simple answer.

"But we don't have any clothes. And they took my bag."

"Then we'll dress in their clothes," Giuseppe grumbles angrily.

So, despairing at the antics of the "crazy Americanos," they dress in the expensive clothing of their employers and exit the house. Stepping out of the gate onto the street, they are surprised to find the road so deserted. It is almost seven and the street at this time is usually filled with traffic. There is also a distinct lack of life in the windows of the villas—the blinds and curtains are all closed.

Shrugging this off, they begin walking down the street

when all of a sudden black-clad men burst out from the alcoves on both sides. Up and down, all along the road, in front of the couple and behind, men march aggressively up, assault rifles pointed right at them, yelling: "GET ON THE GROUND!"

Bella screams. Giuseppe crosses himself. Then complains about his arthritic knees as he's forced down.

Five minutes later both are sitting on the couch inside the living room of the villa. Italian police are all over it, searching the already searched house. Upstairs, they've broken down the attic door and the room is now a crime scene—the murdered man found within.

A tall man with dark eyes and an emotionless face comes before the couple. "My name is Detective Zenoni," he tells them in their native tongue. "I'd like to ask you some questions about your employers."

"Ask away," Giuseppe says gruffly.

"So first of all, do you recognize this man?"

Zenoni flips open one of the passports they found close to the body. The name and all the details inside are fake. The picture is not.

"Si," Bella answers. "That is the Swartz's guest, Charles."

"And when was the last time you saw Charles?"

"Yesterday. I came to clean the house. He was in his room like always."

"So you are unaware that he is now dead?"

Bella places a hand to her mouth, leans toward her husband, who wraps an arm around her trembling shoulders.

"How did he die?" Giuseppe asks.

"He was crushed to death."

"Crushed?"

"Yes. It looks like someone jumped up and down on his chest."

"Who would do such a thing?" Bella gasps.

Zenoni pierces his eyes at her. "You think your Signor Swartz could have done it?"

"No," is her instant reply, the old woman shaking her head.

Giuseppe, on the other hand, doesn't look so certain.

Zenoni looks at him. "What about you, Signor Tomasi?"

"I found something in the shed once."

"What did you find?"

Bella points a narrow-eyed look at her husband. "Giuseppe, it was nothing. Mr. Swartz explained."

"Mr. Tomasi, you must be honest with me," the detective interjects. "What did you find?"

The couple look at each other. Then Giuseppe turns to him and says, "I found guns."

"In the shed?"

"Si."

"Show me."

The old man leads the detective downstairs and then outside. The garden isn't much. A patch of shaded patio with some flowerbeds at the edges in rock planters. A few creeping plants crawling up trellises fixed to the cliff face. Giuseppe guides the detective to a closet that can only be accessed by an outside door. He opens it and shows the detective.

"There's nothing but gardening tools," Zenoni points out.

It is true. All the closet contains are the modest gardening tools needed to keep the villa's minuscule garden.

Giuseppe shakes his head, leans into the shed, pulls to the side a curtain of cables and other loose items hanging on pegs, and pushes a corner of the wall behind it all. There is a clicking sound and the wall opens outwards on a spring. The other side is lined with guns. Shotguns, rifles, assault rifles, a couple of pistols.

"And there are other guns hidden around the house," Giuseppe tells him. "My wife, she often finds them while cleaning."

Bella stands next to her husband with an embarrassed look. She has enjoyed the last year and a half working for Alan and David Swartz (the names they are, or at least were, living under). She has felt a warmth toward them as she's looked after the domesticity of their domain. Sometimes, she even takes her evening meals with them. Alan insisting that she stay and eat with them.

"Signor Swartz is a salesman of guns," she explains to the detective.

"No, he isn't," Zenoni replies in a dead tone.

Bella goes cold.

"What is he, then?" Giuseppe asks curiously.

"We are not sure yet. Alan and David Swartz aren't their real names, though. We also think Alan may be a man wanted in America."

"A criminal?"

"Of the worst variety. They say he is wanted for kidnapping and murder."

Bella's hand is back at her mouth. She is reassessing her relationship with the Swartzes. She admits to herself that there has always been a strangeness about the pair. A distance or coldness to them both. In the two years she's known the father and son, she has learned practically nothing about their lives before they came to Italy. Then there is the way they live. Not just the guns hidden about the place. There are the disappearances. For up to a month at a time, they vanish with no word when they'll be back. She comes to the house twice a week during this time to tend to the plants and the house and hears nothing from them. Simply receives payment directly into her bank account. Then, when they return, they hardly say a thing about where they've been or what they've been up to.

"Do either of you," Detective Zenoni asks, "know where they could have gotten to?"

The husband and wife shake their heads.

Zenoni groans inwardly. Sure that he knows now exactly what the old couple are: innocents caught up in all of this. They've been tricked as much as everyone else. So the detective leaves them in the garden with a colleague and returns to the living room.

Most of the police activity is happening upstairs, where crime scene investigators are photographing and inspecting the body of John Harker. Zenoni nods at an officer who comes in from the terrace and passes through the living room. When he is gone, the detective pushes the door to so that no one can see into the room from the hallway stairs. He then moves swiftly to the light fitting hanging in the center of the room over the couch. A quick furtive check and he gets on tiptoes and feels around the inside of the globe-shaped lampshade. It is exactly where they said it would be.

He removes a wireless listening device stuck inside.

Someone opens the door as he steps down and he quickly snatches the bug into a pocket.

It is the head crime scene investigator. An old man with a crooked spine and bad body odor they call Lurch behind his back.

"The death did not happen upstairs," he tells the detective. "The body has been moved post-mortem."

Zenoni nods and gives one-word answers as the operative provides his initial analysis of the crime scene. The detective hardly listens. He's more interested in what is on the bug.

Having gotten away from Lurch, Zenoni scurries out of the villa and heads down the narrow road.

The second he's locked inside his car, he connects the listening device to his phone and puts it on loudspeaker. He listens to Peter and Michael's discussions as they decide where they're going to go. Listening intently, the detective quickly gathers their plans and makes a phone call.

"They're on the all-night sleeper to Zurich," he tells the person who answers.

SEVEN

MILAN, ITALY - 22:15 CET

IT DIDN'T TAKE THEM LONG TO FIGURE OUT WHICH train Peter and Michael have taken and send two men to Milano Centrale Railway Station. It is a quarter past ten when the sleeper arrives onto the platform.

Anticipation grows in the pair of wet boys.

One is huge. At least seven feet tall and almost four hundred pounds in solid muscle. The other is plain-looking in every category. His only real feature is a milky left eye that looks like a gray-white marble. Long black trench coats hide their bodies and black boleros shadow their faces. They walk with stiff movements and enter the train from opposite ends of the same carriage. Meeting in the middle, where Cabin Number Thirteen is situated, they come to a stop either side of the door and unbutton the fronts of their long coats. Take hold of the Benelli Supernova pump-action shotguns tucked under their arms—A-Tec shotgun silencers fitted to their ends, the guns almost as long as the men who carry them.

They nod at each other. The giant faces the door and pushes it easily in with a huge hand, the metal of the lock twisting and popping, the door flying inwards. Both men rush inside the pitch-black cabin like evil spirits and fire one-two-three buckshot rounds into the beds on both sides. The suppressed guns make strange sounds like compressed air shooting from a cylinder.

They flip the lights on. Feathers float about. The bedding on both bunks covered in holes. No blood, though. And no people, either.

The one with the milky eye uses his phone. "They're not here."

EIGHT

AUSTRIA - 06:00 CET

Peter had spotted the bug in the lampshade the second they'd flipped the living-room lights. Its shadow had been cast on the wall. Not a very smart move by whoever had placed it there.

Using discreet hand signals, he'd informed his son that they were being listened to, and so began the ruse of letting the listener think they were going to Zurich. They had entered the sleeper at Naples—knowing that if their enemy was powerful enough to influence the authorities, they'd be powerful enough to have someone monitoring CCTV—but had gotten off before even reaching nearby Rome. The station in between at Latino has no cameras. A fact that Peter knows from his time checking practically every train station in the area when they had first moved here. This during his time planning possible escape routes.

Good job he did. Even if, at the time, the kid had thought it pedantic overkill.

Getting off at Latino, they walk out into the middle of some woods about a mile from the train station. There they dig up a plastic container buried four feet below the surface of the earth. It contains a hundred and fifty thousand euros in assorted bills. Enough to keep them going for the time being.

They then jump onto another sleeper, this one traveling to Venice, and by the time the two hit men are unloading buckshot at a couple of empty beds in Milan, Peter and Michael are getting off in Venice and stepping onto a sleeper for Vienna, Austria.

Now they can rest.

When they awaken three hours later, they are gliding through Austrian countryside. It is a fine May day, spring warming into summer. The hawthorn is flowering all along the hedges that line the sides of the track.

Neither Peter or Michael see any of it through the closed blinds of the carriage, however. Keeping a low profile, they don't even leave their cabin. Only presenting themselves when the conductor knocks to check their tickets. They don't dare face the restaurant car. Having bought some rolls and other pastries in Venice, they share these in the cabin as they pass cow fields.

"Let's check the news," Peter says after swallowing a lump of bread down.

Michael reaches into a rucksack and pulls out a laptop computer. As well as the money, the plastic container also carried a fully encrypted Apple Mac.

Michael searches the web through a hyper-secure VPN.

"Here it is."

The computer is on his lap. He twists it around so that the screen faces Peter. News stories fill the Google search window. He clicks on one. CNN. The story has gone international. They are both wanted for the murder of John Harker, American journalist, as well as a slew of other crimes including illegal firearm possession, keeping explosives in an unsecure environment, and traveling under false documents. Several grainy CCTV pictures accompany the stories. One has them getting onto the train at Sorrento. Another, changing for the sleeper at Naples. In both pictures they are in disguises, and they've changed since then. Twice. Michael having again complained about the pedantic overkill.

"Well, we can't go back to Sorrento," Michael points out.

"They must be powerful," Peter muses out loud. "I mean, they have the police with them. Or at least a part of it."

"You think it's this 'group' John kept yabbering on about?"

"I don't know. Maybe. Maybe not."

The kid is frowning. "If it is some all-powerful organization, then we've just seriously pissed it off."

"Add it to the list," is all Peter has to say to this.

The two fall silent for a minute. Then Michael leans over the bed and lifts the rucksack up from the floor. He empties it onto the mattress. Picking up Harker's hard drive, he plugs it into the computer.

"Good idea," Peter says.

They haven't tried it yet.

Michael finds that the hard drive itself isn't password

protected, but the files concerning Harker's work are. The only thing they can get into is a diary.

The train is passing a large flat lake that reflects the blue sky as they sit studying the journal. It is bits and pieces about his work. There are lots of figures. After all, he did say that he liked to follow the money. There is also a maze of names. Either people or places—neither Peter nor Michael can decide which. They include "Kay," "Em," and "Dee" pretty often, and especially the word "Cuckoo." On one page of the notebook document is a columned table with those words at the top and different numerical values in US dollars written back and forth along the table.

"It looks like some sort of financing arrangement," Peter says.

"I hope his writing in his blog is clearer than it is in his journal," Michael says.

There is no mention of a "group" or anything concerning a "new world order." In the end they give in to fatigue and fall asleep again. They wake up at Althofen just in time to bundle out and get the morning train north to Salzburg. Another zig.

Piled into a third-class carriage with all the morning commuters, they sit in an atmosphere of yawning mouths and the odor of coffee. Most of the people are off to work and many sit with the same crowd they always travel with. A group of men standing close to Peter and Michael chat about their obviously boring jobs. About who's performing badly or who has taken credit for something they did or whether there's going to be a wave of redundancies coming around the office.

The train rumbles slowly into a land of little wooded

valleys and then to a great wide moor. Gleaming rivers snake through it and high grassy hills lie ahead.

It is almost afternoon by the time the carriage is empty. Just the two of them sitting at the back.

"This next place should be good enough," Peter says.

The next station is in the middle of a bog. There's not even a station house beside the tracks. Just a platform with a tiny wooden shed for shelter. It reminds Peter of Alaska. Of those forgotten little stations in the middle of the wilds. A single-laned road leads out of it and they pass an old woman digging in her garden. As they stroll by, she looks up from her work, smiles a hallo, and then goes back to her cabbages. Soon they are emerging onto a tight lane that straggles over the hilly moor, a row of gray mountains ahead of them.

It is a stunning spring day. Every hill and mountain shows as clear as cut gray diamond against the crystal sky. The air has a faint smell of earth in it, but is as fresh as the ocean. Even though they've been on the run for a day now, it has the effect of lifting them, and soon there is an effervescence in both their steps as they trek along dirt lanes through hilly countryside. In such amazing surroundings, they forget that they're wanted by the police or that there is some conspiracy they've found themselves tangled up in. They forget it all and just enjoy the trek across the landscape, checking their paper map every so often to make sure they're on the right track. Michael even begins whistling.

In a secluded glade that they wade into, they cut walking sticks out of some hazel branches, and then are on their way again, treading along a path that follows the bank of a busy stream.

"The key is to keep moving," Peter had told his son at

the start of their journey. "Stay away from big cities until we have to get to Rome."

They reckon they must be far ahead of their pursuers.

"We can't be too cocky, though," Peter warns his son as they climb a set of steps carved into the rock of a hill. "Even though we don't look like the images in the news, they'll still be looking everywhere for two men matching our height and size."

"Then we should have used the pregnancy belts."

"Too heavy for hiking. We need to be light."

At a set of stepped waterfalls they spot a cottage up on a hill. It is hours since they ate the rolls on the train and the pair of them are very hungry. Using the field glasses, they spy on the moderately sized house from a nook in the rocks. Soon, an old woman with plump hips comes waddling out with a basket of linen and begins hanging it out in the warm breeze.

"Follow my lead," Peter says, stuffing the binoculars back in the rucksack.

The two of them walk across to meet her. She sees them clearly, as there are no trees surrounding it and the little wooden house is open on the hillside. She is at the gate shielding her eyes from the sun with a hand when they reach her.

"Hallo," Peter says.

The woman replies likewise in a warm tone.

In German, Peter tells her that they are a couple of Australian tourists who have come camping in Austria but have unfortunately run out of food, and, expecting to find a general store or something to stock up at, have found themselves too far from anything.

This is actually true. Well, except for the tourist bit and being Australian. Peter had been expecting to find something closer to the tourist routes.

"General store is about six miles up the road," she tells them in English. Being that practically every Austrian speaks it fluently.

"Oh," Peter says, gazing off in the direction of the road.

"Are you both hungry?" she asks.

Michael turns to her with a smile. "Very," he says.

"Then I have a stew on the cooker. Would you like some?"

"Yes, please."

The next thing they are sat around a wooden table eating bowls of lamb stew inside a snug kitchen. The house smells like pine. While they devour the food, the old woman sits opposite drinking a cup of coffee.

"So you've come all the way out here to do a bit of father and son camping, then?"

"Yes," Peter answers.

"Should have got yourselves more provisions."

"We couldn't fit any more in our bags."

"Should have taken bigger bags."

Peter smiles at her. "I'm afraid we always camp lightly."

"That why neither of you appears to be carrying a tent?"

Peter swallows down some stew. Michael, too.

The kid answers her. "It's survival training," he tells her abruptly. "I'm training for special forces."

"In Australia?"

"Yes."

"I have to say," the wily old Austrian says next, "that neither of you sound very Australian. More American."

"We emigrated," the kid replies, before averting his eyes and dipping his spoon back into the stew.

"Yeah," Peter adds. "We only moved to Oz seven years ago."

"Ah," the old woman says, leaning back and sipping her coffee.

She insists upon them spending the night with her at the cottage. Since her husband died last year, she's been all alone out here and it would be nice to have some guests. So they agree to stay.

NINE

THEY SPEND THE EVENING PLAYING POKER WITH the old woman, who wins a tidy sum off the both of them. Never does she check a phone or switch the television on. Instead, she spends the entirety of the late hours exclusively with her guests. At about ten they retire, lie down in nice fresh linen, and neither of them open their eyes again until five.

Gerta, the old woman, insists on them not leaving before having a hearty breakfast of sausage, eggs, bacon and English muffins. Afterwards, she refuses payment.

"After all," she says with a cheeky smile, "I won almost a hundred euros from you both last night. The least I can do is send you off with a full stomach."

The old woman lets out a little cackle, before the pair hug her goodbye and move off. Their plan is simple. They intend on walking for the next six hours until they reach the town of Liezen. There they will catch another train and head in the direction of Linz.

It is another clear spring day. Mist rises up from the lowland, like the untethered souls of the dead leaving their graves. They pass a field of horses that watch them as they stroll by. Over a long ridge of meadow they find their path. It skirts the side of a steep hill. Hedges filled with nesting birds make a racket as they go by and many of the rocky fields are covered in the white specks of sheep.

"You know something," Michael says as they tramp through a copse of ash trees.

"What?"

"I haven't felt this good in a long time. You know what I mean?"

"I do. All the slackness of the past year is slipping away. We'd gone to seed, Mikey. Training once a week and working out in the gym isn't enough. It's the fear that sharpens the muscles and the brain."

Michael gives a coy smile. "I quite like being in danger," he confesses.

"We haven't really faced it yet," is Peter's solemn answer to that.

———

THIS IS A HUGE JOB. Of that Georgia is positive.

Of the hundred and fifty men and women in her surveillance unit, all of them are on this job. Split between Italy, Switzerland and here—Austria. Whoever this Azrael guy is, he must be very important, otherwise Georgia wouldn't have been taken off the job she'd already been on: watching a certain important family in Vienna.

Red alert! Ex-CIA agent and his son wanted. Find them!

Make a positive ID on the man and his boy. Report it to your handler. Do not approach. They had been pretty firm on that last part. "Do not approach under any circumstances" having been the actual wording. Just call it in.

Georgia's certainly not bothered. She's not a fighter, at least not anymore anyway, only a watcher. A set of eyes instead of a set of fists. Or a gun. Tasked with spotting the target and staying with them only up until the point when surveillance is taken over by more hands-on personnel. As a matter of fact, her most accomplished skill—or at least the one that gets her the most praise from her superiors—is her ability to stay with a target without them ever knowing she was even there. As for the name Georgia, it's no more than a codename. Her real name lost somewhere. Hidden behind a facade of false ones.

Their intel said Azrael was an expert in countersurveillance. He'd certainly slipped the net in Italy. So Georgia is sure that he and the son will be disguised. Her estimations are that they'll stay away from major urban areas and places that have heavy use of surveillance cameras. This is the reason Georgia volunteered for Austria rather than Italy or Switzerland. With their heavy use of CCTV, those last two countries make it harder to disappear. She's sure Azrael would take this under consideration when picking somewhere to hide.

The thorough intelligence report she'd been sent also claimed that the two may attempt to contact someone to decrypt the hard drive. Georgia thinks that will come later. For now they will concentrate on simply disappearing, and that means abandoning anything remotely attached to themselves.

This is good for them, Georgia thinks as her keen eyes scan the people stepping off the carriage of a train. Because a room full of highly trained computer hackers is currently surveying every bank account and digital trace of Azrael. It was good that he didn't go to Zurich, too. A kill squad is still in the city waiting for him at the location of his bank, just in case. As for his safe houses or any contacts that he or Michael may have—all are being surveyed. The hacker team worked very quickly unearthing everything on them.

Georgia thinks Azrael knows all this. He won't go anywhere near any of that stuff. He'll stay away from banks, property and contacts. Use untraceable guns and money; some secret cache he's buried somewhere. Even the disguises will have been pulled from there. Command thinks that they'll stay close to Rome. That they'll attempt to travel there in a month's time, when the NATO summit is being held.

Georgia wonders if this is what this is all about. The NATO summit. Because she certainly doesn't know any more about the targets except that they are highly trained and must be found within the next month. As everything in her unit is on a need-to-know basis, and Georgia is essentially on the bottom rung of the ladder, she has been let into no more than a detailed description of the guy and predicted patterns of behavior.

Georgia has some predictions of her own.

She thinks that they'll head into the Alps. It's where she would go. And she thinks that they'll travel by train. Not the main lines, but the little ones that feed the hillside villages.

That's why she and another five of her colleagues are watching the railway lines in the Alpine districts of Austria.

Traveling the trains and scanning every single face they see; especially two men who fit the basic profile of Azrael and the boy. She had spent the previous day until midnight doing it. Then, at five this morning when the trains started up again, she was back at it, zigzagging the train lines, so etching she'll do until she spots the targets or they're spotted somewhere else and she's pulled to another area or another job.

But some feeling inside tells Georgia that today could be her lucky day. That she may be about to get the six figure spotter's fee for finding them.

———

FIVE AND A HALF hours after leaving Olga's cottage they reach a swell of flat land streaked with rivers that glint in the sun. A mile off they spot the town of Liezen.

The train station is similar to the one they got off the day before; no station house, nothing except a wooden shelter for a waiting room, a little shed for a ticket office, a single strip of concrete platform. No CCTV that they can see. In fact, the biggest reason that Peter has picked Austria for their flight is because a nationwide application of CCTV does not exist here, neither in the public nor in the private sector. And there is no automatic face recognition system anywhere in the country.

It would appear that Austrians don't like being watched.

At the ticket office, they pay for a return trip to Graz. Not that they intend on reaching the city.

The bored-looking woman behind the counter hands them their tickets and change, and they wait in the sunshine.

The train is less than twenty minutes and soon they are

on board. Only four carriages long, they take the one at the back. It is empty for the first three stops, but at number four a tall man and his Doberman get on. He takes a position at the other end of the carriage to them, relaxing into the seat, and before long both he and the dog are asleep.

While he snoozes, Peter and Michael study the man. He's mid-to-late thirties, looks like a hiker. Wearing a red woolly hat, big brown boots, a waterproof coat.

While he sleeps, they take the laptop out and search the news. Olga didn't have the internet and the hike to the train station took them into a mobile blackspot, so they've yet to check things over.

In Il Napoli, the local press in Sorrento, there are a few columns about Bella and her husband Giuseppe being questioned by police but let go. Peter has already made sure to place a thousand euros in their bank account for the trouble, as well as paying them for the rest of the year. Hoping, of course, that the police haven't gotten a warrant for the couple's bank accounts. He and Michael are pretty sure they wouldn't have gone to that type of trouble.

In the Corriere della Sera, the Italian national, they read a little more information. The hunt for them is continental. It is believed that they have headed north, possibly Switzerland, maybe Austria.

Both are somewhat dismayed at the accuracy.

Even so, it is the American news which alarms them most. Though there is nothing about Anthony Eustice or his upcoming trip to the NATO summit, there is some unnerving news about themselves. It appears that someone has tipped the Americans off that Alan and David Swartz are none other than the wanted felon Paul Adams and his kidnap victim Michael Henderson. The article goes on to describe their living arrangements in Italy, including the claim that both of them have been working as hit men. There's a whole bunch of spiel about how Paul Adams must have coerced Michael over the last four years he's had him captive. That Michael must be suffering from some type of Stockholm syndrome—blah blah blah.

"Who the fuck writes this stuff?" Michael blurts out.

"This isn't the Italian police," Peter observes. "There's nothing this detailed in the Italian press. No. This is someone else. Someone who has access to far more information than the police."

"The group?"

Peter frowns. He's not willing to become a true believer just yet.

"A group of something at least," he says.

"Whoever it is, they figured out who we are pretty quick."

Peter sighs. He turns to the window, stares at the passing countryside. A village streaks by and he realizes they're approaching the next station.

With them beginning to slow down, he turns his attention to the windows that side of the carriage. The track curves into the station, giving a good view of it from the train as they pull towards it. The platform is practically empty. All except two men.

Even from this far, Peter can tell what they are.

He nudges Michael. The kid looks up from the laptop.

"Two men on the platform."

The kid looks that way. Instantly slaps the top down on the computer and packs it into the rucksack. Both of them have Sig P938 pistols concealed in their jackets. Unzipping the pocket of his, Michael slips a hand inside.

"Take it easy," Peter says with a shake of the head. "It might just be two normal guys."

"They don't look normal."

Michael is right. They are dressed in long black trench coats and black boleros. One is medium height. The other is huge.

The train creeps toward them, the brakes screeching, time slowing down as the doors of the carriage come to line up with the men on the platform.

The father and son are sure now. From this close they can easily see the outlines of guns under the men's long coats.

The train stops and both brace themselves.

Peter gives the rest of the carriage a last-second scan, and it is then that he spots the hiker staring at them from the other end. And not in a friendly way. His dog starts to growl; a low, guttural snarl, its eyes as unfriendly as its master's. And not just that; there is a gun in the hiker's hand.

The two men on the platform.

The hiker and his dog.

A three-man team?

The hiker gets up, one hand holding the gun, the other holding the dog leash, the Doberman pulling on it so hard the leather creaks. He is about to speak when he glances momentarily out the window of the carriage and spots the two men at the door. He goes completely white and quickly tucks the gun away, hisses something at the dog, and retreats back to his corner, the animal standing down.

Peter allows himself a wry smile. The guy with the dog and the men on the platform are separate.

"You seeing this?" he whispers to Michael as the doors hiss open.

"Uh-huh."

Two opposing teams.

The men get on. The giant having to duck. They hone straight onto Peter and Michael and take seats on the opposite side of the aisle, facing them.

The hiker sits with his dog at the other end, studying the scene with caution. Peter gathers that until these guys turned up and ruined things, he was about to frogmarch them off at gunpoint.

Probably to the VW panel van that's waiting in the train station's parking lot.

It's at the bottom of an embankment from the tracks, allowing Peter the perfect view. Beyond the windscreen are the silhouettes of three occupants. They are clearly watching the carriage, the VW idling as smoke floats from the exhaust.

The automatic doors close, shutting them all in together. The two men opposite never stop staring at Peter and Michael. The smaller one has a milky eye that resembles a marble. The larger one is simply huge, and Michael can't help staring at his massive hands.

Peter hopes that these two have no idea about the others.

Eyeball goes to speak when the driver comes over the tannoy, interrupting him. In German he announces, "I apologize for the delay. But we're currently waiting on a signal change."

Peter figures that either these two or the hiker or the three in the van have disabled it. But which one?

"Take your hands out of your pockets," Eyeball growls, before leaning forwards and adding, "And let go of your guns."

All the while the hiker continues to watch.

"Or what?" Michael asks.

Eyeball swivels his good eye on the kid. "Or," he says ominously, "I'll give the signal for our snipers to fire."

The red spots of lasers suddenly appear. One floats about Michael's temple. The other hovers over Peter's heart.

Both of them slowly release their weapons and retract their hands from the pockets.

"Keep them where we can see them," Eyeball says.

Peter now knows who's messed with the signal. These two. It's so their snipers don't run the chance of losing a moving target when the train leaves the station.

Okay. So if that's who disabled the signal figured out, then who do the three goons in the van belong to? The idiot who came armed with a dog? A very unpredictable thing to bring to a gunfight. Or these two guys who look like they're at the higher end of the professional scale?

"Where are the files you got off Harker?" Eyeball wants to know, pointing his snake-eyes at the rucksack by their feet. "Are they in there?"

Peter needs some deviation. "I'm guessing it was this guy who killed Harker," he says, turning to eyeball the giant.

"Yeah," Michael adds with a chuckle. "The one as big as a fucking refrigerator."

All the while Fridge stays as silent as a rock. Hell, he looks like a rock. Or at least carved from one. Some half-finished sculpture made of granite.

Eyeball leans forwards. "I bet you don't even know who

John Harker was, do you? Just like you don't know what is on his hard drive. I hope for your sakes that it is in that bag. I wouldn't want to have to get my friend here to stamp on your son's chest until you told us where it is."

Unfortunately for Peter and Michael, it is in the bag. Peter would prefer it wasn't. Because if they had to torture them, it would, for obvious reasons, not be done on this train—whether that's stamping or something else. They would have to take them to another location where they wouldn't be interrupted. They would have to walk them down the platform, the hiker and his dog following; walk them all the way down the embankment and past the men in the van. That's when they would find out who those three belong to. These two goons; the hiker glaring at the scene through pierced eyes; or a third party.

"You think we're dumb enough to bring it with us?" Peter puts to Eyeball.

"That's what we thought," the goon says. "That you've hidden it. That's why you're going to come with us now. Nice and peacefully. Remembering at all times that our snipers have you under their watchful scopes."

Peter looks sideways at Michael. "You ready?" he asks in a low voice.

"Why not?" is the kid's reply.

They stand up, the red dots following them, their hands kept above their waists. Eyeball leans forwards, dips a hand into Peter's jacket pocket. Takes the Sig Sauer. Fridge does the same with Michael. His meaty paw so big it rips the edge of the jacket pocket as he squeezes inside.

Fridge then pats them down; relieving them of several knives and a wire garrote.

While his partner searches them, Eyeball turns to the hiker. "Wir sind die Polizei," he says with authority.

We're police.

The hiker nods gruffly and looks away. His foot tapping nervously up and down. The dog just as restless.

Eyeball grabs the bag and the laptop. Peter is glad that he doesn't search the rucksack here. Doesn't open it up and find the hard drive right there with the spare magazines and food.

Once they've left the carriage the hiker resumes his staring, following them all the way as the foursome pass the windows. He waits for them to get a few yards up the platform, then scrambles off the train. Him and the dog.

The first thing he does as he steps into the sunlight of the platform is look in the direction of the van in the parking lot and make several gestures with his hands.

It is Peter and Michael's lucky day. It looks like the guys in the van are with the hiker. More simple if it's just two opposing teams.

"How'd you find us?" Peter asks as they move along.

"Does it matter?" Eyeball says.

The platform sits on top of a steep embankment. A set of steps lead down to the parking lot. It just so happens to be right at the other end. Despite it being a relatively barren station the platform is almost a hundred yards.

"Surveillance? Professional spotters?" Peter goes on. "I guess someone's getting their bonus this month."

"Not us," Eyeball grunts.

"So you're not private, then. Government?"

Neither of the men answers.

"CIA?"

"Shut up."

A concrete shelter marks the halfway point of the platform. As they approach it, Peter notices the doors of the van opening. A platform mirror hangs from a post about ten feet ahead of them. It gives the perfect view of what's happening behind them. The hiker has left the train and is following at a distance of three yards. The Doberman strolling beside him.

The three men slip out of the van. They are wearing boiler suits and black ski masks. They carry IWI Tavor TAR-21s; Israeli bullpup assault rifles with a selective fire system.

Peter and Michael walk side by side, keeping their pace as slow as they feel will be permitted. Behind them at a distance of three yards are Fridge and Eyeball. Another three yards and you've got the hiker and his angry-looking dog.

The men in the parking lot fan out. One heads for the steps at the end—the same ones they walk towards. Another heads to the opposite end of the platform to come up behind them. The third heads straight for their position. Two and three begin climbing the grass bank.

"Wait!" Peter says, coming to a sudden stop.

He turns swiftly on their captors—who take immediate steps backwards, their hands already inside their coats, reaching for their weapons.

"Turn back around," Eyeball growls.

"It's on the train," Peter says.

"What is?"

"The hard drive. It's on the train. I hid it there, and I'd rather tell you now instead of having you beat it out of me and my son later on."

Eyeball is frowning. Fridge still looks the same: impenetrable. Behind the two goons, the hiker looks confused. Peter is staring right at him. The hiker catches a quick glance over his shoulder at the train. Not sure if this is a ruse. Not sure whether to run for the carriage.

Eyeball doesn't look convinced. "You're fucking with me, right?"

"No, I'm not," Peter replies, his gaze back on him. "I just came to the realization that I don't give a rat's ass what any of this is about. The only reason we ran from Sorrento was because the police came. We're wanted men and would rather avoid detection. As far as your mission goes, we have no interest in any of it."

Eyeball thinks about it. His huge pal doesn't appear to be thinking about anything. In the background, the hiker watches, the dog growling. All while the three men creep up the embankment.

"It's in the carriage?" Eyeball says.

"Yes. I hid it under the seat when I saw you and your friend on the platform."

Eyeball breathes in, then out. "Okay. Take us to it."

He and Fridge step to the side.

Michael gives Peter a look. It is an "I hope you know what you're doing" look.

The two of them turn around and begin walking back to the carriage. The hiker stands there. Not sure what to do. Whether to run back to the carriage and check under the seat. Wait on the platform for them to do their thing and then attack. Or just carry on and join his three pals.

He spends a second too long thinking about it. Because instead of doing any of these things, he just stands there as Peter marches right up and shoulder barges him. It smashes him harder than Peter's pace suggests. The dog goes nuts, the hiker staggering backwards. Peter gets ahold of him, pulls him upright, stops him from going down.

"I'm so sorry," he says as he manhandles the guy.

"Get off me!" the hiker shouts, pushing Peter away.

He speaks in English. English with an American accent.

The two goons are immediately suspicious.

"Keep an eye on them two," Eyeball says to Fridge as he approaches the hiker. "You are American?" he asks, coming to a stop a couple of feet from him.

The dog is snarling.

"I asked you a question," Eyeball says.

"Y-yes. I'm out here hiking. Are you American?"

Eyeball says nothing. Instead his eyes narrow to terrible slits. It is like watching a crocodile's third eyelid come down as it dives underwater.

"Is that your dog?" he asks as the Doberman begins barking.

"Yes."

"Can you tell him to shut up?"

The hiker shouts a command and the animal quietens down.

"What is your name?" Eyeball asks.

"John. And you are?"

The hiker looks back over his shoulder. The men are almost on the platform.

"Where is your bag, John?"

"My what?"

"Your bag. You said you're out here hiking. Where is your bag?"

The hiker is sweating. He turns to his pals. Eyeball

follows the look. Spots the three men closing on their position.

When the hiker turns back to Eyeball, there is a gun in the guy's hand and it is pointing at him.

Quickly, he reaches into his pocket. Finds nothing where a Beretta M9 should be.

Now he knows why Peter shoulder barged him. It was a classic pickpocketing technique.

There is a single pop of suppressed gunshot. The bullet hits the hiker right where his heart is.

"Ah fuck!" he gasps, dropping to his knees and grabbing at his chest. There is a distinct lack of blood.

The bullet is buried in a thin sheet of Kevlar. So Eyeball sends a bullet into his forehead where there is none, turning him into a crumpled heap next to his dog—which goes crazy.

"Three men," Eyeball shouts to his massive colleague. "Coming up the—Aaah!"

The Doberman has taken advantage of the distraction. Highly trained, it knows how to take out a weapon, and its jaws are accurate. It has ahold of Eyeball by the wrist and is mauling him; the two becoming involved in a violent tug of war. The dog trying to pull his arm out of its socket.

Fridge forgets about their captives for a moment, whips out his Glock, goes to shoot the dog. That's when the Tavors explode. Bullets punch a litany of holes into the train carriages right above their heads. They are lucky the men below are at too steep an angle.

Planters made from railway sleepers dot the platform. Fridge heads for the cover of the nearest one, sending a barrage of bullets at the hiker's pals as he stomps across the concrete. The men doing their best to tuck into the hill.

Peter and Michael are kissing concrete. With the world descending into chaos around them, they begin crawling toward the train. Inside, the driver is ducked down in his cab. The few passengers are on the floor.

Fridge turns to them as they reach the edge of the platform but is quickly distracted when the Tavors begin to hit the planter he hides behind.

Within the cover of the next planter along, Eyeball is ducked down with the dog, a foot against the Doberman's chest, blood dribbling out its mouth and down his arm, the two involved in a tug-of-war.

Peter and Michael jump down onto the tracks, disappearing into the gap between the concrete bulkhead and the train. Peter is gripping the hiker's Beretta M9 in his hand.

"I need a gun," Michael complains as they move along.

"You should have grabbed the rucksack."

"The big guy had it. I wasn't going to risk getting within his reach."

"Well, you should have. All our stuff is in it."

"At least we're alive. Better to live another day and all that."

Peter is frowning. "What does that even mean?"

"It means forget about it. Our priority should be getting out of here."

They shuffle along within the gap. The train is inches from their backs, pressing them into the platform. They pray it doesn't start moving.

Peter leads. He spots movement above them farther ahead. The man at the far end has made it onto the platform and is moving from planter to planter toward Eyeball and Fridge.

The gap is large enough to see down if you stand within a few yards of the platform's edge. The assassins pull up and wait as the guy leaves the planter, runs toward the carriage— happens to glance right at the two men as they look up at him from the tracks. Swinging his Tavor around, he is about to fire when Peter sends a bullet into his masked face.

The guy goes down with his momentum, like he's stumbling. He lands close to the tracks. Michael is lightning quick as he lunges up onto the platform, grabs the fallen Tavor and the spare mag dangling from the pocket of the guy's boiler suit, and gets back down like a retreating rat.

The kid checks the weapon over. He's used one before. The guns feel comfortable in his hands. Pulling the mag, he finds that it's almost full.

"You ready?" Peter asks when Michael looks up from the Tavor.

"As I'll ever be."

In crouched positions, they sneak along the edge of the platform, opening up the distance between themselves and the gunfight. They begin to hear faraway sirens. The police on their way to join the action. They really do need to get out of here.

They reach the end. Cautiously check things out.

The men are busy with each other.

Peter and Michael lift themselves up and sprint across the platform to the embankment steps. They don't take the stairs. Instead they take the sloping grass of the embankment.

They run toward the panel van. The engine still idling.

Jump in. Peter puts the VW in gear and does a one-eighty. Then he guns it out of there. As they drive away from the station, five police cruisers come charging in the other direction.

"We need to dump this van the first chance we get," Peter says as they head for the hills.

Michael's eyes are on the wing-mirror. "Who were those people?"

"At a guess I'd say they were all American. But two groups."

"US Government?"

"I don't know."

"Mercenaries?"

"I don't know, Mikey. This is making less sense by the second. But one thing is for sure."

"What?"

"We're not taking the train anymore."

TEN

THEY PULL OFF THE HIGHWAY ONTO A DIRT ROAD.
It leads them deep into hilly woodland. Two miles later Peter
stops within the shadows of tall pine. They are well enough
hidden to keep out of sight of the police helicopters they can
hear flying about in the distance.

Peter slumps forward over the steering wheel, resting his
forehead on the grip and swearing through clenched teeth.

"Come on," Michael says softly. "It's not so bad."

"Not so bad?" Peter says, raising his head and turning to
him. "Do you not realize? We just left all our money and
possessions at that train station. We now have no weapons.
No documentation to travel with. No laptop. No disguises.
No encrypted dongle for hidden access to the internet. We
don't even have Harker's hard drive. So we also have... no
way... What?"

Michael is grinning at him.

"That's where you're wrong," the kid says.

Peter frowns.

Michael shoves a hand down the front of his pants and pulls out the flat, cell phone-sized hard drive. Peter's eyes shine.

Michael tells him, "I hid it the second I spotted those two goons on the platform. I shoved it where my dick is hoping that the one that patted me down was such a homophobe he'd go nowhere near my Johnson. I was right."

"I'm glad you were," Peter adds dryly.

Michael goes to hand it to him, but Peter doesn't reach for it.

"Maybe wipe it down first," he says with a grimace.

The kid rolls his eyes, before turning his attention to the van itself. "What else have we got?" he says as he leans forward and pulls open the glovebox.

To his great disappointment it is empty.

"There'll be nothing here," Peter says. "The van will be clean, the plates leading to nothing. As for the dead left behind, you can guarantee it'll take the cops a long time to identify them—if they ever do. Those..."

They both go cold the second they hear something move behind them: in the back of the van.

They look at each other, then slowly turn to the partition separating them from the back.

Outside, Peter rips the side door open. Michael is stood five feet back, the Tavor tight to his shoulder.

Terrified eyes stare back at them from the darkness. A man sits on the flatbed with a filthy cloth stuffed in his mouth. His hands are zip-tied behind his back. Peter leans forward and pulls the gag out.

"Please, don't shoot me!" he cries out.

"You're American," Peter observes.

The guy frowns. "You're not one of them?"

"One of who?"

"The Group. That's who."

"Slow down," Peter says, holding a hand up. "What's your name?"

Instead of answering, the American turns to Michael and says, "Do you mind lowering the gun?"

The kid looks at his father.

Not taking his eyes off the stranger, Peter holds a hand up to Michael and gives the hand signal to stand down. The kid lowers the weapon, while still maintaining it in a ready position.

"You didn't answer me," Peter says to the stranger. "What's your name?"

"Ron Chambers."

"And who is Ron Chambers?"

"I worked with John."

"John Harker?"

"Yes. I was his editor at the magazine he writes for. Are you the guys he was staying with?"

"Yeah. That's us."

"Oh, great," Ron Chambers says with relief, shuffling forwards. "Can you cut me out of these ties, then? They're really biting into my wrists."

Instead of answering, Peter asks, "So you worked with John Harker?"

"Come on, man. Get me out of these and I'll answer all your questions."

"You worked with John Harker?"

The guy rolls his eyes. "Yeah. I worked with John Harker."

"And that's how you ended up in the back of this van?"

"Yeah. They picked me up this morning."

"And who are they?"

"The Group. Or at least I think so. I never saw any of their faces. They spoke in English but never used names."

"How'd they pick you up?"

"I got a call from John two days ago. He was real upset. Wanted to give me something. Said it would change the world."

"He tell you what it was?"

"No. Said he couldn't speak on the phone. Just told me to meet him in Rome. But I never made it. These guys snatched me right off the street outside the airport. Just jumped out of a van and scooped me into the back. At first I thought they were gonna kill me. They started asking loads of questions about John. Started beating on me. Then they began bawling about some hard drive. Started asking about files. Accusing me of having them. But I haven't got anything."

"That's because he didn't send it to you," Michael says.

Peter throws the fist back up. Shut up.

"We've got it," the kid adds.

"Mikey," Peter warns.

But Michael ignores his father. "Did John ever tell you the password to his hard drive?"

"Yeah," Ron Chambers says with a narrowing of the eyes.

"Then we need to get you to a computer."

ELEVEN

THE GIRL IN BLACK LEATHER GRIPS THE handlebars of her Ducati Panigale V4R as she throws the forty-five-thousand-dollar superbike down serpentine mountain roads. Her slender body pressed tight to the bike, she is one with the powerful machine, the two of them weaving in and out of traffic, the engine exploding between her legs.

She comes upon a coach filled with tourists on an almost vertical descent. About a hundred yards ahead is a hairpin turn that veers a sharp left. The sun is coming in from the east, and before she sets off around the bus into the opposing lane, she checks the road ahead.

A sheer rock face blocks the turn, and when she spots the long shadow of a truck stretching out along the tarmac from around the corner, she stays tight behind the coach as the aforementioned truck comes bulldozing around the bend with its forty foot load.

The second the truck is past, she twists back the throttle, swerves into the opposing lane, and bursts past the coach like a comet—the schoolchildren onboard cheering as the bike rockets down the mountain.

She enters a short tunnel, the roar of the Ducati's engine filling it. When she emerges the other side, she has a good view of the valley below—and, essentially, the train station.

The track runs across the flat center of a vale; the station in the middle, on the edge of a village that is no more than a scattering of little white cottages that look like breadcrumbs on a lawn. On the other side of the tracks, police helicopters hover around hilly woodland.

She reaches level ground, heads down a road that winds alongside a river and enters the village, slowing her speed so as not to attract attention. She reaches the police cordon and pulls into the side of the road. Using a police scanner built into the bike, she listens in on their radio conversations through AirPods.

Her German's a little rusty but she soon begins to get what the chatter is all about. It certainly sounds like Azrael and his boy. Sounds like the type of carnage they'd leave behind. And it looks like they got to leave it behind, too. Because she quickly works out that amongst the high turnover of dead, the two assassins are absent. She discovers that they managed to escape in a panel van their supposed attackers had brought.

Before today, Azrael and his boy had no idea what they'd gotten themselves into. If they thought they could just go hiking up the mountains to escape the heat coming after them, then they sure as hell don't think that now.

The Girl in Black switches the scanner off and makes a telephone call.

"Girl in Black?" a man's gruff voice answers.

"Avenger."

"Challenge word Godfrey."

"Reply..." She has to think. "Reply kidney."

"Good. What've you got?"

"Looks like our friends engaged with Azrael and his boy."

"Was it Jack or the others?"

"Both, I think."

"Carnage?"

"By the looks of things. From the scanner, I heard a lot about a big shootout between two groups. At least six dead including two cops."

"But Azrael and the boy got away?"

"Yes. They got away. None of the dead fit their description."

"What's your plan from here?"

She sighs into the helmet, steaming the tinted visor.

"Two men escaped in a van," she tells him. "I'm guessing that was Azrael. It was seen leaving the scene. I'll head in the direction the cops were talking about. See where it leads."

"Okay, you do that."

She goes to cancel the call when Avenger says, "Girl in Black?"

"What?"

"There's something else."

She groans. "What?"

"I've just found out that the Russians have gotten word."

"Great. That's all we need. More players in the field."

"Try not to let it affect your search and update me when you have a development. Avenger out."

The call goes dead.

TWELVE

PETER CALCULATES THAT THE POLICE HAVE PUT UP a fifty-mile cordon. They'll have to stay away from roads and public transport, as well as houses or any other thing that has people anywhere near it.

Great!

Thankfully, the landscape is there to protect them. On all sides they're encircled by vast swathes of open country. A brown river forms a radius around them, and high hills and low mountains make a northern circumference. There is not a sign nor sound of people, only the hissing water of the river and the occasional cries of the birds.

Nevertheless, for the first time since this began they feel the genuine terror of the hunted. Knowing the police were coming after them didn't really fill the assassins with terror. More an urgency.

But the ones coming after the hard drive, the ones who know its secrets—Peter is sure that these people will hunt them with a keenness and vigilance not shared by any law enforcement agency in the world.

"So what do you know about this so-called Group?" Peter asks Ron Chambers as they clamber up a hillside.

"Not much," the journalist says, to both Peter and Michael's disappointment.

"What's not much?"

"Just what John told me. That there's this group of super-rich families who've been..."

"Controlling society since the dawn of civilization," Michael finishes for him. "Yeah. He wouldn't shut up about it."

"Anything else?" Peter asks.

"Like what?"

"Any names?"

"He told me he hadn't cracked the cipher on it all yet."

"What about you—you think you can crack it?"

"Maybe."

Peter looks back over the landscape. The sun glints off the steel cables of power lines as they travel overhead from one huge pylon to another. In the distance are the shadows of mountains, and in the air eagles glide upon the thermals in loops. You couldn't find a more peaceful sight in the world. But something is up. Something that makes Peter cry, "Run!"

They burst into flight. He leads the others to the top of a ridge and into a natural gully overshadowed by elderberry bushes, the three of them crawling into the tangles of vegetation, slipping into deep mud created from drainage. It is the mud that has attracted Peter; it will hide their heat signatures.

Lying flat within the sludge, Peter scans the valley in the direction of the railway line, moving his eyes from east to west across the panorama.

"What is it?" Michael whispers.

"Can't you hear it?"

All the kid can hear is Ron Chambers' heavy breathing.

Peter's hawk-eyes can make out nothing moving against the landscape. So he looks west beyond the ridge, scrutinizes an area of flat valleys latticed by the faint lines of roads. His gaze moves into the blue sky above, and it is there that he sees it: a dot glinting in the sunshine—a UAV (Unmanned Aerial Vehicle).

As it gets closer to their position, he recognizes the UAV as an MQ-9 Reaper: a hunter-killer. The first UAV designed for long-endurance, high-altitude surveillance. Not to mention attack. It can carry up to four Hellfire missiles and two 500lb GBU-12 Paveway II laser-guided bombs.

"I see it," Michael says.

The Reaper climbs up to the heavens, and Peter gathers that it has lost sight of them. That it is trying to get as good a vantage over the whole landscape as possible to try and find them again.

"You sure it's them?" Chambers asks.

"Who else would own a Reaper hunter-killer drone?" Peter puts to him. "Now stay hidden and keep quiet."

"Keep quiet? Can they listen in on us with that thing?"

"No. But you're annoying me."

For an hour or so they watch the Reaper from their pit of elderberries and mud. It flies low along the jagged hilltops, then in narrow circles over the valley that they'd come in by.

Then it appears to change its mind, rises up to a great height once more, and flies off south.

"Great," Peter complains when it is gone. "I'm thinking now that maybe the countryside's not such a good refuge."

"These hills are no good for cover," Michael puts to him. "We'll need to stay within trees."

"Even that won't protect us for long," Peter says. "No. What we need is shelter."

———

IT IS STARTING to get dark when they come around the ridge of a steep hill and spot the white ribbon of a road in the distance. It is winding up the hills on the other side of a narrow vale. They follow along the edge of a rye field, ready to jump into it if they spot the drone again, and eventually enter a plateau of woodland where a solitary two-story house occupies a clearing overshadowed by tall beech and fir.

The three of them eye the place from the edge of the trees—their weapons stashed beneath bushes not far from where they now stand.

All the windows of the chateau are open and wild animals run around the muddy yard; pigs, chickens, a goat. A woman with long brown hair saunters around a corner of the house and they shrink back into the trees. She is wearing denim cutoffs, an olive green vest, and carries an axe in one hand and a struggling chicken in the other. The men watch as she marches up to a slab of wood, plonks the chicken down on it, raises the axe, and—a short clucking shriek later —dinner is killed.

It is as she strolls back to the house that she comes to a sudden stop. Ron Chambers has just taken a step back onto some broken branches and tripped. Falling onto his ass, he makes a racket.

She turns a pleasant and sunburned face on them, cocks an eye, the headless chicken leaking blood down onto her tan desert boots.

Peter, annoyed at the clumsy journalist, emerges from the trees. "I'm sorry," he says loud enough for her to hear from thirty feet away across the yard. "We're lost."

All three are covered in dried mud.

"It would appear so," she observes in English.

"We lost our stuff in a river," Peter adds. "Lost our map and phones."

A wry smile is rising up on the woman's face.

"You are American?" she asks.

"Yes."

"And you're lost?"

"Yes."

Peter takes a few steps toward her. She squeezes the handle of the axe. So he comes to a stop, having closed the distance between them to about ten feet.

"My companions and I," Peter says, "were wondering if there is somewhere nearby we can perhaps stay the night."

They have no money except for the few euros' change in their pockets, but they can think around that later on. For now it is just about surviving the next moments.

The woman appears to relax.

"Not really," she says.

She then spends a few seconds weighing them up. It

would seem that Peter asking about places to stay has put her at ease. The three of them probably come across as the usual bunch of ill-prepared tourists that often come hiking this way during the season.

"Saying that," she goes on, "my own home here is a guest house. I'm not open until the beginning of June, but I guess I can squeeze in three guests if they aren't too worried about the state of the place."

"No, ma'am," the three men say one after the other.

"Come on," she says, walking off to the house. "Follow me. I'll show you the rooms and you can perhaps clean yourselves up."

She marches confidently into the house with the chicken and they follow. It is one of those chateaus where the rooms are really tall and spacious. Sunlight shines through huge latticed windows, scattering the wooden floors with squares of light. Wood paneling covers the bottom half of the walls and mounted animal heads stick out at them here and there; a gazelle, a tusked bore.

"These yours?" Peter asks the woman as they pass along a corridor lined with horned deer heads.

"No. My father was the hunter. I just stick to chickens."

She leads them to a spacious scullery with a huge open fireplace.

Michael spots nothing except the young woman chopping vegetables at the rear of the room.

"This is my daughter Lena," the woman informs them.

The men smile at the girl. Especially Michael.

"And your name?" Peter asks the woman of the house.

She blushes. "Of course, I forgot. How silly. I am Clara."

Peter steps forward and offers a hand. "I am Peter."

She places the chicken down on a countertop. Her hand is warm when he shakes it. As she looks up at him, her green eyes sparkle, until she goes even redder and looks away.

"And these here," Peter says, not letting go of the hand, "are my son, Michael, and my friend, Ron."

———

THE MOTHER and daughter eat with them—chicken schnitzel with ratatouille—and afterwards they sit around an old wooden table in the dining room. Almost the entire end of the room is taken up by a huge window that has been thrown open onto the night. A pleasant breeze breathes into the house, and a view of moonlit hilltops spreads out beyond. A tepid light is provided by the glowing embers of a fireplace and the few candles dotted about the table. Along with the wine it gives the scene a pleasant, snug feel.

"As you can see," Clara says as she pours Peter another glass of dark red burgundy, "we're quite isolated out here. The nearest neighbor isn't for another eight miles, and without access to a computer or TV, we're nicely cut off."

"You don't have a computer or a television?" Ron Chambers asks.

"Nope," Clara says, settling back into her chair. "Just a telephone that we take bookings on."

"But you have the internet, right?"

"Yes. We have the internet for our guests. But we don't use it ourselves."

"It's pretty cool you being off grid like this," Peter says.

And not to mention lucky for us.

At the other end of the table Michael and Lena are involved in a chat of their own.

"It's amazing, the two of you living out here with no link to the outside world," Michael says as he leans back in his chair trying to look cool.

"Yeah. Mom and me feel blessed," Lena replies. "We were living in Vienna before. I was at university and Mom was an accountant, if you can believe it." She sighs. "We didn't know it, then, but we were slowly dying inside."

"You were bored," Michael points out before pressing his glass to his lips.

"Yeah," Lena says nodding. "Really bored. Like soul-destroyingly bored."

Michael smiles and it makes her cheeks burn.

At the same time Clara is telling Peter and Ron Chambers about her late father leaving her the house three years ago.

"My first instinct was to sell it," she says.

"I'm glad you didn't," Peter says.

She smiles. Pours a little more into his glass.

"It was strange," she goes on. "I'd never really liked coming here as a child. See, my grandmother used to live here, and my parents would drive me out in the summer and force me to spend a fortnight with the miserable old bird. Two weeks, every single summer. Back then I found this place so desolate. But when Lena and I came out here after Papa died, I just fell in love with the location, and the house. It was literally on the way back to Vienna that we both decided to move out here permanently. Planned the whole thing during the five-hour drive."

"That's really romantic," Peter remarks. "I'd love to live in a big house like this surrounded by such beauty."

Clara smiles rosy-cheeked at him and sips her wine. Peter, in turn, smiles back, relaxed in his chair. Taking ahold of his wineglass by the stem, he lifts it to his lips.

In comparison Ron Chambers sits with a nervous expression. Shuffling forwards in his chair, he asks the lady of the house, "So you don't even have a computer in the house? One tucked away somewhere just in case?"

She turns to him from Peter, the smile dropping. "No," she says with a gentle shake of her head.

"No laptop or anything?"

"No. Nothing."

Chambers gazes at Peter. "We really need to check our emails," he says with a widening of the eyes.

"We can leave it till tomorrow," Azrael tells him.

"Lena can take you into town in the morning," Clara says. "There's an internet café."

Chambers goes to speak again but Peter holds a hand up and stops him. He then gives the journalist a look out of the corner of his eye that tells him to zip it.

The rest of the night passes by in an atmosphere of chatting and drinking. Around eleven they all begin to feel heavy and file off to bed. On the landing, Clara touches Peter's hand as she says goodnight. The two stare into each other's eyes for a second or two, before she burns up, looks away, and turns around. As she reaches her bedroom door, she glances one last time over her shoulder, giggles and enters her room.

At the other end of the landing a similar scene plays out

between Lena and Michael. They stand facing each other, holding hands.

"Come on, Mikey," Peter calls to him.

The three men retire to their bedrooms. Peter having insisted to Chambers that they all share a room. Three beds line the wall. Chambers in the middle between them.

Because Peter still isn't sure about their new companion.

THIRTEEN

Their room is at the back of the house. A set of windows open outwards like doors onto a wooden balcony. It has a stunning view of the plateau. Woodland surrounds the house, practically hiding it within a shroud of green. Further out, enclosing the forest from all sides, are mountains. A fortress couldn't be any more protected, and from its high position, you only have to climb out onto any given balcony to see if something is coming by air.

A Reaper drone perhaps.

Lena owns a moped. She offers to drive Michael into town to source a laptop from a friend of hers—the offer of the internet café having been rebuked on the part of them needing to access a storage device. So the daughter had come up with a friend of hers who owned a laptop and sometimes loaned it to Lena when she needed it.

Michael goes to get on the back of the Vespa when Peter stops him.

"You can't go," he tells his son in a hushed voice.

"Why not?"

"Use your head. You can't risk anyone seeing you."

Michael groans. "I was planning on spending a little one-on-one time with her."

Peter grins. "I know you were, you dirty little dog."

Michael makes his excuses and Lena goes off alone.

She returns an hour and a half later. The three men thank her for the Hewlett-Packard laptop and retire to their room. A little later they get into the hard drive. The password is Curly-Fry.

"It was John's dog when he was a kid," Ron Chambers explains.

Their excitement pricked, the three are set for instant deflation. The cipher on it isn't any little old cipher with a keyword that helps find out what each symbol refers to in respect to the alphabet. It is a cryptographic code that may vary from word to word. Meaning that each word or image of the document has its own code.

"This is serious stuff," Peter says. "When I was with the CIA, I only ever knew of them using such a cipher for the most delicate files."

Ron Chambers looks the most disappointed of all of them. "We're gonna need the decryption algorithm," he states.

"And how do we get that?"

"With a much more powerful computer and a much better hacker than me."

"And where do we find those?"

"I know a guy out in Vienna."

"Vienna is too dangerous," Peter points out.

"But it's the only way to know what is written in these files."

They resolve to go the next morning.

So, after finding their way blocked on the hard drive, they check the news. The shootout at the station is all over local media, some of the international press as well. They check CNN and the rest and find no real updates on Harker's murder, or anything on their various aliases.

Peter then checks the Ben Knight story. Police are still searching for him. No real updates.

"This again," Michael says.

"What's this?" Chambers asks as he stands in a corner of the room.

"A guy Peter used to know in the CIA. Killed his family."

"You knew Ben Knight?" Chambers puts to Peter.

"We worked some jobs together. He always came across as a standup guy. If it wasn't for the fact he's a wanted man, I'd have thought he'd be a good guy to go to with this."

"Shame he's a mass murderer, then," Michael quips.

When they go downstairs to the kitchen, they find Lena relaying to Clara something her friend had told her. The mother sits brooding over it when she spots Peter and the others and a big smile creases her lips.

"Come have some coffee," she tells them.

Peter and Chambers join her around the table while Michael returns the laptop to Lena. The kid strolls over to her like he's the coolest cat in the alley. His manner eliciting a roll of the eyes from Peter.

"Lena was just telling me," Clara says as she pours their drinks, "about trouble not far from here. About ten miles across the valley. A big shootout yesterday. Six men dead, including two policemen. Another three of them in hospital."

"You know what it was over?" Peter asks discreetly.

"The papers are saying it's gang related."

It is true. When they'd checked the news themselves there was, for some reason, no mention of Peter and Michael's aliases. Nothing about Paul Adams, or Alan and David Swartz. Nothing connecting what happened at the train station to the death of John Harker in Sorrento.

"I didn't realize Austria was known for its gangs," Peter observes.

"It's not. Especially this far from the cities."

Peter then happens to glance out the window right at the moment a plume of dust is kicked up by car tires about a hundred yards up the dirt lane that leads to the house. Next second he spots the silver grille glinting in the sun. As the low rumble of its engine reaches the kitchen, Clara turns to the window.

Something about it raises the hairs along Peter's neck. His instincts go haywire. He slips a hand across the table and when she feels its warmth on top of hers, Clara turns to him from the view. At first she is smiling. But it drops when she sees the grave look on his face.

"Peter," she says softly, "what is the matter?"

"Please protect us, Clara," he breathes.

The lady of the house suddenly realizes that Michael has come away from Lena, and by proxy the window, just as a silver Mercedes pulls up in front of the house.

"What is wrong?" she asks.

"Men will harm us if they know we are here. They will

harm you and Lena, too. But if they think we're not, they'll leave you be. Please, I beg you, Clara, get rid of them."

She stares at him for a few seconds before nodding.

Peter lets go of her hand, nods at the other two, and the three of them retire upstairs. As they close themselves quietly in their room, the sounds of Clara explaining things quickly to her daughter float up through the airy floor-boards. Outside two men in long black trench coats and boleros climb out of the car.

The bedroom is at the back of the house and all the talking is done in the hallway at the front. It means they're unable to listen in. They consider creeping onto the landing, listening from the top of the stairs, but the house is old. Its whining floorboards and creaking hinges will give them away.

Three minutes later they hear the engine of the Mercedes rumble back into life. It is parked on their side of the house. Peeping from behind the curtain, Peter catches sight of the two figures. One is slim, the other irregularly large: the men from the train station.

As the Mercedes disappears around a bend in the lane, Clara knocks on the bedroom door. When Peter opens it, her green eyes shine with agitation.

"They said they were from the police," she whispers. "But I don't think they were."

"Why not?" Peter asks.

"Firstly, they weren't Austrian."

"How could you tell?"

"Their accents were foreign. They sounded Scandina-vian maybe."

"Not American?"

"Maybe. I don't know. The one with the bad eye wasn't Austrian anyway. The big one I don't know. He kept quiet the whole time. Just stood there staring right into me."

"Did they have identification?"

"Yes. They showed me police IDs. But I got the feeling they were fake."

"What else did the one with the bad eye say?"

"Said they were investigating what had happened at the train station yesterday. They say that both you and your son are very dangerous. That you killed two policemen and four innocent bystanders."

"Liar!" bursts out of Michael's mouth. He comes away from the alcove that he is standing in. "We'd left before the police even arrived, so there's no way we shot or hurt any of the cops. And as for innocent bystanders, Peter shot one guy —and he was one of the attackers. The guy was about to shoot us."

Clara turns to Peter. "They left their number. Told me I was to call them if I happened to see any of you in the area."

"And are you?"

The two stare at each other from across the threshold.

"I don't know," she says. "Depends on how you answer my next questions. Who were those men just here?"

"You want the truth?"

"It would be nice." The green eyes shimmer at him.

"The truth is, Clara, I don't know. See, me and my son have come into all of this accidentally. Will you let me explain it to you?"

She takes a few seconds to come up with the answer. Then. "You have five minutes."

IT TAKES ALMOST the entire five minutes but Peter gives Clara a general account of the last two weeks; making sure to leave out the whole professional hit men, former CIA agent backstory stuff.

Clara is sitting down on one of the beds by the tale's end.

"Do you believe me?" Peter asks.

Looking up at him, she says, "It is too crazy to be untrue, I think."

Peter is about to speak when he's interrupted by a knock at the door.

"Mama?" Lena's voice whispers from the landing.

"May I tell my daughter?" Clara asks.

"It's best to keep it just between us. Look, I am sorry to put you in this situation."

"You said before that we were in danger."

"Only if we stay here."

"Then you must leave." She is looking right at him.

"Mama," comes Lena's voice again.

Clara moves toward the door. Peter takes hold of her wrist and she turns to him.

"I need your help."

She stares at him. Then. "What help?"

"I need you and your daughter's cooperation."

"In what?"

"I need you to take the Vespa and stay in town tonight. Give me the use of your house."

"You must be joking."

"I'm not. Those men will be back. And they won't just be asking next time."

Her lips screw up, and Peter wonders if she isn't wishing she still had that axe to hand.

"Let go," she says.

But he doesn't. He can't.

"I spotted a car under a tarp out in the yard," he says. "Does it work?"

"Yes. It is my little Citroën. I use it during the winter when it's too cold for the Vespa."

"Can I borrow it?"

She narrows her eyes at him. "You don't look like the type of person that returns things you borrow."

Peter does his best to look solemn. "When all this is over," he says, "I promise I will repay you."

Clara sighs. Then tugs her wrist out of his grip. "You wouldn't be the first man to break your promise to me," she spits before leaving the room to join her daughter on the landing.

FOURTEEN

MEN COME FOR THEM JUST AFTER THREE A.M. A minivan skids to a stop at the bottom of the dirt driveway that leads uphill through trees to Clara's house. Five men in body armor and ski masks sit inside. Each feels their Brügger & Thomet MP9 submachine gun as if it were an extension of their arm.

They leave the van, spread out into formation as they climb the hill toward the house. Each MP9 has a silencer on the end and a folded stock extended to their shoulders. Hip holsters carry Glock-17s and harnesses over the body armor carry both flash and frag grenades.

It is a dark night. Clouds cover the moon. As they glide through the trees, they snap down night-vision goggles.

"Five hundred meters," the commander whispers into his comms.

The wind picks up, sweeping across the hillside, making the trees creak. Giving the driveway a wide berth, they almost reach the chateau. It looms up at them like some lonely witch's house hidden in the middle of the woods. None of the lights are on, and it looks abandoned.

Stocks pressed against their shoulders, sights just below the eyeline of their night-vision, each man takes a position along a ten-foot perimeter of the house.

"Number One," the commander whispers into his comms, "I need you at the front door."

One moves silently into position.

"What we got, people?" the commander asks.

"Three in position on the west side," comes through the comms. "I got a ground-floor window. No sign of movement."

"Four in position on the east side. Two ground-floor windows. No sign of movement."

"Two in position at the back. I got a back door. No movement."

"Okay," the commander says. "You each have entry. Wait for us to go in the front first, then follow. And remember who we're dealing with here. You're gonna need your A game tonight, boys."

The commander pulls a frag grenade from his armor and creeps toward the front door. One is waiting at the side with a Benelli shotgun loaded with a breaching charge.

The commander gives a hand signal. You ready?

One gives the signal back that he is.

The leader holds his fingers up. Three-two-one—

Boom!

One fires the breaching load directly at the lock. The door bursts inwards in a shower of splinters and lands on the hallway floor. The commander is on one knee, rolling the grenade into the house underarm. It skittles along the wooden floorboards—once, twice...

The gentle sounds of this secluded little paradise are broken into by the almighty racket of the grenade exploding. Its blast area hits the bannister of the stairs and sends shards of wood into the air.

Number One charges into the hallway while the commander stays outside. Three and Four smash the windows and dive into the house. Two remains at the back door keeping guard for anyone that should try to escape that way.

Having penetrated the house, each man lets out a burst of controlled fire as they enter each room. Not taking any chances with the man they now know for sure is the feared assassin Azrael—as well as his young apprentice. One and Two go upstairs, splitting at the landing and taking a side of the house each.

All clear in the rooms, they try the attic.

Nothing.

Once the three men searching the house are sure it is empty, they confirm with the commander, before asking him and Two if there's any sign outside.

"None," comes back from both men.

All five begin to worry.

"They should be here," the commander says.

Suddenly the sound of a car engine coughing into life comes from the far corner of the yard. The commander wheels to his right just as headlight beams illuminate green tarpaulin. A car jerks forward, bursting out from under it.

The commander dives out the way as a burst of gunfire comes from one of the back windows. He's hit in the elbow. Injured. But nothing deadly.

Lying in the dirt, he watches the Citroën 2CV disappear over a slight rise.

———

PETER DRIVES the Citroën down the dirt driveway as hard as it will go, tearing along the uneven ground. Chambers sits in the passenger side, Michael in the back with the Tavor bullpup.

Before dark Clara and Lena took the Vespa and are currently staying with friends in the nearby town of Hallstatt. Annoyed at the disturbance to their peace, but unharmed and not in danger.

In forty seconds they reached the highway. The men sent to kill them have parked their black minivan at the point where it meets the driveway. Peter pulls up alongside it and Michael leans out the back window. He sends a burst of gunfire into both tires on that side. Knowing that if they've got a spare, they won't have a second.

Then they're on their way. Heading northeast toward the capital: Vienna. Aiming to change cars as soon as they can.

———

AN HOUR later they still haven't come across a potential change of vehicle.

The needle on the V2's speedometer rattles at seventy. It's as fast as the rickety little Citroën will go. The steering wheel shakes mercilessly within Peter's grip. Paranoia chases them, and he continuously glances at the mirrors, before turning anxiously back to the empty highway ahead.

Their main worry is whether their attackers are in league with the police. Whether a vague description of the car has been handed out to law enforcement and every traffic cop for the next hundred miles is looking for them. He hopes not.

Just in case, he keeps to the loneliest roads, staying away from either the West Autobahn or the Pyhrn Autobahn. It is coming up to half past three when they join a road that straggles a tributary and takes them along steep hills. It begins to corkscrew and climb over a pass.

"We're heading too far north," Chambers points out.

He sits with a road map open on his lap.

"Then get me onto another road," Peter says.

"Okay. Take the next right."

They enter a long straggling village, the place dead at this time. A few more turnings and they find themselves cruising through a broad valley.

"This should take us south a little," Chambers states. "Then once we reach—"

"Shh!" Peter snaps.

He's spotted something in the mirror.

The sun is emerging from the horizon and the world is drenched in dusk. In the lightening sky Peter can make out a shadow that is hovering about—and lo and behold there is their old friend the Reaper; flying low, about three miles to the south, moving rapidly toward them.

"Mikey," Peter calls into the back, "that UAV is behind us. Six o'clock."

Michael looks.

"God darn it," he mutters under his breath, grabbing ahold of the Tavor and tugging back the cocking arm.

While on flat, open land they are at the hunter-killer's mercy. Only by reaching the cover of nearby woods will they have any chance of escape. Peter spots a gap in the stone wall that edges the road and guesses correctly that it leads to a dirt lane—one that will take them all the way to the forest bordering the top of the field.

The V2 scrambles up the rutted dirt track, the chassis bouncing violently on its springs, tossing everyone about. Michael uses the sunroof as a shooting nest. Wedging his feet against the backseat to keep himself as steady as he can, he props the Tavor on the roof and begins firing controlled bursts at the UAV. The Reaper takes aversive maneuvers, twisting and spinning in the air.

"How many rounds you got left?" Peter cries at him.

"Not many," the kid replies.

There's another fifty in the spare magazine he snatched at the station. After that, it'll be down to the Beretta with the three bullets left that Peter robbed off the hiker at the train station.

As the Citroën reaches the trees, the Reaper rights itself and fires off a Hellfire missile. Michael sets the bullpup on full auto and lets off a stream of bullets at the approaching rocket. It explodes right as it reaches the forest canopy, lighting up the trees and making the kid wince from the heat blast.

Peter veers left and heads down nothing more than a

clearing barely big enough for the car, no sign of any path or track, the V2 smashing through vegetation. Peter is just about able to see, his eyes constantly checking the mirror for the Reaper.

Michael sees it. The UAV has gotten higher. He pulls the trigger of the Tavor. It fires twice before the bolt holds open —a feature of the Tavor when the last round has been discharged.

He slaps in the second magazine and tugs the cocking arm.

Fifty bullets left.

The forest floor descends sharply and Michael is almost thrown out of the car. Down they go like greased lightning, Peter wrestling with the steering wheel, momentum more than anything propelling the V2.

"You see it, Mikey?" he shouts.

"No. I've lost it."

"There!"

Ron Chambers is pointing through the windshield. The Reaper has come around them and is now in front. Another Hellfire shoots from its launcher and Peter twists the wheel right.

"Hold on!"

Michael almost loses the Tavor. The Citroën lurches violently sideways and then down. The gun's strap comes lose from his neck and for a moment the bullpup is flying away from him—and he just manages to grab it by the cord and reel it back in.

The missile arcs after them through the trees—hits one. For a second time the dark wood explodes in flames and light.

Michael spots the Reaper behind them. He lets off more controlled bursts and spots sparks coming off the UAV. In the trees the hunter-killer can't pull so many aversive maneuvers. It goes to climb back up, but as it shows its underside, Michael lets rip with the Tavor and penetrates the outer shell right where the receiver is. The Reaper begins tipping to the side. Michael puts the Tavor on full-auto, concentrates his fire on the same spot as the Reaper tumbles and lurches, trying desperately to get to a higher altitude.

The UAV's operator, realizing that the craft is lost, puts it into full throttle and aims it at them.

"Peter, you need to turn!" Michael shouts.

"I can't."

There is a solid row of trees on both sides.

"Peter! It's coming right for us!"

"I know," his father replies, one eye on the mirror.

"Peter, you GOTTA—!"

They're in the air. The forest rising up behind them. The Reaper hits the edge of the cliff and explodes in a burst of light and fire. The kid braces for impact and is thrown back into the car as they hit terra firma. Everyone feeling the landing in their bones.

Peter plunges a foot down on the brakes and brings the car to a clanking, smoking stop in the middle of a cow field. Then, as bits of burning debris float down from the sky, they catch their breaths.

"You good?" Peter asks his son.

Michael is lying in the footwell. Instead of speaking, he holds a thumb up.

"How about you?" Peter asks Chambers.

The journalist is completely white, his fingers pressed

into the soft upholstery of the dashboard. When Peter asks him again, he just nods.

Smoke and steam rise out of the V2's hood. Peter goes to start the engine but it's dead.

"Looks like we're walking," he says.

FIFTEEN

VIENNA, AUSTRIA - 07:34 CET

VICTOR MILONOV IS NERVOUS AS HE SITS INSIDE his hotel suite waiting for the call. He hasn't been this anxious since his early days running assassination missions for a clandestine hit squad of the SVR—Russian foreign intelligence. His leg jogs up and down and he keeps picking at a fray on the cuff of his steel gray suit jacket, a habit that only occurs on the rarest of occasions for the assassin.

After almost two decades' experience, he shouldn't be like this. But he can't help it. Because the target, or potential target, is none other than Azrael: a man responsible for the deaths of many men Victor has known personally. Men whose skill he admired.

While staring at the screen of his phone, Victor perches on the end of an unslept-in bed, hoping that when they get him the address, there's a place for a sniper's nest nearby.

Of Victor's 178 confirmed kills, the vast majority have

been long range. Only thirty-three have been up close. He doesn't want to get up close to Azrael. Especially after what the American did to Semyon Mikhailov. The Hunter.

Whatever, Victor thinks. That was him. This is you. Keep your mind on the job in hand. You have your mission. Stay alert, stay alive.

Control has no idea how Azrael and his band will be arriving in the city. In what vehicle and from where. Not even when he will be here. Where he will stay.

What they do know, however, is who he will be making contact with. So, importantly, they know where Azrael is going.

Victor is simply waiting for the contact's name and address.

The phone vibrates in his hand.

"Control?"

They have the address.

"Give it to me."

Victor memorizes it.

As well as being one of Russia's best snipers, he is also gifted with an acute memory. Not quite photographic, but good enough to recall with a one hundred percent accuracy most information that is given to him.

At the end of the call, he places the phone in his pocket, gets up from the bed and leaves the room. Making sure to grab the trumpet case from beside the door. The one with the broken-down VSS Vintorez hidden inside.

SIXTEEN

THEY STOLE A VOLKSWAGEN SEDAN FROM A NEARBY village and drove diligently for the remaining two hours.

The sky is turning pale with morning when they arrive at Vienna. The Danube sparkles in the early light and the domes of the stone buildings are catching the first rays of sun.

They enter a narrow boulevard of four-story terraces and get rid of the Volkswagen. They park it in the shadow of some scaffolding and make their way through the city on foot. They can't meet Ron Chambers' contact until tonight, so they'll have to find somewhere to hide for most of the day.

Peter knows just the place.

It is one of the more rundown areas of the city. A street known for its crime rather than its art. On an alleyway of broken lives, and buildings, they pile into a dirty little hotel that usually charges by the hour. The man behind the counter is almost dead. He sits in a chair with an oxygen mask cupping his thin, gray face. A yellowed plastic tube feeds his nostrils with air that comes from a big black bottle that stands behind him like the Grim Reaper. Every so often, he peels the mask off so he can take a drag of his cigarette.

His dirty brown eyes watch the three men as they approach the counter.

They take a room, the shriveled-up clerk coughing the whole time they fill the book out with false names. He never asks for identification, and soon they stand within the confines of a cramped room that stinks of mildew. Three single beds squeezed into it.

"I need to contact my man," Chambers says. "Let him know we're in Vienna and see where he wants to meet."

"We'll go with you."

"You look tired," the journalist says. "I can go on my own."

"No," Peter snaps.

Michael places a hand on his father's arm. "He's right," the kid says. "You do look tired. I'll go with him. You sleep. You had to drive all night."

Peter has to admit that he is deeply fatigued.

"Okay," he says. "But take the Beretta."

Michael lifts his jacket to reveal the pistol stuffed in the front of his pants. "Already thought of it."

And with that, they are gone.

Peter wastes no time in lowering himself to one of the sagging mattresses. Turning to the filthy wall, he shuts his eyes.

———

DRESSED in baseball caps and sunglasses they'd borrowed from Clara's, Michael and Ron Chambers work their way through the backstreets of Rennbahnweg; a district on the eastern side of the river. Though not exactly rundown, it isn't as quant or as nice looking as the historical center. No Hofburg or State Opera House to please the aesthete in you.

They find an internet café and Chambers takes to one of the booths. In the meantime, Michael situates himself at a booth on the end. From it, he has a good view of the rest of the place; as well as being close to a door at the back with the words Nur für Personal (Staff Only) written across it. There is no lock, and when a staff member opens it, Michael can see all the way along a short corridor to the alley that runs along the back of the building, the fire escape wide open.

"I'm done," Chambers says ten minutes later, having made contact via an encrypted email server.

They walk outside into the daylight and begin making their way back to Peter.

"When do we meet your guy?" Michael asks as they move along.

"Tonight at six in the Café Alpine, near to Rauthausplatz."

"Why so late?"

"He's out of town until then."

"And we can definitely trust him?"

"Of course we can."

Trust. It is such a funny thing. You find a man bound and gagged inside the back of a van and you think he must be an enemy of your enemies. But in the world of espionage, trust is the first casualty.

They are no farther than ten yards along the sidewalk when a car comes screeching up on them and before Michael knows what's happening two men are jumping out of it and approaching him. Michael grabs the Beretta. But as he draws it, one of the guys smashes his hand with a baton and he drops the pistol as searing pain rushes up his arm.

He wheels around to Chambers and is about to shout "run" when he spots that the journalist is just standing there watching. The men grab Michael and his gun and soon he is being bulldozed into the back of the car and driven away. Ron Chambers having gotten into the front passenger seat by his own volition.

———

THE CREAK OF A WHINING FLOORBOARD. Outside the room.

Peter's eyes snap open.

It came from the stairwell across the hall. Someone is creeping up those steps and has stopped right at the top, probably cautious of the sound they are making. It registers because everyone else in this stinking place thumps up and down that stairwell without a care in the world for who hears the warped wood straining under their feet.

Peter grabs the first thing to hand, a dusty bedside lamp, and is off the bed, his back flat to the wall beside the door, listening.

Creak. It is closer. Not far now.

Peter waits, holding his breath.

Footsteps. Rapid; thunking across the hallway.

The door crashes in. Peter pushes it back, throws all his weight into it, clamping the guy against the doorframe. He smashes the china lamp over the head that pops through, lets fire a rapid succession of fists, then tears back the door, hits the guy with a headbutt that sends him careering back into the hallway, then grabs him by the hair and yanks him back into the room, throwing him onto the floor. The guy lands on his back, and the next moment, Peter is on top of him with a shard of the lamp pressed into his chin, a little bead of blood running down it.

A Beretta M9 with a silencer screwed to its end lies close by on the floor.

Peter back-kicks the door closed and listens for signs of more people on the stairs. Silence. Then he goes to ask the guy if there's anyone else, but his eyes are flickering and he passes out before Peter gets the chance. It must be from the crunching headbutt, which has cut a gash into his right eye.

He checks the guy's pockets, finds a wallet. Opening it up he discovers various credit cards and IDs. But he's no closer to knowing who it is. Each ID holds a different name —always the same face, just a different name. The credit cards have similarly different owners.

He's a professional.

Peter gets up from the unconscious hitman, picks up the Beretta.

He ties the guy to the bed with electrical cord he pulls from the bust lamp, shoves a piece of ripped bedsheet in his mouth, leaves the room.

He moves slowly along the dimly lit hallway. Stops. Stands motionless. Listens.

A burst of laughter comes from the stairwell. Peter presses his back to the wall, gun poised. The laughing trails off as a young couple pass by going upstairs.

At the staircase he cautiously starts down until he reaches the bottom. The hallway of the first floor is almost silent.

Almost.

A sound. Scratching. Polyester rubbing against wallpaper. Someone hiding in one of the recessed doorways on the right. Without breaking the rhythm of his walk, Peter shifts the Beretta to his left hand—

An arm appears, a pistol on its end. Peter fires once. Hits the hand at the fingers and blows three of them off at the knuckle. The gun spills out onto the floor and the man lurches involuntarily into the hallway. Peter fires a second shot into the guy's thigh and he collapses.

Like a bird of prey Peter swoops down. He shoves a hand over the screaming mouth before the guy can alert anyone. After all, all three shots were silenced.

"How many more?"

He slowly removes the hand. "J-just the t-two of us," the guy whimpers.

"Are you sure?" Peter asks, the Beretta shoved into the guy's ribs.

The hitman nods.

"Who sent you?"

The guy hesitates. He's going to lie. "A man named Avery."

"Avery?"

"Uh-huh."

"Avery who?"

"That was all. The job came via the dark web."

"You don't work for anyone?"

"No. This was a private contract."

"And that's all you've got—Avery?"

He nods.

Peter gets angry. Presses the hot end of the silencer into his cheek. "You're a liar. You know exactly who you work for. Now tell me."

The man's expression darkens. With absolute solemnity, he says, "You'll have to kill me."

Peter groans. "Typical. Next question. Where's your car?"

"Outside."

And with that, Peter pistol whips the guy into unconsciousness, grabs the car keys from his pocket, the other Beretta from the floor, and leaves the building.

He spots the car immediately. After all, it is the only BMW 4 Series parked along the road of shabby vehicles. He unlocks the door with the key fob and opens it. Climbing behind the wheel, he adjusts the seat to suit a larger man, then tucks the Beretta in the door sleeve and starts the ignition.

The engine thunders into life and he sets off.

———

MICHAEL FEELS sick as the Fiat guns its way through Vienna. They are heading back to the hotel. To get Peter and the hard drive. Only keeping the kid alive in case they have to negotiate.

One man sits in the back with him. The kid's hands

hover at shoulder height where they can see them. A silenced Beretta is aimed right at him. Chambers sits in the passenger seat right in front of Michael while the other man drives.

"You should see your face," Chambers says.

"I'm guessing you're not really Ron Chambers," Michael replies.

The guy grins. "No. Ron Chambers is no more real than John Harker. You can call me Jack."

"Okay, Jack. So what is this here, then? You working for the two goons on the train or the assholes whose van we found you tied up in?"

Jack's eyes narrow at him in the rearview mirror. "You and your old man really have no idea what is on that hard drive, do you?"

Michael says nothing.

"I don't know why I'm going to bother telling this," Jack goes on, "but what the hell. All that bullshit about a group is just that: bullshit. The man you refer to as John Harker obviously didn't trust you and your old man enough to tell the truth. See, there are men who will pay billions for what you have on that hard drive. I work for a group of mercenaries who like to get themselves involved in such things."

"So you were with the guys in the van, then?"

"Yep. I was coordinating the attack, but when you and your old man jumped in and drove away, I had to think quick. Amazing what a man can do in the back of a van while he's being driven at speed. Stuff like shoving a cloth in his own mouth and zip tying his own wrists behind his back."

A smug smile reflects back at the kid from the rearview mirror.

Michael says, "You've been looking for an opportunity to get the hard drive away from us."

"Yeah. But your old man keeps it on him at all times and sleeps with one eye open. I need help."

"And the UAV?"

"That's not us. You think I'd have my own people firing missiles at me?"

"Then who is it?"

The smile is back. "Oh, kid. You have no idea what you and your old man are in possession of. What we will soon be in possession of."

Michael shakes his head. In a serious voice, he says, "No, Jack. It is you who has no idea. Whoever you've sent to kill my father is already dead."

Jack shrugs it off. "Then it doesn't matter because we have you as collateral."

"Do you?"

"Do I, what?"

"Have me."

Michael's eyes burn at the mercenary through the mirror.

"Break one of his fingers," Jack suddenly commands.

The big guy moves quick for his size. He shoots a powerful arm over Michael's shoulders, vicing his throat within the crush of his bicep, the gun jammed into the kid's side, just below the ribs.

The driver pulls the car into the curb, and no sooner have they come to a stop than he has twisted around in his seat and is leaning into the back. Then, while his pal holds Michael still, he grabs the kid's right hand, takes ahold of the forefinger, and in a rapid whip-crack movement snaps the bone.

The kid refuses to cry out.

The car is quickly moving again. The driver back facing forward. Breaking someone's fingers as natural to him as popping the cap on a bottle of beer. They swing into a side street, heading north. Michael is collapsed in the seat, pushing the pain away. Everyone else is back in their normal places.

It is then, while they speed down the narrow street, that they pass a BMW going the other way. The two cars appear to recognize each other and both screech to a stop.

"The others?" the driver asks.

"They would have called," Jack says.

Everyone is gazing out the back window at the tailgate of the BMW. While they do, Michael takes his chance. He lurches forwards. Reaches to his ankle, his left hand fumbling at the leg of his pants.

He feels it. The handle of the small paring knife he took from Clara's kitchen. The one he's taped to his ankle.

"It's him!" Jack cries out as the BMW does a hasty U-turn. "Drive!"

Right at the moment the driver puts the car into gear, the man in the back grabs ahold of Michael, pulling him back onto the seat. Michael's hand comes up—level with the attacker's chest.

The guy widens his eyes as the blade is forced right into the guy's heart. Michael's other hand, the one with the broken finger, grabs the gun as the fingers go weak and the guy arches back in the seat, dying.

At the moment Peter rushes up on them in the BMW,

Michael swings the Beretta around the seats, jams the suppressor into Jack's neck.

"Tell your guy to get his hand off the gun," Michael says coolly in his ear.

The driver has his left on the wheel. His right is dipped into his jacket and is touching his own Beretta.

Jack looks at the driver through the mirror. Nods. The hand comes away. Both hands on the wheel.

"You don't want to kill me," Jack says.

"No," Michael says watching the road. "Pull up here. On the left."

"Only I can get that thing unencrypted for you."

They drift past the parking space the kid had meant.

"Hey!" Michael shouts. "I said the space on the left. Pull over."

Instead of slowing the driver presses his foot down on the gas pedal. The road is clear ahead and soon the parked cars that line both sides are whizzing by.

"Slow down!"

The BMW is racing up behind them.

"You crazy bastard!" Michael shouts, wedging a foot in the footwell and using his free hand to put his seat belt on.

There are traffic lights ahead. The needle is up to a hundred and twenty kilometers an hour.

"You need me," Jack hisses. "You and your old man. We can split the money the Russians are offering. Work together."

"The Russians?"

The engine is screaming. The lights are red. Traffic flows from side to side across the junction. People skip along a crossing.

"No more information," Jack says. "You let us live and we work together. What do you say?"

"Stop the fucking car!" Michael cries, shoving the gun into Jack's neck.

"Without us, you have nothing. All my man here has to do is crash the car. We all lose."

"We all lose," the driver repeats with a clenched jaw.

"Fuck this!"

Michael puts a bullet through Chambers' neck and turns the gun on the driver. The guy jams on the brakes. The car lurches, sending Michael into the back of Chambers' seat, crushing the dead man into the dashboard. In the scramble, the driver gets hold of the gun, rips the Beretta out of the kid's hand, but loses it as it spills into the passenger seat footwell.

The driver dives to fetch it. Michael rips him back, grabs him by the neck, presses a thumb into his windpipe, yanks him back and up off the seat. Then he uses his right to thrust a thumb into the guy's face and gouge his left eye. As his opponent reels back, Michael releases the throat and makes a dive for the Beretta. He gets a hand around it, flips over, and from the footwell is aiming the gun at the driver.

But he doesn't pull the trigger. Because the driver has his own gun on the kid. The one from his jacket.

"A Mexican standoff," Michael says.

"It would appear so." The driver cocks the barrel. Then adds, "What's a kid like you doing in this game anyway?"

"Family business."

"Yeah. Well, now it'll be just your—"

The bullet enters the back of the driver's head, obliterates his brain, and exits through his forehead, shattering the passenger side window above Michael. The dead man then tips forward onto the kid, revealing Peter in the broken driver's window behind him.

Peter tugs open the door and drags the body out. Then he holds a hand out to his son.

"Come on," he says. "We need to get out of here."

SEVENTEEN

Victor spots the kill squad's gray VW Transporter parked on a corner of Engerthstraße. Two men sit in the front. Another two, Victor knows, are in the back.

The street is lined with five-story apartment blocks. Some restaurants and cafés line the bottom floors.

Victor walks up to the driver's window of the minivan. The man sitting there rolls his eyes and winds down the window.

"You're in a no-parking zone," Victor tells him in Russian.

"We'll move if we're asked."

"You'll draw attention. Move it now."

The guy glances down at the trumpet case dangling at the end of Victor's arm.

"You do requests?" he asks with a smirk.

His companion in the passenger seat chuckles at the joke.

"Here's a request," Victor says in a cold tone. "Move the fucking van."

"Where are we supposed to go?" the guy complains. "There is nowhere to park."

"Find somewhere. Just not here. Now move!"

Victor walks away, only mildly aware of the guy giving him the finger to his back. He'll report the fucker when he's back in Russia.

If he gets back to Russia.

Head in the game.

Control has given Victor two addresses. The café where the meeting will take place, and the address of the contact. The Russian has decided against staking the café out. During their digital reconnaissance, they spotted that the place is in a crowded part of the city well known to tourists. Any tall building within range will be locked up and heavily guarded. No. Better it should take place at the contact's apartment, and only when there is confirmation that they have the hard drive on them.

Victor looks left and right when he reaches the gate of the building site. Once he's sure no one is looking, he drops the trumpet case, flips it open, and removes the medium-sized bolt cutters. These get him through the padlock on the chain.

He skips into the site, applying his own padlock, and locks the gate back up. The construction of the seven-story block of flats was abandoned long before any doors, windows or internal walls had been put into place. Inside it is bare brick and concrete. Victor had spotted it on satellite imagery when scoping out the area.

Thankfully they finished the stairwell before the company in charge filed for bankruptcy last month. It means Victor can climb up to the third floor and set the VSS Vintorez up in one of the empty window spaces.

Reaching his desired spot, he cuts two holes in the plastic sheeting that covers the cavity: one for the scope, the other for the barrel. He then sets himself up behind the gun, and so begins the spider's wait.

———

IT'S ALREADY all over radio news. Three men found dead in a car at Melangasse. Two shot in the head. One stabbed in the heart.

Other than the guns, they took a cell phone that the driver had on him. It contains texts from a contact. A person named Gustav. He appears to be the contact that Jack/Chambers had been talking to Michael about. Apparently he hadn't lied when he'd told Michael they were meeting at six in the Café Alpine near to Rauthausplatz. After all, he'd not expected Michael to live much longer—so why bother lying to a dead man?

No. The texts confirm it, and when Gustav texts for confirmation of their appointment, Peter texts back in the style of Jack and the meeting is set.

It is now five fifty-nine p.m. and they sit in a booth of the Café Alpine, facing the door, the broken finger on Michael's left hand strapped up.

"We should be a million miles away," Peter complains as they watch the entrance.

Jazz plays on speakers. The decor is all dark wood paneling, low, arched ceilings, cozy little booths, candlelight flickering everywhere. It feels like a cave. A stench of coffee hangs in the air, but most of the patrons are now drinking wine. Peter and Michael stick with the coffee.

"The only way out of this," Michael says, "is to get to the bottom of it."

"It's what we might find at the bottom that bothers me."

A waiter approaches. When he offers them refills they decline and he leaves. All the time they watch the door.

"You think this guy is what Chambers said he is?" Michael asks.

"Only one way to find out. Ask."

Right then Peter spots a face. A small one on a large head, the man's features sunk into the pink flesh. It waddles in on top of a heavy body. But it isn't his size or odd features that mark the man out from the rest of the people entering the café. What marks him out is the nervous look he wears as he scans the interior.

"That's our guy," Peter whispers as the fat man takes a booth close by.

The man sweats profusely into a gray suit and matching Panama. When he raises a hand to call the waiter, dark patches show at his armpits.

The two assassins let him order coffee. Then, once the waiter is gone, they hurry from their seats and join him. Peter slides in opposite, while Michael squeezes in next to him. Before he can utter a word, Michael is pressing the silenced Beretta into the guy's crotch.

He goes stiff and swallows.

"You're not Jack," he observes in English.

He sounds Austrian.

"No we're not," Peter replies in a cool tone.

The fat man brings a hand up to his face and uses a finger to wipe away the sweat from the edge of his thin-lipped mouth.

"Are you friends of Jack?" he asks. Before adding, "You don't look like friends of Jack."

"How do you know Jack?"

"Is this an interrogation?"

Michael pushes the gun further into the guy's groin. "A very quick interrogation," the kid assures him. "So hurry up with your answer."

The fat man turns to the door before refacing Peter. "I do some freelance work for Jack."

"What type?"

"I work in computers. I supply certain digital tools for him and his crew that are illegal on the open market."

"And is that what you're here today for?"

"Yes."

Peter looks at Michael. "So he told the truth about that, too."

"Look," the man starts blathering, "whatever this is, I can..."

Peter interrupts. "You were going to sell him an encryption device, weren't you?"

The man exhales a sigh. "Yes. He said he needed to translate some files from their cipher format."

"That's it?"

"Yes."

"And you have the device needed?"

"Not on me."

"Where?"

"Back at my place."

"And where's that?"

"You know Leopoldstadt?"

"Yes," Peter replies. "Do you have a car?"

"It's parked in the next street."

"Then we'll take yours."

———

THE GIRL in Black and her Ducati arrive on Melangasse, pulling up about ten yards from the police cordon. A news reporter is being filmed in front of it. The car with the dead men is beyond. CIS operatives in white coveralls are all over it, like ants on a spilled Danish.

The Girl in Black has been waiting all day in Vienna for something on the scanner and now she has it. Three men found dead in an abandoned car.

The narrow residential street is cut off at both ends by cordons for about a block and a half. Parked fifty yards from the crime scene, she flips the visor of her helmet and places a small pair of field glasses to her eyes.

They're only now removing the bodies. Two paramedics carefully pull one man from the passenger seat. The Girl in Black recognizes him.

She makes a call.

"Challenge Rupert," the man on the other end says.

A few seconds to think. Then. "Reply esophagus."

"Talk to me, Girl in Black."

"Jack's dead and so are his buddies."

"It was only a matter of time. Any sign of Azrael?"

"He's long gone, but I sense he's still in the city."

"He may be trying to meet Jack's contact. Get to the bottom of the hard drive. That's my guess."

"What about the Russians?" she asks.

"I'm looking. But I've got nothing at the moment. Keep listening to the scanner. If the Russians do get anywhere near him, it'll create a lot of noise."

EIGHTEEN

They force the fat man to drive. Peter in the passenger seat. Michael in the back, right behind the driver, the suppressor of his Beretta poking into the seat in front, enough so the hacker can feel it digging into his spine.

The Austrian stares forwards out the windshield. Beads of sweat glide down his face. His heavy breathing is audible. Earlier he told them his name. It's Gustav Drecker.

As they drive in silence, both Peter and Michael can't help going over in their heads the things Jack had said in the car, the kid having divulged all of it to his father.

The mercenary had blurted out that the "Group" was a lie. John Harker spinning a yarn because he didn't trust them. That even Harker wasn't real. Or at least as real as Ron Chambers. He had also said that the Russians would pay a billion.

What would the Russians pay a billion for?

And what about the stuff concerning Anthony Eustice and the NATO meeting? Is that all lies now as well? More of

Harker's subterfuge? And if Jack/Chambers had nothing to do with the UAV, then who in the hell sent it after them? And what about the two guys at the station?

The curved front of the Hofburg rises up in the red early evening sky. The footlights have just been switched on, casting the Archduke Karl monument in eerie shadows.

They drive past the sprawling Wasserwiese park—full of strollers and dog walkers at dusk. The streets are crowded, people crossing at intersections.

"Are you going to kill me?" Drecker finally plucks up the courage to ask.

"That all depends on you," is Peter's reply. "Now keep your eyes on the road."

They reach Leopoldstadt and Drecker turns onto Kafkastraße where his flat is. New and old apartment blocks share the avenue. Old stone competes with polished glass. The character of the older flats battling against the utilitarian nature of the contemporary ones.

They come up on a neat row of five-story flats with little stunted balconies poking out of them.

"I live up there," Drecker points out.

"Which one?"

"The third floor at the end."

"Drive past real slow," Peter instructs him. "But don't stop. Not until I tell you."

Drecker passes his place at about fifteen miles an hour. Peter watches every window for an outline; someone looking out. It's no good, though. All the curtains are closed.

Across the wide street is a construction site. The brick and steel shell of a half-finished tower block. Plastic sheeting ripples over the cavities of incomplete windows and balconies.

"Drive around the block," Peter says once they've gone by. "And keep it slow."

———

VICTOR WATCHES the contact's car go by, the driver's side facing him. All he can see of the kid in the back is his legs—Michael staying as far back in his seat as humanly possible, out the way of the window. As for Azrael, Victor can see nothing except Drecker's sweating melon of a head, the hacker completely blocking the way.

There hasn't been confirmation that they've got the hard drive yet, but even if there was, Victor is highly unlikely to make the shot. Sure the VSS boasts enough caliber (nine by thirty-nine) to make it through Drecker's wide body with sufficient power to kill someone on the other side. But that doesn't take into account the change in trajectory that would occur as the bullet passed through Drecker's bone, muscle, organ tissue and fat. A man that size could alter a bullet's course by inches. That would mean losing any chance at getting the kill shot Victor knows will be required for Azrael. Because the Russian understands fully that those who fail against the assassin with the first shot don't usually live to take a second.

———

As DRECKER DRIVES them around the block Peter studies the area carefully with his hawk-eyes. He is especially concerned with the possibility of men sitting in parked vehicles or occupying upper-floor windows.

There are none.

Not in the nearby vicinity, anyway.

They park on a street adjacent to Drecker's. Peter exits the car first, ordering the fat man out next. As he does, Michael opens the back door and slips out with him, keeping the aim of the Beretta on the guy's spine, the gun and hand hidden inside the pocket of his jacket.

"Please," Drecker suddenly says, "don't kill me."

"Shut up," Peter growls. "I told you. Give us what we want and you're safe."

He maneuvers the fat man so that Drecker acts as a meat-shield for the two of them. "Keep tight behind him," he barks at the kid at one stage. "Like we did in training with the dummy."

"Yeah. Yeah," Michael groans.

"You train him?" Drecker says as he walks. "Shouldn't he still be in school?"

"Senior year. If you can believe it."

"Then why—"

"He's homeschooled," Peter snaps. "Now shut up and hand me your keys."

The house key is on the same ring as the car key. A set of stone steps rise to the recessed entrance of the apartment block. Mailboxes line the wall by the door.

"What number are you?" Peter asks.

"Seven."

Peter checks the name on box number seven. There's only a number. A small key hangs on the ring. Peter uses it to open the mailbox and pulls some letters out. Bills, junk mail. Gustav Drecker written across most of it.

Okay. So he didn't lie about his name.

Peter opens the door and stands to the side while Michael shoves Drecker through the opening.

No sooner are they in than Peter grabs him by the shoulder, pulls the hacker to the wall, and waits. From above come the sounds of voices. Peter and Michael listen carefully.

They are thankful it is nothing more than a friendly conversation between two neighbors as they enter their respective apartments on the next floor up. Ended by the sounds of closing doors.

"Go," Peter snaps.

They march up the stairs, Drecker in front. The stairwell is pretty featureless, as is the hallway landing—straight walls painted a sickly green, no alcoves or recesses for waiting assassins to hide in.

On the third floor they move to the door of apartment Number Seven. Peter opens it with the key, stands to the side. With a nod of the head he signals for Drecker to go in first. The two assassins are once again using the hacker as a shield, should there be anyone waiting inside.

There isn't. Not that there's not plenty of places to hide. The flat is an absolute tip, garbage and computer parts strewn all over the place. The acrid stench of cat urine hits them the moment the door closes them inside like an airlock. Further evidence of felines comes when they spot a litter tray filled with months old fluffy little turds.

"Can we maybe crack open a window?" Michael asks with a grimace as he raises an arm across his face.

Peter ignores him. "Where is it?" he asks Drecker.

"In the bedroom."

"You lead."

They follow him, stepping over mounds of dirty clothing that reek of damp.

"My cleaner has been ill," the Austrian says, embarrassed.

"I bet they have," Michael replies sardonically.

They reach the bedroom. It is the worst room yet. The bed is covered in computer parts and clothing. A space has been cleared one side of the mattress, enough room for Drecker to sleep.

At the end farthest from the door is a computer station with a wing-backed comfy chair in front of it. Three flatscreen monitors spread out in the center of a solid-looking desk, and several portable air coolers sit around a large stack of servers that churn away at the side of it all. Peter and Michael quickly realize this is no ordinary computer.

"So where's the thing that's going to crack the cipher?" Peter asks.

Decker points at the computer. "This is it."

"I thought you were going to supply a program to crack it. That was all."

The nervous Austrian shakes his head. "That's not how this works. I need to link the hard drive up to that." He points at the station.

"And what," Michael says, "make a copy of it? Send it to someone?" The kid's eyes cut at him.

"No. Nothing like that. But to run this decryption program you need a certain type of computer. A powerful computer. Like the one here. You access that program on any normal PC and you're gonna find yourself in prison within the next twenty four hours when they track you through your IP."

"Why?" Peter asks.

"If what I think is on that hard drive, you're going to need this computer."

"And what is it that you think is on the hard drive?"

"American intelligence files. That's why you need that." He is pointing once more at the computer. "Because CIA code changes in real time, you have to communicate with the Pentagon mainframe to break through it. Pretty sophisticated, because to crack it, you have to log into their servers. Risk getting caught when they spot your IP during the session. That's why you need an extremely powerful computer to run the type of encryption that keeps you hidden while you're rooting around the CIA servers running their decoding programs."

"How long will it take?"

"Depends. Could be an hour. Could be a minute."

"Make it quick."

Peter hands over the hard drive and the fat man plants himself down in the comfy chair, the springs wheezing as it drops several inches. Then he begins, fingers jabbing rapidly at the keyboard.

In the meantime the two assassins slip their guns into the waistbands of their pants and relax as much as they're willing to. Michael cracks a window, making sure to keep the blinds closed and his face away from the pane. They take seats on the edge of the musty-smelling bed. Sit and watch.

To fill time, Peter tries a little small talk. "So how does a guy like you end up working with a guy like Jack?"

"Before Jack went all mercenary," Drecker replies, "he was a hacker. A good one. I know him from then. Back before he started hooking up with ex-special forces guys and robbing people of their secrets."

"What does he do with the secrets?"

"Isn't it obvious? He trades them on the black market."

"He mentioned Russia in the car," Michael adds.

"Makes sense," Drecker says.

"He tell you much about what's on that thing?"

"No. Just that he'd pay me handsomely if I could—Was zum Teufel?"

"What's the matter?" Peter asks, getting up off the bed and coming behind the chair.

"It isn't CIA," Drecker says. "It's something else."

"What?"

"I don't know, but the CIA encryption program is incompatible."

"Can you get into it another way?"

"I think. I've got other programs I can run. But it'll take even longer."

"Just do it."

———

VICTOR HAD WATCHED them go in. Until now he'd been hoping that Control's intel was incorrect. That it wasn't actually Azrael and his apprentice who have the hard drive. But having watched the pair march Drecker to the front door of his apartment, the Russian now knows for sure.

Not once did Drecker leave the line of fire between Victor's rifle and the two assassins. As the Russian had gazed through the crosshairs of the Vintorez, he'd not for a single second been able to drop them on the two killers. They had used the hacker's wide body to shield them the whole time, keeping him between themselves and the construction site.

Victor had to commend his opponent. Azrael knew by instinct that if a sniper had set up in the area, he'd be here at the unfinished apartment block. Easy access, no one around to bother you, perfect view of the apartment's only entrance.

It was a shame. Because Control had been in touch right before the three of them had walked around the corner of the adjacent street. Telling him that it was confirmed: they had the hard drive on them. The kill was his.

But, like before, there was no way he'd be able to hit them with any force through the fat man.

As he scans the windows of the apartment through the scope, Victor ponders getting the kill squad to storm the building, but decides to hold back.

No, he eventually says to himself. Azrael will welcome it.

The five of them have already been over the floor plans of Drecker's apartment. Only one entrance. They'll essentially be funneled at the stairwell. A line of ducks for Azrael and his boy to shoot.

Not good.

So he'll wait. Let Azrael think all is well. Follow him if need be. Then, when he least expects it, a bullet with his name on will slam into his head and Victor will rip the hard drive from his dead fingers.

Smiling at the thought, Victor presses his comms.

"Sasha, you there?"

"Yeah," comes back in his ear.

"Stay alert. Azrael is in the fat man's apartment."

"Who else?"

"Only the kid. I don't see the mercenary."

"Maybe he's one of those three guys they found earlier in Melangasse."

"Could be. I asked Control to look into it. They haven't got back yet."

"You want us to go into the place?"

"No. I told you. It will be suicide. Hold tight. I'll let you know if I need you. Over."

"Da," Sasha grunts back despondently.

———

FOR THE NEXT hour Peter and Michael sit watching Drecker move his thick fingers at rapid speed over the keyboard, the man continuing to sweat profusely, even with all those coolers churning away beside him.

As the minutes tick by, they become bored. Michael daydreams about the young Italian woman he's been seeing lately. Her smooth, bronzed skin brings tantalizing prickles to the back of his neck. He recalls a month ago when he took her away for a week on their boat the Mother-Magda. Took her sailing around the Mediterranean. God, he wishes he was with her now. The boat and the girl.

Sitting beside him, Peter's own brain chugs away. Always the obsessive, he can't help going over recent events. He'd suspected Chambers from the start. Back at Clara's, the mercenary had asked several times to use the laptop to contact his family. Claiming that he needed to let them know he was alive. Peter had given him a categorical no each time. Telling him the reason was in case his family were being watched. The truth was he didn't want Chambers alone with the computer because he didn't trust him not to send a message to someone. By the time they reached Vienna, however, his guard had lowered through fatigue. Otherwise he would never have allowed him to make the contact himself. Would have insisted that Michael operate the computer under Chambers' supervision.

"Whoa!" Drecker gasps.

Both assassins rush up and crowd around the back of him.

Spotting the characters, Peter observes, "It's in Mandarin."

"And it's not computer files," Michael points out.

He's right. Instead of computer files it is pages and pages of scanned paper documents. Meaning that whatever they have, it is from before people routinely did everything on computer.

"I can run a translation program through it," Drecker says. "It might be a bit sketchy because it first has to make a digital copy of each scan and then try and work it from there. Some of the documents are handwritten. So that may be a problem."

"Get it done."

While Drecker goes to work, Peter and Michael flick through the pages of scanned documents. They are accompanied by pictures. Black and whites of young men. Some are Asian looking. Others European. Without understanding the words accompanying the pictures it's hard to know exactly what they're seeing, but whatever it is, it happened a long time ago.

"By the look of the clothing," Peter muses out loud to

his son, "and the grainy quality of the photos, it could be the seventies."

"Maybe."

Drecker soon finishes with the translation and the two assassins become glued to the screen. It is at this moment that the hacker gets up from the chair, ostensibly to give them room to look. But essentially for something else entirely. Their attentions occupied, he stands watching them for a moment. Then, he begins moving furtively toward a shelving unit in the corner of the room.

Peter turns sharply.

Drecker has a hand inside a rucksack that hangs on the corner of the unit. His eyes are fire, the glistening face contorted into a powerful scowl. The hand bursts out, in it a Ruger Mark IV .22, and before Peter can pull his own gun, Drecker fires. The shots come rapidly. Peter dives to his right, dragging his son with him. Michael is hit in the shoulder, filling it with ice-like pain, while another bullet skims Peter's arm. Two additional shots miss.

"Fuck you!" the fat man screams as his erratic aim follows them around the room.

Peter and Michael draw their weapons. Fire. Two hit the fat man in his oversized head. Another three burrow into his chest, at least one of them reaching his heart.

The shots knock Drecker back. He slumps against the shelving unit, the gun trickling out of his fingers, and, as he falls, he brings all the shelves with him, a waterfall of junk cascading down on top of him. A gurgling hiss and he's dead.

———

VICTOR HEARD the distinct crackle of the Ruger firing. An eye pressed to the cup of the scope, he scans the third floor of the apartment block.

No movement behind the closed curtains.

"Sasha?" he whispers into his comms.

"What's up?"

"Are you close?"

"A few blocks."

"Get your team over here. I've got gunshots in the apartment."

"They killed him?"

"I don't know."

"I told you we should have set up a camera inside the place."

"We didn't have time. Now hurry up."

Victor concentrates the crosshairs on a large rectangular window that covers the landing. There's one on every level and they give a partial view of the stairwell. It's the only way in or out.

They have to pass this window.

———

"OH GREAT!" Michael mumbles weakly as he drops onto the bed, grasping hold of his bleeding shoulder.

"You can breathe all right?" Peter asks.

Michael nods.

"Then the bullet hasn't punctured the lung and the bleeding doesn't look heavy enough for the artery."

"What about your arm?"

Peter looks at the deep gash running along his forearm.

"Flesh wound," he says dismissively.

They rip up the cleanest T-shirt they can find and secure their wounds. The little .22 slug is still burrowed in Michael's shoulder. He can feel it burning away within the flesh.

Why the hacker tried to kill them, they don't know. They were willing to let him live. Maybe it was something he saw on the files. Whatever it is, they'll soon find out. The hard drive is decrypted and translated. All they need is somewhere to read what's on it. Not here. The Ruger's not the loudest gun, but it is loud enough to alert neighbors in an apartment block.

Peter helps Michael limp quickly out of there. Doors begin opening up and down the landings. One resident steps out from his apartment and attempts to take their photo with his smartphone. Before he can, Peter has grabbed it from his hand and thrown it so hard onto the ground that it shatters into pieces.

"Mutterficker!" the guy shouts.

Peter doesn't hear him, though. Every sense except sight goes momentarily numb when he sees what's across the street: the silhouette of a man behind the plastic of a window on the construction site.

"Sniper!"

The second he pulls Michael into the man's apartment, muzzle flash lights up the unfinished tower block. The landing window explodes and the neighbor screams the second the bullet hits him in the left shoulder, slamming him to the floor like he's been hit by a car.

Inside the apartment a woman pokes her head out of a bedroom door, sees two men staggering into her home and screams, before noticing her husband lying on the ground outside their doorway, bleeding out.

Peter and Michael enter a living room with tall windows down one side. The blinds are open. Bullets punch through the glass, hitting the furniture and chasing them back into the hallway.

"There!" Peter cries out.

They throw themselves inside a bathroom and lock the door behind.

————

VICTOR WATCHES the apartment block through the VSS Vintorez's scope.

No sign in the living room.

He scans left.

No sign of them on the landing.

Tendrils of panic begin to spread out inside of him. His heart beats a little faster, his breath a little shorter.

After all, the first shots have missed. Not good.

He should have waited for them to leave by the front door. But the second he saw a glimpse of the assassin in the landing window his fear pressed him into pulling the trigger. And now Azrael knows.

"Sasha?" Victor barks into his comms. "Where the fuck are you?"

Sasha's voice comes back, vexed. "You told us to park in the closest place we could find a space. Well, that was the other side of the river. Now we're caught in traffic."

"Fuck! Time?"

"ETA five minutes."

"Make it two."

"How, Victor? The van doesn't fly."

"Gah!" the Russian sniper cries out.

The operation is going to shit and Victor knows it. Azrael knows where he is and Victor has lost visual.

Azrael knows where he is, repeats in his head.

It is then that Victor realizes he needs to move.

"Changing position," he says into his comms as he picks the VSS up.

————

THE DROP from the second-floor window into the alleyway wasn't far. They spill out of the passage, turn left onto an adjacent street. Keeping tight to the edges of the buildings and in single file, they move south, away from the construction site.

"We need a car," Michael says weakly.

"I'm on it," Peter replies, his hawk-eyes scanning their environment.

At an intersection the lights are red. Several cars queue up waiting for them to change.

Not the convertible, Peter thinks as they pass a Mazda MX with its soft top down, before spotting a silver Mercedes S-Class. The specifications of the luxury sedan come to him: 429 brake-horsepower. 0–62mph in just 4.2 seconds.

The driver doesn't lock his doors. Too bad for him. He's on speakerphone when the two men slip into his car. Michael into the back, Peter into the passenger seat.

The phone is in a holder on the dashboard. Peter cancels the call. The gray-haired, middle-aged driver goes to protest but stops the second he realizes Peter is pressing the barrel of a Beretta into his leg. All the color drains from his face.

"Drive," Peter growls in German as the lights turn green and the traffic ahead of them begins to move.

The driver swallows, then asks, "Where to?"

"Forward would be a good start."

"Then where?"

"Just—!"

Hot blood explodes in Peter's face, getting in his eyes. When he's cleared them, he finds the driver sitting there holding his neck, blood gushing through his fingers.

Peter and Michael are as low as they can get. Another bullet passes through the car and hits the driver in the shoulder through the back of the seat, throwing him forward onto the steering wheel.

The sniper has moved.

They're three hundred yards from the shooter. Another hundred and fifty till they're out of range of the VSS.

Another shot hits the back of the driver's headrest with a thud. Peter pops the dead man's seatbelt, then leans over him and opens the door. He pushes the Austrian out the car, puts the Mercedes in gear, and pushes the gas pedal down using his hand as more shots echo in the distance.

A hundred and fifty yards up the road, Peter lifts himself up and jumps into the driver's seat, pulls the door shut. Raising his eyes to the rearview mirror, he spots the sniper moving along the rooftop of the construction site. Pushing his foot down, Peter guns the S-Class out of there.

It isn't long before they have company.

Seconds after passing a side street on their left, a dark gray minivan comes flying out of it, pulls a ninety-degree skid, tires shrieking, and is soon coming up fast behind them like a lion on a gazelle.

Peter checks the men in the van through the rearview mirror. The one in the passenger seat is getting ready to lean out of his window; a Glock-18 fully automatic 9mm machine pistol in his hand. Before Peter can take this in, the side door of the van opens and out leans another man with another machine pistol.

"Keep down, Mikey!" Peter cries out as asterisks of muzzle flash spread from the barrels of the guns.

Bullets skirt up the back of the car, sounding like stones in a dryer, punching holes across the tailgate, the back windshield long gone, the kid lying across the seat covered in glass.

Peter dodges left around slow-moving traffic. The van follows them into the opposing lane. A bus heads straight for them. Peter plays chicken with it. Waits until the last second before pulling back onto the right side.

The minivan just makes it, tires screaming as it tilts to the side, the bus's horn blaring. The guy hanging out the side door is thrown onto his back, almost sliding out, his buddy grabbing him just in time.

They are fast approaching an intersection, the lights red. On the left, several blocks to the east, Peter can see the tall tower and suspension cables of the Donaustadt Bridge looming up over the buildings. He swings the Mercedes into the opposing lanes, races onto the intersection, tugs the wheel left and leans the car in a curving arc that takes them skidding sideways through a small gap in the crossing traffic. The next thing they are heading for the bridge.

The chasing VW veers across the junction like a hippo

chasing a cheetah, smashes side-on with a panel van, the men in the back thrown about mercilessly. By the time the driver manages to correct its course, they've lost considerable ground on the S-Class.

Peter doesn't take the bridge. It is too clogged with traffic. Instead, he swerves right and heads down the causeway, the van lumbering to keep up, only just spotting the Mercedes cut in front of another car and exit the road via the off-ramp.

———

"I GOT A VISUAL," the Girl in Black cries into her comms as she races down the center of the Donaustadt Bridge, cutting through the middle of the jammed traffic, handlebars almost clipping the never-ending row of wing-mirrors.

"What about the Russians?" Avenger asks.

"Them too."

The road they're on, Wehlistraße, curves around the bend of the river, heading left from her position. Only problem: the Donaustadt flows over the Wehlistraße. She needs to get off this bridge, and every second she can't, the Mercedes and the van get farther and farther away from her. The frustration burrows under her skin. She might lose them.

The Girl in Black thinks quick. She spots a gap in the two-lane traffic and swerves the Ducati to the edge of the bridge. Lifting the front wheel up onto the curb of the sidewalk, she cuts off a couple walking arm-in-arm across the bridge, almost knocking them over.

"Was für ein Idiot!" the boyfriend barks, having almost spilled his Starbucks.

The Girl in Black ignores him. She parks the Ducati, leaning it onto its stand, and jumps off. Attached to the superbike along the length of the seat fairing is a custom-made saddle bag about twenty-five inches long and narrow.

The boyfriend goes to press the matter, stepping up angrily to the Girl in Black while she removes a custom-built Bergara B14 HMR sniper rifle from the bag. It is fitted with a collapsible stock and sliding barrel to shorten its storable length from forty-three inches to twenty-two. The boyfriend watches in awe as the Girl in Black extends the weapon, the barrel clicking into position on a smooth mechanism.

It is at this point that the boyfriend decides to leave it.

A round already in the pipe, the Girl in Black leans the Bergara on the wall of the bridge, sets her eye to the scope.

Takes in a short breath.

Holds it.

———

THE BACK of the S-Class is covered in bullet holes. In front, lumbering traffic blocks their progress. Peter slams his fist on the horn to get a loitering family sedan out of the way. The decrease in speed allows the van of Russian killers to catch up.

Wehlistraße is a three-lane expressway. Peter does his best to use all three, to maintain the Mercedes as a moving target, swerving the car from left to right across the lanes like a pendulum.

But it's no good.

Fifty yards ahead the lights of an intersection are fixed on red. All three lanes are blocked by thick traffic at least four cars deep. Added to this: a concrete barrier traps them one side, and the river traps them the other.

"Mikey," Peter says, glancing up at the rearview, "we're gonna have to get out. Do the next part on foot."

His son lies across the back seat, covered in glass, barely conscious.

"I'm not sure I can do that," he mumbles weakly.

"Just stay alert, kid. Follow your training. How many times have I taken you out to Fang Island after you've been awake for days?"

Michael says nothing.

"How many?!" Peter shouts.

Michael shakes himself. "About twenty-seven, I think."

"So you know what it's like to perform while fatigued. Now grab your weapon and get ready. This is it."

Peter pulls the car off the road and onto the sloping grass bank of the Danube. Bringing the bullet-riddled Mercedes S-Class into a sideways skid, so that it is side-on to the road.

"Time to stand and fight, Mikey," Peter says, wrenching the handbrake and bringing them to a stop. "Mikey?!"

The kid snaps his eyes open. Nods. Uses every ounce of ebbing energy left in him to pull himself out of the car and take a position alongside Peter behind it. They both unscrew the suppressors from the Berettas to increase their accuracy from range. Then they wait.

"This isn't good, Peter," Michael mutters as he aims the pistol. "I can hardly see."

"Keep your focus."

The Russians get to within fifty yards of them and the pair open fire. The minivan goes into a skid, comes to a stop. The four men exit, having pulled ski masks down over their faces and replaced their machine pistols with SR-3MP nine-by-thirty-nine millimeter compact assault rifles. As well as this, they have the high ground.

The men fan out, using the static traffic as cover. When some of the people in the vehicles see the armed men moving in between them, they become animated. Many of them take their phones out to record it. Nobody, by chance, bothers to call the police.

Peter fires at a head bobbing along the top of a car, sending the owner of it into a dive. Then he loses sight of the Russian.

Like dogs on a fox they are trying to outflank them. Creeping in between the cars. Four against two.

"Mikey?!"

The kid's nodding off. Peter grabs ahold of his wounded shoulder and gives it a squeeze. That does the trick, Michael's eyes bursting open.

"Focus!" Peter snaps at him.

Gunfire comes in from the front, forcing the assassins to duck down behind the S-Class. Two of the men begin pounding them with sporadic fire while the others sneak around the edges.

Peter ignores the two in front, concentrates on the sloping bank his side, keeping real low behind the Mercedes. That's when he spots a pair of feet moving purposefully up on them through the gap underneath the car. The owner is about ten yards up the bank. Peter fires two shots. One in each ankle. The guy screams out as he drops down and Peter sends another two shots into his chest once he's on the floor.

He hears gunshots directly behind and whips around. Michael hasn't spotted the guy coming from the left. The Russian has a clear shot and is about to take it when his face is turned into an exit wound by the .308 Winchester that's just torn through it.

Peter searches the horizon. His hawk-eyes quickly pick out a figure on the bridge, about four hundred yards away.

To get the shot from that range, even with zero wind, that person has to be either an Olympic athlete or a professional of the highest order.

Another shot crackles from the bridge and Peter watches one of the men in front take a bullet through his shoulder that plants him straight on the ground. It grabs all the attention of the last Russian standing and Peter isn't going to waste the opportunity.

"Mikey," he cries out, "we're leaving."

He grabs ahold of his son and practically drags him along the bank. A set of stone steps leads up to the intersection. They come across an abandoned VW Passat with the doors flung open. For the first time Peter notices all the people shouting and screaming. Notices that they aren't the only ones sprinting from the scene. A large crowd of people having taken to their feet.

The keys are still in the ignition and the engine is running.

Michael throws himself into the back and Peter jumps in the front, shoves the car in gear and guns it out of there, sirens wailing in the background.

"Who the fuck was that?" Michael mumbles.

"I don't know," Peter says. "Maybe more mercenaries."

They pass several cops going the other way—a haze of flashing lights. Peter glances into the rearview at his son. The kid is almost out, his eyes rolling.

"Hey, Mikey?! Stay awake."

The kid shakes himself. Rubs a hand down his face.

"I'm good," he says in a scarcely audible voice. "Just... get us out of this city... before someone else... tries to... kill us..."

That's when he finally does pass out.

———

THE ENTRANCE to Drecker's apartment block is wide open. On the second floor a man in round-rimmed spectacles is performing CPR on another man who is laid out along the landing. There is a hole in one side of his chest. In the open doorway of a nearby apartment the eyes of a watching woman stream mercilessly with tears as she clenches a hand over her quivering lips.

Victor floats past them like a shadow. Not one of them notices the lithe Russian go past. As for the rest of the apartments, they're closed up, the residents cowering inside.

At Number Seven, Victor crouches before the door, opens the trumpet case, uses a lock pick he takes from inside to get in. He instantly grimaces from the overpowering stench of cat urine. There is another scent too. The odor of a fired gun.

He heads straight for the bedroom. There, he stands over the dead body of Gustav Drecker. The computer hacker sits at the base of a broken shelving unit, a Ruger .22 lying beside the outstretched fingers of a hand. The computer is wrecked. Shot in the crossfire. The servers gently smoking.

"Ty idiot," Victor grumbles at the corpse. "You were supposed to stick to the plan."

The SVR have—or at least had—been running Gustav Drecker for the past three years. He was the one who tipped them off about an American contact of his, Jack, having gotten in touch about some government files on a hard drive that he wanted decoding. The fat man hadn't known what was on them, but his Russian handler had recently put him on high alert for anything that came to him regarding a hard drive. When Jack contacted him yesterday, Drecker immediately sent an email to the SVR's Dark Web account. The plan had been for the Austrian to decrypt the hard drive, make a secret copy, and leave the rest to the Russians. But Drecker had gone beyond his remit. It wasn't the SVR who'd armed him. No. The Austrian must have sourced the Ruger himself. They certainly hadn't wanted a low-level informant to engage the likes of Azrael and his cub.

"You should have followed orders," Victor spits.

He lurches forward, boots the corpse hard in the gut, then turns and marches through the stinking apartment to the front door.

However, as he crosses the hallway, a key rattles in the lock and the door begins opening inwards. Victor doesn't have enough time to turn around and hide somewhere in the dirty flat. All he can do is stand in the middle of the hallway. Wait for the door to open.

The police officer jumps the second he sees the tall, morose-looking man standing there holding a trumpet case, looking more like an undertaker than a jazz musician.

The cop's hand scrambles for his pistol, and Victor waits patiently for him to eventually get it out.

"Hands where I can see them," the officer shouts in German once his eyes are back on the Russian.

"I'm a neighbor of Herr Drecker's," Victor says in perfect German. "I heard gunshots and came here to see if he is all right. My name is Herr Dreisler. I live in the apartment next door."

He says it in such a friendly way that the cop loosens his grip on the gun, lowers his aim. He glances over his shoulder. Probably looking for his buddy.

If the Russian had a weapon to hand, this man would already be dead.

"Have you got any identification, Herr Dreisler?" the officer asks.

Victor smiles. "Why yes, I have. It's in my case."

"I'd like to see it."

"Of course."

Victor drops the trumpet case and crouches before it. He makes sure to angle it so that it's side on to the cop—so that when he lifts the lid, it shields the guy's view of the contents.

"Have you ever fired that gun at a person, Officer?" Victor asks in a voice as calm as the ocean while simultaneously cocking the suppressed MP-443 Grach pistol inside the case.

"W-what?"

"I thought not."

Victor stands and shoots him in the head. Then twice more in the chest as he collapses. The shots are as silent as compressed air and don't alert the man's partner on the next landing down.

As Victor passes the second floor, the other cop has his back to him. He is gazing through the broken window at the end of the landing, speaking into his radio and trying to determine the ETA of the ambulance.

It is when Victor reaches the bottom floor that the woman in the doorway screams out above him and the man in the glasses announces to the cop that her husband is dead.

Victor feels nothing as he glides across the road and heads for his car three blocks away.

"Sasha?" he says into his comms.

Nothing but static comes back for a moment. Then. "This is, huh, Sasha." He sounds out of breath.

"Do you have eyes on the target?"

He can hear vague swearwords said under breath. Then. "No."

"Why not?"

"We were ambushed. We had the target cornered but he had help."

"From who?"

"A sniper. So I didn't get a close look. But whoever it is can shoot a bottle cap off a bottle from half a mile away."

"What about the others?"

"Vasily and Igor are dead. Yusuf is badly injured. I left him in the road. He probably won't make it."

"Where are you now?"

"Getting the fuck out of here."

Victor can hear sirens on the other end of the comms.

"Okay," he says. "Get yourself out of the fire. I'll contact you when I'm also clear. Victor out."

Police cars race down the street as Victor turns a corner

and heads for his car. It is parked at the other end. Not a single person notices him walk by. The Russian nothing more than a dark cloud floating over. Covering everything in shadow as he passes by.

NINETEEN

MICHAEL CAN HEAR VOICES ABOVE HIM. SHAPES
and outlines gradually come into focus. A spill of table
lamps illuminates it all. He is in a large room, in bed, a thin
single mattress on a carved wooden frame. Two people stand
at the other end of the room with their backs to him. He
recognizes Peter but doesn't straight away recognize the
woman who stands at the window with him.

"I really shouldn't have let you in last night," she is
saying. "You saw what they did to my place."

"I am sorry," Peter mumbles apologetically back.

"So you keep saying."

Michael realizes it's Clara.

"Look, I need to go," she says.

She breaks away from him and leaves the room, closing
the door quietly behind her.

When she is gone, Peter turns to Michael. Seeing him
awake, he makes his way over and seats himself in a wooden

chair next to the bed. Michael goes to sit up, but Peter places a gentle hand on his chest.

"You're hurt pretty bad," he says.

Michael turns to his right shoulder. It is heavily bandaged and there are red spots showing through.

Peter adds, "It took me almost two hours to get the bullet out and secure the wound. You lost a lot of blood. But give it a few days' rest and you should be good."

Michael goes to speak but instead coughs. Peter takes a glass of water from the sideboard and hands it to him. The kid takes a few sips and speaks.

"You brought us back here?"

"It was the only place I could think of going once I dumped Drecker's car and stole another."

"Seems a tad stupid."

"They'll never suspect that we came back."

"What if they're watching the place?"

"Why should they?"

Michael stares at him a moment. Then. "You think we can trust her?"

"Who—Clara?"

"Yes. I mean, the last time we were here we didn't exactly leave a good impression."

Peter glances off to the side. Groans. "There was nowhere else I could think of taking you. What could I do?"

"I guess. Where's Lena?"

"She's in town staying with friends. Clara said she was really shaken when she came back to the house and saw all the damage."

"Yeah. I guess seeing that would have that effect." Michael is gazing at a great big black mark that covers part of the wall and carpet close to the door. It is where someone has thrown a stun grenade into the room. "You think she might come back?" he asks when his eyes are back on his father.

Peter goes to answer when he is stopped by a knock at the door. As their gazes turn that way, it opens and Clara peeks inside.

"Peter," she says, "may I speak with you?"

It isn't really a request as she doesn't bother to wait for an answer. Just closes the door again and waits for him on the landing. When he meets her she speaks with him in a hushed whisper.

"I think," she says, "the least you can do is give me an explanation."

———

THE EXPLANATION HAPPENS DOWNSTAIRS in the kitchen. On the way, Peter surveys the damage.

Part of the ceiling in the hallway is exposed. Walls are blackened. In places, great big chunks of masonry are missing. There are bullet holes covering the walls in several of the rooms, as well as some of the furniture.

"Go on, then," Clara says as they take seats around a solid oak table. "Who are you really?"

"Until four weeks ago," Peter begins, deciding to be absolutely honest, "I was a retired hit man."

He tells the tale of himself and the kid. Leaves out the more gory parts. Leaves in the stuff that's more likely to sway her benevolence. Then he once again gives her the lowdown on the last few weeks: the tale of John Harker. About what happened after they left for Vienna. Everything up until this point in time, including what has become of her beloved Citroën V2.

Afterwards she spends a few moments thinking it over.

"You're really innocent in all this?" she says before correcting herself. "What I mean is: are you innocent in this latest stuff? All the other stuff, I guess not," she adds in parenthesis.

"I am."

"You appear to be the type of person who attracts trouble."

"My whole life."

"And you wish to stay here until Michael is well enough?"

"Yes."

She takes in a deep breath, studying him all the time with her jade colored eyes. "You know," she says, "you really shouldn't put your son through this."

"Through what?"

"Being a contract killer or whatever you are."

"I told you. I gave him a choice. He chose this life."

"And what type of father lets him choose that?"

He feels her eyes burn into him.

What type of father lets him? Peter thinks.

The type of father that would be lost without the kid at his side. The type who knew it was wrong to accept Michael's choice—or to even give him one in the first place. The type of father who couldn't let him go, knew the kid would choose the gun. A selfish man in need of human contact is the type of father who would accept his son choosing to follow him into fire.

But Peter says none of that. Instead all he can do is mutter that he doesn't know.

Clara sees the growing sadness in his eyes. Feels the loneliness in his voice. Her expression softens and her demeanor changes.

"But then how could you be anything else," she says softly. "After the life you've had, how could you be normal."

When he'd arrived in the dead of the night with a blood-soaked and unconscious Michael in the passenger seat of a strange car, the V2 nowhere to be seen, she hadn't hesitated; she'd immediately helped Peter carry the kid inside and place him upstairs. Then she had aided Peter in undressing him and dealing with the gunshot wound to his shoulder. Watched in awe as Peter had removed the bullet and sewn his own son up; his own child. Then done the same to himself —stitching up the gash on his forearm. She couldn't believe a man could do that to his own son and then himself without a single sign in his expression to say that he was under any type of stress, or that any part of it wasn't a normal day in the life of Peter Black.

Afterwards, they had been too exhausted to talk about it and had gone to bed in silence.

Waking up this morning Clara was amazed that this man, having taken her car and brought so much trouble to her house, had turned up out of the blue with more trouble, and she hadn't considered turning him away for a single second.

There has to be some reason for that, Clara gathers. Some reason she hasn't turned him in to those men, and didn't turn him away last night.

She thinks she knows what that reason may be.

Clara gets up from her chair, comes around the table and stands over him.

"Who are you?" she whispers.

His gray eyes shine up at her. "I just finished telling you who I am. Weren't you listening?"

"But that doesn't explain the look I see in your eyes, or the way I feel around you."

"You shouldn't feel like that. I'm not a good person."

Clara reaches down and takes ahold of his chin.

"I know what I see," she purrs. "What I feel."

"And what's that?"

"Good," she breathes, leaning forwards, closing her eyes. Kissing him.

TWENTY

CLARA GETS THEM A COMPUTER FROM TOWN, AND they spend a whole day going over the files on the hard drive. The translation program that Gustav Drecker ran wasn't exactly the best. The text is grammatically all over the place, impossible to read in sections. They consider running another program from the internet, but decide it is unsafe to log on from this IP address. Someone could be watching digitally.

Regardless of the poor translation, however, it is pretty obvious that the files are from Chinese intelligence. Many of them have the Ministry of State Security (MSS) stamp on them. And one thing's for sure. These are internal reports of the highest security. Only members within the top echelon of the Chinese Communist Party (CCP) would normally have access to what they're seeing. Just a shame the translation is so foggy.

John Harker obviously hadn't trusted them with the truth. And with Jack and his band of mercenaries on his tail, who could blame him. All that stuff about a "Group" was straight up bullshit. The type of conspiracy theory that helps keep the masses from the actual truth: that behind all of the war and destabilization is the usual state-sponsored crap. One nation pecking at another: elites-versus-elites, always trying to keep hold of power, or increase it their grip on it. The rest of us caught in between while they do.

Because of the poor wording, they don't get the whole thing. But the gist, they do. The latest dated files are all about one thing: the 30th of May. Last day of the NATO Summit in Rome.

Whatever is going to happen will involve Anthony Eustice, Secretary of State for the USA. That much of Harker's story is true—or at least is backed up by what they read in the files. On one they find detailed building plans of the Pratica di Mare Air Base where the summit is to be held. Other files contain all sorts about staffing, security, layout. To Peter it looks like the plans for an assassination.

Though they find no direct mention of it, they do wonder: Are the Chinese planning on assassinating the US Secretary of State at the Summit? It would be an act of war.

Nevertheless, they gather from the files that the Chinese don't intend on taking any blame for the assassination. They intend to have it blamed on something else—on a lone wolf. They find lots of stuff detailing a secret association with an American far-right white supremacist group. There's evidence of the CCP covertly financing domestic terrorists. It would appear that they've infiltrated the group with at least ten individuals who are funding their activities, along with helping it tactically.

Peter and Michael can't help thinking: why kill Eustice if

you're just going to blame it on someone else? What does it achieve pinning it on other Americans? And why not the president?

It makes no sense.

They find other building plans. A large house. Looks American from the layout. Large five bedroom in the Georgian style. There's nothing that details its location. Or if it does, the wording is unintelligible because of the program. There are schedules of people. What time they leave their house; when they exercise; where they take their coffee. It looks like surveillance notes. Surveillance of a whole family. Anthony Eustice's name all over it.

It is then, after finishing with the files on the Secretary of State, that they discover something even more interesting. Something that appears to be the crux of it all.

The file is codenamed Agent K. It contains the black and white pictures they saw at Drecker's filthy flat. Going through them, they find the earliest dated photos: 1986. Chinese men, athletic men, stand before the photographer, lined up as if on parade. They are in their underwear, their muscled torsos impressive to see. Thirty men lined up in front of a red curtain with the hammer and sickle of the Chinese Communist Party across it.

From what Peter and Michael work out, these young men have been chosen for a very special mission. They are the cream of the CCP; the cream of China. Reading the poorly translated files they learn that all thirty men possess an IQ higher than 140, have 20-20 vision, and have shown athletic prowess. They are all the sons of high-ranking officials in the CCP. They are all between five-feet-ten and six-feet-six in height.

"Wait," Peter says as they read. "That's the ideal height requirement for the US military. Between five-feet-ten and six-feet-six."

"That's interesting," the kid remarks.

They go on.

Next, the men undergo reconstruction surgery. The following photos show varying stages. The first: the men have had blepharoplasty; an eye surgery that "corrects" monolids to make Asian eyes look more European. Next comes a thinning of the nose. Then skin pigmentation surgery. Hair transplants. Until, by the end, each man looks as European as Peter and Michael.

Following this, in 1988, each of the thirty is placed within the US, and it becomes quite obvious what these men are: sleeper agents. And already in the US for over thirty years.

The rest is practically incomprehensible. Some bits stick out. Stuff about two specific agents climbing higher than the others. An Agent K and an Agent M. Other parts state that at least four of the agents have been killed or simply died while in action. Others found themselves stalling in their respective military careers. A few have gone AWOL. There are no names. No dates. No addresses. All codewords and serial numbers. Agent K, M and the rest of those thirty men lost to the wind.

"This is huge," Peter says once they've finished.

Just then the sound of the Vespa reaches their ears. Clara is back from town.

"Close that up," Peter says.

Michael collapses the laptop down.

Straight off the back of the moped, Clara comes inside

and marches upstairs. Peter exits the room as she crosses the landing. She doesn't notice him until he calls out to her. By this point she's at her bedroom door, a hand on the knob.

Clara freezes, her back to him. He is sure the skin up her spine twitches underneath her blouse. She takes in a breath, and when she turns to him, she is wearing a crooked smile.

"Are you okay?" he asks.

"Yes," she says, like she's not. I just met up with Lena is all."

"Is she okay?"

Clara goes to answer, swallows. Then. "She's fine. Just worried for me, is all. She practically begged me to kick you both out of the house. So we had a little argument about that, and, I guess, I don't like arguing with her. It reminds me of my relationship with my own parents."

"If you want us to leave," Peter tells her in all seriousness, "you only have to say."

"No. No. It's fine." She tries to put more life into the smile. Her eyes gleam. "It's all good." She leaves the door and comes to him. Placing her arms around his waist, she looks up into his eyes and adds, "I'm a big girl."

And with that, they kiss.

———

THAT NIGHT, Clara lies within Peter's arms, head on his chest, the two having made love not long ago.

She slips back from him and raises herself up on an elbow so that she can look him in the eyes. Then she lays a hand on his sweat-frosted chest, keeps it there, his heart beating through to her palm.

"You know it's only a week until the summit," she says. "What are you going to do?"

"Most likely avoid it," he says. "Me and Mikey were going to send the files to the Justice Department and be done with it. Just include a cover letter explaining about John Harker."

"What about taking it to a diplomat?"

"You mean take it to the US embassy in Vienna?"

"Yes."

"It's too risky. The Chinese could be watching. As a matter of fact, if I was them, I'd be watching the US embassies specifically."

"But you need to get it to the Americans in a way where they'll believe it all and act, right?"

"Obviously. That's why we're not even sure if the Justice Department will take it seriously. Being that it'll be all anonymous."

"So you need someone who can take it to them for you. Someone who will be believed."

"Yes. But who?"

"David Powell." She says it like it's the answer to everything.

"David Powell? Who's he?"

"He used to be the American ambassador to Austria. Afterwards, he set up a company here and stayed in the country with his Austrian wife. They live not far from here. Just outside Linz."

It gets Peter thinking. "Do you know him?"

"Not personally. But my old company used to do his accounts. Every year he'd invite us out to his place. He lives in this huge converted mill on the banks of the Danube. It looks like some old castle, and it even has a working water-wheel. A pretty wunderschön place."

"And he still has connections in the US Government?"

"Of course he does. His company connects American businesses with the European market. I'm sure if he went to them with those files, they'd listen to him."

Peter runs a hand along the stubble of his chin. "Yeah," he muses out loud, "that just might work."

TWENTY-ONE

PETER AND MICHAEL CAN'T CALL AHEAD. CAN'T make an appointment. Can't just turn up at the door. No. To do this in a way that won't see them instantly set upon by either the police or one of their enemies, they'll have to intrude on the former ambassador. Catch Powell on his own and force him to listen to them.

It is night when the assassins descend on the former mill the American lives in. Dressed all in black and wearing ski masks, they come unarmed; a definite gamble, and one they've not taken lightly.

Having reached the decision that they only want to speak with the man, they realized that if they arrive waving guns, it will probably weaken any chance they have of persuading David Powell to become their ally.

About a hundred yards up the river is an outhouse that is linked to the main building by a tunnel. The door is sealed but not impregnable. Someone has merely screwed a wood panel over the top and secured it with some long screws into the frame. It takes them less than five minutes to clear it all. Next, they check to see if it is wired to an alarm. It isn't.

The outhouse takes them into a narrow passage that smells of mouse feces and dust. It's not long. At the end, a set of wellborn wooden steps rise to a hatch in the ceiling. Back when this was used as a mill, this would have been the route the flour took to reach the boats moored along the river.

The hatch is unlocked and nothing is stored on top. They lift it, and climb out into a basement filled with dust and junk—boxes, wooden crates, some bicycles, a canoe.

There is sound above them. A soccer match playing on a television somewhere. The assassins think a goal has been scored. The crowd on the TV is going crazy. Several men begin grumbling in German. The two assassins count at least four—and suspect by their tones that it is the opposition who have just scored.

Emerging from the basement into a hallway of ornate wood paneling, Peter and Michael begin creeping toward the sound of the game, and the men, when all of a sudden a door opens ten feet away on their left and a man emerges.

Lucky for them, he isn't paying attention. His eyes are fixed to the smartphone in his hand. They duck through an open door on their right before he looks up, and enter an empty room. Soundlessly shutting themselves inside, they pray this isn't his destination.

It isn't. He is visiting the other men. They ask him where the boss is, obviously meaning Powell, and the newcomer tells them he's upstairs in his study. Then the guy takes a seat amongst the rabble, and it's five men watching the soccer instead of four.

The assassins open the door and leave the room, stalk along the hallway like shadows. The door is open on the soccer game. Peter and Michael observe all five men. They line a long leather settee, backs to the door, watching the game on a huge flat screen.

They look like security.

The kid frowns at Peter. He uses hand signals to ask why there are so many. Peter doesn't have an answer.

Both drift away from the door, hit a staircase, pass three Andy Warhol prints of Marilyn Monroe along the way. Always mindful of the men they leave in their wake.

They are deep within the bowels of the large house. At the end of a thick carpeted landing is a door that lies wide open. Across the threshold is a pleasant study. A tall window looks out onto the surrounding hills. Bookshelves teeming with leather-bound volumes line most of the walls. More books exist inside an inner chamber, the giant study divided into two by shelves. Museum cases stand against some of the walls. Inside are old coins and other artifacts. One case is filled with ancient guns, some muskets line a wall, and there are swords as well.

A fat desk occupies the end. Powell sits at it with his back to them, some open volumes at his side, his fingers working the keyboard of a desktop computer. They gather that he comes here purely for work, never entertaining. Because there are no other chairs in the room except the ergonomic one he sits on.

Michael coughs into a hand. Powell stops typing. He looks up from his work and slowly swivels around in the chair.

His face is round and shiny. A pair of thick-lensed glasses

cover his eyes, enlarging them. The top of his head is as bright and bare as a crash helmet. He reminds them both of an owl. For a full thirty seconds he doesn't move a muscle. Just stares at the intruders like he's considering if they're real or not.

Eventually, he asks, "And who do we have here?"

"It doesn't matter," Peter says. "I need to ask you some questions."

"If you wanted an interview you should have made an appointment with my assistant. I can get you his number if you'd like."

"This is deadly serious."

Powell looks Peter up and down. At the ski mask. The black clothing. The severe look in his eyes.

"I don't doubt that for a second," he says.

Something about Powell both puzzles and terrifies Peter. He is too at ease for the assassin's liking. People with five-men security teams who find their work interrupted by masked men don't react this way. It is almost like David Powell has been expecting them.

"Look," Michael says. "We're not here to hurt you. But we couldn't just stroll up to the door and ring the bell. Give us five minutes to explain things and I'm sure we'll all be on the same team by the end."

"Okay," Powell replies in a dubious tone. "You have five minutes."

Michael then explains things. Lays it all out to him. While he does, Powell watches the kid with a pair of intelligent eyes.

Except it's not just their intelligence that Peter sees.

There is something else about them. Certain memories flash back to him.

"So what you're saying," Powell says, the skin across his forehead crumpled, "is that these agents have assumed positions within the American government?"

"Yes," Michael says.

"And you think Anthony Eustice is in danger?"

"He could be. Maybe if we get a better translation of the files, we'd know for sure what's up."

Peter continues to watch Powell, an uneasy feeling growing to a crescendo inside of him. Then it explodes when Powell takes his glasses off to pinch the top of his nose. A flash of something John Harker said comes back to him. He had told them about "a man with deep-set eyes ringed in black"; a man he believed was behind it all somehow. Was this another of Harker's partial truths? Because without the glasses to hide them, Peter observes that David Powell's eyes are deep-set and the skin surrounding them is dark to the point of looking bruised.

The blood goes cold in Peter's veins.

"And this hard drive," Powell is saying, "you have it on you?"

"Not on us," Michael replies. "But we can get it."

"Tell me where and I'll have one of my men fetch it. I have a computer program that may help translate the files better."

Michael goes to answer, but Peter holds a hand up to him and he keeps quiet.

"You're one of them," Peter says.

Powell frowns at him. "One of what?"

Michael is looking at his father strangely.

"One of the agents," Peter goes on.

Peter is going over the thirty agents in his head. The shots of them after plastic surgery. This isn't K. He's sure of that. Their facial features are too different. Peter's photographic mind reels through the men in the pictures.

Which one? Which one?

And then he finds it.

"Agent M," he announces.

Thirty-five years ago he'd had hair and the rings weren't so dark. But his eyes have always been deep-set. Before and after surgery. This must be who Harker referred to as "Em" in his notes. The man he believed behind it all. Agent M.

A twitch runs up the stretched skin of David Powell's face.

"That's you, isn't it?" Peter says. "Agent M."

Powell doesn't immediately speak.

Michael looks at his father, then Powell.

"We came right to you," Peter says. "This is where that UAV came from, isn't it?"

A smile curls the lips of the man opposite. Not a nice smile. One that looks like it enjoys cruelty. Peter is aware of movement behind them. He wheels around to find two men standing there—gripping Glock-17s.

Michael looks confused. "What the—?"

It is the two men from the station. The ones who came looking for them at Clara's. The one as large as a refrigerator and the one with the gray eyeball staring out of his face like the eye of a rattlesnake.

The assassins appraise the situation.

Without the guns… maybe. The huge one is definitely Peter's. But with the Glocks and in such a tight space? No.

Both he and Michael will be dead before they've completed a single step forward.

Peter catches Michael looking at one of the glass cabinets. Especially at the WW2 bayonet inside of it.

"Easy," Peter says out the side of his mouth.

"I am. I am," Michael whispers, removing his eyes from the cabinet and refacing the armed men.

Behind them David Powell is standing up from his chair.

"Turn around," Eyeball commands.

They do as he says—the man with the gun always being the one in charge—and face Powell. He looks smug.

"The woman did well," he says. "Led you all the way to me. Did she drop me into conversation after sex like I told her to?"

And, with that, Peter knows.

"You took her daughter, didn't you?" he says. "You took Lena."

Powell is smiling. "Obviously. We've tried coming at you loud, and it got us nowhere. This time we decided to use subterfuge. We took her daughter two days ago."

It is the day Clara came back distraught.

"Then," Powell continues, "I met with her and explained exactly how she would get the girl back."

"Peter," Michael says slowly, "has Clara double-crossed us?"

"Shut up for a second, Mikey."

"It's a shame you recognized me," Powell says, "I was hoping that you'd lead me to the files John Harker stole."

"He stole them from you?"

"Yes. He found out about me somehow. Came in disguise offering his services to my company. Little did I know that he was a fake. He introduced himself to me as Jack Clemente. Said he was a PhD in global economics. But he wasn't, was he? He was just some computer hacker."

"Aren't you just a mercenary?" Peter puts to him.

Powell's eyes burn. "I'm a patriot," he snaps back. "Everything I have done, I have done for China and the Party."

The telephone on his desk begins ringing, cutting what was meant to be a longer speech on the subject of his patriotism.

"Just a second," he says, holding a finger up.

Powell answers it and immediately Peter can hear Clara's voice on the other end. She is frantic. Telling Powell that she can't find it. Obviously looking for the hard drive.

Peter is glad he hid it away from the house and didn't tell her.

"Okay, okay," Powell says to her down the phone. "It's okay. You got them to us, at least. No need to worry. We have other ways of finding out where it is."

He is staring straight at Peter when he says this, and there is a terrible cruelty in his ringed eyes.

"Now come to the house," Powell tells her. "You've done your job. It's time to collect your daughter."

At that moment Peter steps forwards and shouts:

"Clara, RUN! DON'T—!"

The big one pistol whips him in the back of the head. It's like being hit with a wrecking ball, and Peter collapses onto his knees, everything slowly fading to black.

TWENTY-TWO

PETER WAKES UP WITH A SUDDEN COUGH. IT IS SO hoarse it sends sharp pain erupting through his ribcage, cutting off his breath.

He takes a moment to get it back. Then lifts himself up from the hard, cold floor with a muffled groan he does his best to hold down.

The kid sits opposite. Everything in their cell is drenched in the incandescent glow of strip lighting. They are both naked. Their hands are secured behind their backs with handcuffs, the metal eating into their wrists. The details of a bloody nose, black eye and cut lip have been added to Michael's features since Peter last saw him, and the bandaging covering his right shoulder is dirty. There is fresh blood showing through.

"What happened to you?" Peter asks.

"Nothing out of the ordinary. At least for us. Just a little bit of everyday torture."

Peter studies his own body. Bruising and grazes cover his flank, thigh and lower back.

"They dragged me here?" he asks.

"Yeah. And not nicely, either. There were steps."

"I can still feel them," Peter says. Before adding, "They searched us pretty severely, then?"

"Yeah," the kid replies. "Even took our clothes in case we had GPS or anything stitched into the seams."

"But did they search us severely enough?"

Peter is looking earnestly at his son.

Michael shakes his head.

"Good. That's something at least."

Peter surveys his environment through a bludgeoned haze. They are locked in a damp windowless storeroom—concrete floor, brick walls, a space no larger than your average prison cell. A stench of mildew hangs in the stale air, and the only furniture is a set of half-rotten wooden shelves that line one of the walls.

"They beat you?" Peter observes.

"The big one pulled my stitches out."

Michael nods at the fresh blood coming through the bandage.

"At least they put the bandage back," Peter observes.

"Yeah. That's something. At least."

"You told them where it is?"

"No. But they'll soon be back, after they realize the place I sent them was a ruse. I bought us maybe half an hour."

"How much of it is left?"

"About five minutes. You've been out a while."

Peter rubs the back of his head. Feels the coagulated blood going stiff in his hair. His skull rings like a bell.

"Chances of escape?" he asks.

"The door's thick oak," Michael replies. "A block placed across it on the other side. There's no windows, and the walls are solid stone. Just like the ceiling and floor."

"So that's a no, then," Peter says gruffly.

"That's a no. Unless you have something which can burrow through concrete."

"I don't."

The pain in Peter's head makes him feel mildly sick. Still, it isn't as sick as the double-cross does. His instincts had been going wild since Clara had returned that day from town. He should have listened to them. But she had hit a blind spot in Peter—that is now crystal clear. Deep down he'd known something was up, but he'd pushed it away. Told himself that her behavior was nothing more than the result of general stress. No. He had hoped that it was no more than stress. Hoped that her feelings for him were genuine. In a way, they were. It had certainly made the lie easier for her. The lie that had brought them here; to this concrete store cupboard.

"Any sign of Clara?" Peter asks.

Michael groans. "Nope."

Peter raises both eyebrows at his tone. "What?"

"Why didn't she tell us Lena had been taken?"

"She was scared."

"Not scared enough that she didn't have the where-withal to trick us into coming here, though, huh?"

"They had her daughter. The first thing they would have told her would have been, 'You tell anyone, she's dead. Any sign that he knows, she's dead.' Clara's a good mother. She'd do anything to save her child."

"Well, by not coming to us, she's put Lena in the grave."

"Watch your mouth, kid."

"It's true."

"But you don't have to be so cold."

"If she'd come to us in the first place we could have helped her."

"Doesn't matter." Peter changes the subject. "You were saying something about them not searching us thoroughly enough."

Michael goes serious. Nods.

"You retrieved yours yet?"

A second nod.

"You tried it in the lock?"

A third nod.

"It works?"

A fourth.

"Good. Give me a minute to get mine. Then hopefully they'll come and take us somewhere else for the torture."

"Hopefully," Michael says dryly.

Peter maneuvers his bound hands so that he is ostensibly sitting on them. "And there," he groans, "was you... thinking... I was being... pedantic again." He breathes out this last part like a sigh of relief.

Having retrieved a metal tube about a centimeter in diameter, he uses a thumb and forefinger to unscrew the lid. Then he slips out the thin piece of metal inside. About two and a half inches long, it has several teeth on it and is perfect for picking handcuffs.

The staccato echo of approaching footsteps makes Peter quickly conceal it within his hand. Peter and Michael stand up, take positions in the middle of the room, brace themselves. There comes the grating of the old bolt being slipped back on the door. It opens and two men enter the room, come to a stop two feet from the door. Out of reach of the two assassins. It is the man with the eyeball and his refrigerator-sized friend. Both carry their Glock-17s.

The rattlesnake eye glares at Peter. He half expects a forked tongue to flick out the mouth.

Eyeball holds two pairs of overalls in the hand not holding the Glock.

"Get dressed," he says, tossing them over.

The two get into the boiler suits. The heavies then escort them through the building. As they walk barefoot along thick carpeted hallways, the aim of both Glocks remain firmly fixed on Peter and Michael's backs.

The frog-march ends under the vaulted ceilings of a library. It takes up a whole floor of the converted mill. Two stories if you consider that this entire room originally housed a whole other level. A giant semicircle window covers almost the entire left side wall. The nighttime valley spreads out beyond, the stars and the house lights twinkling away. On the right are bookshelves going all the way up to the high ceiling. Halfway up is a wrought-iron mezzanine that travels along the midsection of the colossal bookshelves. Small mahogany desks are dotted about, shining under the glow of green table lamps, and in the center of the library is a huge antique Qum silk rug depicting a sultan in his palace surrounded by various concubines.

Two aluminum bistro armchairs wait for them on the other side of the rug.

"Go take a seat," Eyeball barks at them.

They move across the library toward the chairs. The five

guys who'd been watching soccer earlier now line the way on either side of the rug. Each of them holds an AK-47. Not the weapon Peter would have chosen. Not in such close quarters.

The two of them are shoved into the chairs, their arms yanked behind them, the handcuff chains clipped to the back of the seat by a snap hook, holding them there. Peter is glad the hook is non-lockable. That it'll only take a quick maneuver of thumb and forefinger to release it.

Once they're hands are fixed behind them, the chairs are tipped back and both men are dragged to the window. They come face-to-face with the night. Somewhere in the distance is a road. Yellow and red dots, headlights and taillights, meander around distant hills, resembling fireflies.

David Powell walks into the room. Peter recognizes his overpriced cologne. Soon, the owl-like double agent is standing before them. His bald head shines under the intense lighting, and the big eyes glare at them from behind the thick bifocals. He's around five-feet-eight, the lower end of the US military scale, and gone a little to fat in his old age. It looks like these days he gets other, fitter men to do his dirty work. Like Eyeball and Fridge, whom the assassins sense are hovering behind them with their Glocks.

Powell holds a finger up. "The hard drive," he says, "isn't where your boy said it was. He lied." His eyes go even darker; as though he is drawing them further into his skull. "It'll be the last one he ever tells."

A door opens at the rear of the room. Powell flicks his lizard eyes over their shoulders. He smiles at what he sees; convincing Peter to twist around.

It is Clara.

She looks distraught. Obviously. Her blonde hair is a mess and her eyes are red.

Peter can't believe how well she had kept it together earlier on. When she'd hugged and kissed him as he and Michael had left to come here, he had felt no stiffness in her; going off to meet Powell with hopeful feelings.

She had played her part to a T.

"I just want my daughter," Clara says. "You promised me if I..."

She stops talking the second she makes eye contact with Peter as he looks at her from over his shoulder.

She swallows. Turns to the guy who's brought her here. "Where is she?"

"Come, Herr Muller," Powell says, his loud voice resonating and filling the room. "I would like you to stand beside me."

"I'd rather just get my daughter and leave," Clara replies. "Please. Where is she? Where's Lena?"

"My man will fetch her." Powell nods at one of his cohorts, who immediately begins leaving the library. "Now come," Powell adds, turning his attention back on Clara. "Come stand beside me. These men are safe where they are. They won't hurt you."

"I just want my daughter." Clara practically sobs it.

Powell goes red. He stamps his foot and screams at her. "COME HERE!"

Clara is frozen in shock. She suddenly becomes aware that the man closest to her, the one who'd delivered her to the library, is aiming a pistol right at her.

The man steps forward and the look on his face tells Clara to join Powell.

Trepidatiously, she comes before the bound men, and once she is close enough, Powell grabs her roughly by the arm, pulls her close to his side. She stands there, shaking all over, eyes on the floor. Powell's claw-like fingers trapped around her arm.

Even though this woman has double-crossed them, Peter still feels like breaking those fingers. Still feels a rush of hot blood course through him at the sight of a man physically hurting a woman. Whatever she has done, in Peter's eyes, she has done for her daughter. Her motives aren't wrong. Even if her actions have condemned them.

"You shouldn't have come, Clara," Peter tells her.

She finally looks up at him. Whimpers, "They have my daughter."

Another door opens and this time it is Michael who turns in its direction. Lena is marched in. She looks disheveled—her hair messy, clothing scruffy.

"Momma!" she announces.

They allow the girl to run to her mother, and the two embrace not far from Powell, who has let her go for now.

The whole time those deep-set eyes of his glare at Peter.

"Do you want to spare them their lives, Azrael?" he asks.

The women hear this and look sharply at Powell. Then Peter.

"Only you can do that, Agent M," Peter says.

"You're wrong," Powell retorts. "Even in that chair you can spare these women. All you have to do is tell me where those stolen files are and who you have shared them with."

"No matter what I tell you," Peter replies in a cool tone, "those women are already dead."

Looks of absolute shock erupt on the faces of Clara and Lena.

A grin wrinkles the corner of Powell's mouth. His lips part, showing his tiny little teeth. "Good point," he says.

Powell turns to Eyeball and nods.

"Take Cheng," he tells him.

Eyeball comes out from behind Peter and takes hold of Clara by the arm. Another man, Cheng, takes hold of Lena.

Clara turns to Peter. "Tell them," she begs.

"It won't matter, Clara."

"You'd let us die?"

"I'm chained to a chair and this man is never going to risk his mission by allowing you and your daughter to live."

"But we don't know anything."

"You know enough."

Clara turns to Powell. "Please. I don't know anything."

"Take them," he tells his men.

Eyeball starts dragging Clara away.

"Peter, please! Tell them!"

"You should have come to me," Peter tells her.

"Take them!" Powell snaps.

Before either woman knows what is happening, a pistol has been pressed into her ribcage and they are being marched out of the library.

While listening to Clara's diminishing wails, Peter stares into those deep eyes of David Powell—aka Agent M.

"You've killed that woman and her child, you know," Powell says. "You should never have gone back there. We didn't think you'd be so stupid. But as it goes—"

"Just get on with it," Michael interrupts.

Powell swivels his eyes the kid's way, snorts a rapid breath in through his nostrils, and turns back to Peter.

"Sure. Why not," he says. "After all, the object of all this is to find out what you've done with those files. Whether you've sent them to anyone you shouldn't have."

Something big moves behind them. It is Fridge. They can feel the air shifting around them. The giant joins his boss at the front. In one of his colossal mitts he holds a black satchel.

He unzips it.

Peter thinks he already knows what's coming.

From the satchel, the thick fingers pull two surgical masks out. He hands one to Powell, then places the other on his face. The elastic barely stretches far enough to get around the backs of his jug-handle ears. They should have gotten one made for a horse.

"Stand back," Powell tells the others in Mandarin as he places his own mask on. "You don't want to breathe any of this in."

Fridge pulls from the satchel a glass vial, followed by a metal tube no larger than a slide whistle. He pulls a rubber stopper off the vial and begins tapping white powder from it into the device via a loading hole at the top. This finished, he hands the loaded contraption to Powell.

Waving it about, Agent M says, voice muffled by the mask, "I take it you know what this is?"

"A blowgun," Peter answers.

"And you know what's in it?"

"Scopolamine."

Powell shoots a finger at him. "Give that man a prize."

"I'm trained to withstand its effects," Peter tells him.

"But is he?" Powell turns his eyes on Michael. "Scopo-lamine hydrobromide," he goes on. "Some call it the truth drug. But its results are a little up and down to say the least. Often the subject is so drugged they are incapable of real thought—no good if you want detailed information off him. Nevertheless, one thing that is for sure, is that its effects can be devastating on the human mind. It has been known to turn the subject into a complete zombie. Permanently."

Peter and Michael are glad that Eyeball and Fridge aren't behind them anymore. They are also pleased that the other men have gotten further back to avoid the possibility of breathing in the drug. Fanned out around the outer edges of the library, they aren't paying particular attention to the bound hands of the two captives.

Powell comes toward Peter, looms over him—thumb resting on the blowgun's trigger.

"I know of a man in Hong Kong," he whispers, "who used it to rape women. It's said that he would keep them for months as sex slaves. Giving them doses of scopolamine throughout. Make them do terrible things while they were out of it. I wonder if your boy would be so susceptible to this sort of behavior."

Michael and Peter aren't listening. They are too busy manipulating their picks in the keyholes of their respective handcuffs. They've done this many times in practice, timing each other and having little competitions. Michael has the quickest time, but Peter is the only one who has had to use the technique in the field.

"Last chance. Where are the files?"

Powell brings the blowgun right up to Peter's face. Mere centimeters from his nose. Peter holds his breath.

"Come on," Powell hisses. "Otherwise—"

Peter launches himself up off the chair. His hands whip out from behind him. His left grabs ahold of Powell's wrist, trapping the hand with the blowgun. With the steel cuffs wrapped around his other fist, he fires a quick one-two. The first jab smashes Powell's cheek, sending his glasses flying off his face. The second hits his paunch of a stomach, winding him.

The Fridge goes for the Glock in his underarm holster. But his fingers grabs nothing but air. He looks down sharp. The gun is gone.

"This way, dipshit."

Fridge looks sideways.

Michael is out of his own chair, holding Fridge's Glock. A handcuff dangling from his left wrist.

The kid fans around the back of him, placing the huge man between himself and the armed men on the other side of the room. Making sure to keep out of Fridge's enormous reach.

Only now are the others grabbing up their AKs.

At the same time, Peter has twisted around the back of Powell. He now holds the Chinese double agent in front like a shield. One made of meat, fat and bone. His left hand holds the hand with the blowgun. His right holds one of the handcuffs like a curved knife; the single strand poking into Powell's windpipe like a claw, the pressure already obstructing his breathing.

The men with the assault rifles line up in front of them. Peter and Michael back up to the window. Glancing over their shoulders, they spot the four-story drop straight down onto a cobblestone courtyard.

Going through the window is not an option. They can literally imagine the sharp slap they'd make.

Beyond the courtyard are the hills, and all the twinkling lights of the villages, the cars and the stars.

"Let me tell you how this is going to be," Peter says calmly. "You're going to let us out of here or these two men will die."

Even though he is winded and his swollen face aches, Powell can still manage a smile. In Mandarin, he tells his men, "Nothing is to jeopardize the mission. The Americans must die no matter what. Shoot through us if you have to."

And with that, he closes his eyes like some martyr.

The men start pulling back the cocking levers on their weapons. Peter and Michael look at each other. Cringe.

The first shot comes. But it does not come from inside the room. It comes from the hills behind them. Not from an AK, either. From a Bergara B14 HMR instead.

A pane in the huge semi-circle window shatters behind them and the bullet hits the man nearest to Peter, travels straight through his forehead and leaves in a puff of pink mist out the back of his head. The remaining four men's attention is taken by it. Right at the moment a second bullet crashes through the window and hits another of them.

It would appear a second sniper is working another part of the hill.

The room descends into chaos. The men run for cover as more bullets fly through the window.

Peter grabs the blowgun from Powell's hand and pushes him away. Michael steps out from behind Fridge and fires off three shots—one-two-three—hitting another of the men as he dives for cover. One in the hip. The second in the shoulder. The third the killer shot: through his cheek and out the side of his head.

The Fridge has had enough. Maybe Michael should have shot him first.

The colossus wheels around on him. He's quick for his size and catches Michael unawares. A huge hand snatches the kid by the gun-wrist—and squeezes. Michael gasps in pain, drops the Glock—grimaces as he awaits the inevitable cracking of bones. But before that can happen, Peter is there, ripping the face-mask off the giant, holding the blowgun right up to his face—and pressing the trigger.

A huge dose of scopolamine explodes from the gun. Hits him from barely two inches away. Fills his mouth and nasal cavity.

Fridge roars, letting go of Michael. He staggers back, trying to wipe the powder off his face, nasal cavity coated in it. Both assassins hold their breath as they move away from the white cloud floating around the giant.

In the meantime, the snipers hidden in the hills have taken out the remaining men except for Powell.

The "cuckoo" is busy hobbling toward one of the bodies, his ribs busted from Peter's earlier punch. He is about to take an AK from the limp fingers of a corpse when a rough hand grabs his shoulder and spins him around. Before he can say or do anything, a powerful squirt of the scopolamine blasts out of the blowgun. Filling Powell's nose and throat.

———

THEY DRAGGED him out of there and loaded him into a VW sedan they found on the carriageway. The keys had been in his suit jacket.

Michael drives at speed. Peter in the back with Powell. The heavily drugged man lying on his back along the seat. His eyes are rolling, jaw clenched, sweat pouring down his pale face. It looks like he's sick, like he's got a dreadful fever. Peter is over him, holding him up by the scruff of his shirt.

"Where now?" Azrael yells.

All Powell can do is hum through his teeth.

Peter slaps him hard. "WHERE?!"

Powell's rolling eyes settle like the reels coming in on a slot machine. When he focuses, he recoils—a look of terror exploding on his face. To his drugged mind, Peter looks like the devil.

"I-I told you," he shivers, his wide eyes fixed to Peter. "Günterlung Forest. It's up in the h-hills."

"There's a turnoff coming up," Michael calls into the back.

Peter lifts Powell to the window, presses his face to the pane.

"Do we turn off here?"

Powell's eyes go in and out of focus.

"WELL?!"

"No. No. It's after the n-next village."

"Günterlung?"

"Uh-huh. Have either of you got any water? I'm really thirsty. And I feel so light. I think there's something wrong with me. Would you be so kind as to take me to a hospital. I think I may be coming down with something."

"You'll get water once we find the two women your men took."

Michael calls into the back again. "I'm seeing a sign for Günterlung up ahead."

Peter shakes Powell awake. "Is this it?"

The headlights illuminate a stretch of hillside road. There is a turning that takes you upwards.

"That's it," Powell says through clenched teeth.

They turn off, find themselves racing through a pitch-black village of wooden Alpine houses with stone chimneys. Barns and other farming buildings speckle the hillsides. The road climbs higher, lifting them out of the village. It's pretty winding, too.

Coming over the peak of a hill, they enter the shadows of a vast forest. The road sinks into it, the car descending into the trees like a submarine diving into an oceanic trench.

Peter is holding Powell up to the window. "Where?" he repeats over and over.

Powell's eyelids close. Peter shakes him violently.

"There's... a turning," the agent slurs when the lids open. "On the right. Past the little... bridge."

A river runs along the bottom of the deep valley they drive through. An old stone bridge crosses it at the bottom, the water rushing by underneath. The road then begins its ascent once more, winding around to the right—and there's the turning: a dirt track leading into the tall spruce.

Michael makes the turn. The hard, uneven ground leads upwards. In the headlights he spots tire tracks.

"How far?" Peter says.

"About a mile," Powell replies.

"Mikey," Peter says into the front, "kill the headlights."

The kid flicks them off and they're drenched in darkness. Keeping it in second, they creep up the hill, their eyes searching the dark woods.

Soon they spot the outline of a sedan further along the track.

Michael stops the car and switches the engine off.

Peter has brought handcuffs with him. He pulls Powell's arms behind his back and clicks them onto his wrists. Then he grabs the Glock he got back at the mill, Michael grabbing the one he took off Fridge, and the two get out.

The sedan is abandoned. No sign of the women, or the two men who took them. That is until Peter crouches beside the car and surveys the muddy ground. There are three distinct sets of shoe prints. Two are men's—size tens and a set of nines. Then a woman's eight. The shoe more narrow than the other two. From the pattern Peter can tell it's a Converse Allstar. Clara wears Converse Allstars. Then there is a set of bare feet; making it four sets of impressions in the sodden ground. Lena had no shoes on when they brought her out in the library.

The two follow the tracks up the hill. About a hundred yards along they spot the first indication of them.

A flashlight beam bobs about inside the trees.

Peter and Michael leave the track and move tentatively into the woods, their eyes taking in everything. The torch beam stops moving and becomes fixed. Shapes move about in the light. The assassins close the distance quickly. A hundred yards becomes eighty, seventy, sixty...

There is a river nearby. A rumble of water fills their ears. It masks the sounds of someone begging. A woman. Lena.

Peter and Michael fan out. They glide silently toward the

light and the obscure shapes that move within it, each step a study in silence.

They gradually make out a single man with Lena. Clara is nowhere to be seen. The young woman is on her knees, begging, her clothing covered in dirt. The man stands over her, his back to the two encroaching assassins, a pistol gripped in one hand.

"Please, don't do this," the girl sobs in German.

The man growls something down at her that they cannot hear over the river. Two shovels lean up against a tree, and two mounds of dirt occupy the space beyond the henchman and the girl. Though they can't see the holes, they are sure that they are graves. Balanced upon one pile of dirt, and pointed directly at the scene, is the flashlight.

Like Clara, Eyeball is missing.

But not for long.

A hand bursts out from the tree to Peter's left. He wheels around with the Glock but the kick beats him to it—sending the pistol spinning out of his hand and through the air. The blow almost breaking Peter's fingers.

"Cheng!" Eyeball shouts as he comes face-to-face with Azrael, keeping his opponent between himself and Michael.

Cheng twists around. His shriveled penis hangs limply out the flies of his trousers. He shudders when he sees the men at the edge of the light.

Before he can reach his gun, Michael fires the Glock twice, hitting him in the chest with both shots. The Chinese operative tumbles backwards into one of the holes, letting out a groaning cough as he falls into the grave.

Michael is cautious. It didn't sound like a death rattle. It sounded like the type of cough you'd let out after being shot wearing Kevlar. Michael can hear him trying to get his breath back inside the pit.

MICHAEL BUSY with Cheng about twenty yards away, the now unarmed Peter is faced with Eyeball.

The Chinese operative has left his gun at the graves, having gone to relieve himself behind a tree. But that doesn't mean he isn't adequately armed. Gripped in his right hand is a Böker Magnum Spike karambit. A stylish and versatile knife, the karambit has its origins as a Filipino fighting knife that resembles a claw. Eyeball even holds it in the Filipino style: his thumb on the back of the blade, using the ball of it to index the razor-sharp edge. He also carries a Szabo Express single-edge knife in a sheath fixed to his hip.

It looks like the guy really likes his knives.

He comes at Peter.

"HELP ME!" Lena screams as she runs toward Michael, her white eyes glowing in the bright moonlight. She gets in the way. Behind her Cheng crawls out of the hole, Michael's shot compromised by the frantic girl.

By the time she is throwing herself at the kid, the Chinese operative is out of the hole and back in the game.

"Get down!" Michael shouts, shoving Lena to the ground.

He throws himself behind the nearest tree right as Cheng fires off five quick rounds. Three disappear into the woods. The other two follow Michael to the tree, smashing into the trunk of the spruce.

Breathing heavily and grasping his chest, Cheng yells, "That really hurt, kid."

Lena is on her belly in bracken, her wet, terrified eyes shining at Michael from the darkness. He stands with his back pressed to the bark. Cheng is already in cover. Ejecting the magazine of his Glock, he snaps in another.

"Michael?" Lena sobs.

"Just stay—"

Another two bullets hit the tree.

"Down," he finishes.

EYEBALL IS A MASTER OF KALI—FILIPINO knife-fighting technique. The claw-like karambit flashes from every direction at Peter, the blade performing a dance in the air. Azrael uses all his balance to skip back and away, kinking his body as the knife comes at him. Every now and then he is afforded a glimpse at the dagger hanging from his opponent's hip.

Sidestepping, Peter pushes up with his right hand and hits Eyeball in his elbow. It pushes him a fraction off balance, but it's enough. As Eyeball repositions his arms and feet to balance himself, Peter is able to reach in and snatch the Szabo Express from his waist.

Eyeball makes a last minute grab for it, but Peter is quick enough to unsnap the clasp and slip the dagger out its leather sheath before the karambit is slashing through the air at him—Peter skipping away and getting into fighter stance.

With both men now armed, things are a little more even. The space between them widens and they begin circling.

Eyeball isn't the only one who is a dab hand at Filipino

knife fighting. During his childhood on the farm Peter had been taught by a Kali master. He too rests his thumb on the back of the blade; holding the knife up at his center line; about chest height.

"Do you mind if I take my shoes off?" Peter's opponent inquires.

"Go ahead."

The night is cloudless and filled with silver moonlight. There is not a town or city within eight miles and the sky is unspoilt by light pollution. The stars spread out beyond the trees. Peter waits patiently as his opponent removes his slip-on loafers, then tugs his socks off—feels the damp earth between his toes.

Peter recalls the words of his Kali master: "When in doubt of your surface, bare feet are best." Peter's feet are already bare. They'd not supplied them with shoes to go with their overalls, and he and Michael had been in too much of a hurry to grab a pair on their way out of the mill.

Eyeball begins siding to the left and they resume circling each other within a clearing. The wet ground is relatively flat, and the universe stretches out all around them. Eyeball has got his shirt off. His solid body is like knotted whipcord wrapped around a skeleton. His karambit glints in the silver light.

He calls out: "Is it true that you and your boy just stumbled on all this? You're not working with CIA?"

Peter says nothing. He feels his muscles unite themselves, become poised and ready.

"To your death, Azrael!" Eyeball declares.

He pounces. Strikes nothing but empty air as Peter whips out of the way, maneuvers himself behind the MSS agent. Eyeball's back is momentarily exposed, but he's quick. Before Peter can reach it with a counter, he is able to twist around and away.

Peter withdraws, taking a low crouching stance. "Where's Clara?" he asks.

Eyeball simply smiles.

MICHAEL IS STILL PINNED behind the spruce. Lena has managed to crawl to another tree and is behind that—on her knees, hands clamped to both sides of her head, eyes screwed shut as the forest shoots up around her.

Cheng is trigger happy, firing off into the woods. He's also wheezing from the two he took in his Kevlar-coated chest. Sounds like a couple of cracked ribs.

Michael has already run out of ammunition. But he has an idea. When Cheng's Glock starts to click, he comes out from behind the tree, drops low, and tear-asses it at the guy.

Cheng gets the mag into the receiver. Lifts the pistol, peels from behind the tree—

Michael is there.

The kid's right takes the wrist of the hand holding the gun. His left takes the elbow of the same arm. Using all his strength he pushes the arm up, at the same time smashing Cheng with a crunching headbutt that he puts all his weight behind.

It sends the MSS agent reeling backwards. He loses his grip of the Glock. Michael grabs it, right as the Chinese lands on one of the piles of earth. The Glock now aimed at him.

Cheng lies there propped up on a mound of dirt, hands raised in submission, fear glowing in his eyes.

"You were going to rape her," Michael says with withering anger in his voice.

PETER HEARS two gunshots in the distance.

Eyeball uses the distraction to attack, rattlesnake eye bulging, his body a yellow blur in the moonlight.

Once more Peter slips away, but is too slow with the counter.

And this continues as they dance about. Each time, Eyeball missing, and each time, Peter's counterblow coming a split-second late.

The two figures in the moon circle each other: Eyeball with the karambit held forward, tipped up slightly; Peter crouched with the Szabo Express held low.

Eyeball pounces. This time he twists to the left where Peter is dodging. Azrael has no other choice but to meet the karambit with the Szabo Express. The knives clash in a swish of sparks. Then Eyeball is gone, twisting away to the right. Landing on his back foot, he springs forwards like a highly trained gymnast, coming at Peter, the karambit back on the attack, Eyeball twisting one way, then the other, a nonstop combination of moves, Peter able to pull nothing out except defense, trying to find an in and finding nothing, slowly falling under the spell of the man's supreme knife skills. Eyeball feints one way, goes the other. Peter is momentarily lost, and before he can withdraw, the end of the karambit is stabbing his knife hand.

· · ·

MICHAEL IS GUIDING Lena through the forest.

She is in shock, shaking mercilessly.

When he'd finished with Cheng, he'd attempted to go off and help Peter, but she'd begged him not to. Begged him to stay with her. He decided there and then to get her to the car.

"Where's Mom?" The girl shivers as they reach it.

She holds on to his hand with both of hers, gripping his fist so tight it is beginning to hurt, her nails digging into the skin. The kid can't help thinking that both she and her mother would have been better off if Clara had chased them out of the garden with the axe that first day they showed up with Chambers.

"Now you need to stay here," Michael says as he lowers her into the passenger seat.

She won't let go of his hand.

"You don't need to worry," he says. "You'll be perfectly..."

Michael doesn't finish the sentence. Because something in the back of the car has caught his attention.

PETER RUBS THE HAND. Blood drips from a deep slash right across the top, the whole thing aching as it holds onto the Szabo Express. His gray eyes are wide and staring. He studies Eyeball with a new wariness in the light of the moon.

"That hurt, didn't it?" Eyeball observes.

Peter says nothing.

"And you're out of breath. You should feel honored. Only one other man has lasted as long as you in a knife fight with me." His expression goes dark. "But he didn't make it for much longer."

Eyeball presses the fight. He circles quickly, changing his feet every so often, as well as changing his knife hand. A two-handed Kali fighter. A new energy has taken hold of Eyeball. He has seen the fear in his opponent.

Once again the words of his Kali master come to Peter: "When you see fear in your opponent's eyes, that's when you give him a moment. Stand back and give it time to work into him; time to turn into terror. A terrified man fights himself. Eventually he will attack out of desperation, and in this desperation will be his mistake. The one which will get him killed."

Peter tries his best to push the fear down. To hold his nerve, wait for the right opportunity, not rush the thing because he is scared his opponent is going to kill him. Keeps telling himself: the fight ends when it ends.

Eyeball leaps into the air, feinting and striking down with his right hand—except the hand is empty. The karambit has swapped to the left. Peter shifts the Szabo Express in a blunted motion, slipping his body sideways, stopping the karambit as it comes to claw his throat out.

Twisted up, his feet are all wrong. The ground comes away from him and he's falling, Eyeball coming down on top.

Peter lands on his back. The weight of the other man presses him into the mud. The Szabo Express is trapped against him, the blade stopping the karambit from reaching his neck. Peter has both hands on the dagger's handle, trying to clear his opponent's weapon away. Eyeball removes a hand from the karambit. He still has enough strength in one to keep Peter busy. After all, he's the one on top. His free hand reaches down his leg to the sheath strapped to his calf. The one holding the six-inch bayonet.

Peter spots it. How many fucking knives has he got?

Just as Eyeball grabs the bayonet, Peter uses every sinew of strength in him to flick the karambit away. But he has to drop the Szabo so he can snatch the bayonet as it comes down on his face.

He catches it between both hands right as the knife reaches his mouth, which he opens quick to avoid his lips being sliced down the middle.

An inch of the bayonet hangs inside his mouth, and the blade begins to cut his hands as Eyeball forces it slowly into him. Blood begins to dribble onto Peter's tongue, sliding down the edge of the bayonet and dripping off its end. Eyeball's onyx eye shines in the moon as he drives it gradually through Peter's hands and into his mouth, inch by inch by inch. Azrael tries biting down on the blade, the steel slowly sliding between his teeth, until it has almost reached the back of his throat, and Peter is closing his eyes, waiting for it to enter the oropharynx and carry on to his spine when two gunshots shake the air around them and the weight on top of him is dragged away, the knife pulled from his mouth.

He opens his eyes to find Michael standing over him.

Eyeball lies nearby with half his face missing. The last beats of his heart push a steady flow of blood from the cavity where his right ear used to be and then stop.

Peter sits up. Studies his bleeding hands. Looks at Michael. Asks, "What took you so long?"

"I was taking Lena back to the car."

"You could have helped me first," Peter says, sitting up in the bracken.

"I thought you had this handled," the kid replies.

"Well I didn't have it handled," Peter grumbles. "Did you find Clara?"

Michael goes solemn. Swallows. "Not exactly."

"What does that mean?"

"I'll show you."

CLARA LIES in one of the graves. Killed minutes before they got there. Two gunshots to the head, execution style. A cruel way to go. Peter can't help thinking that once again he has brought death to an innocent person's house. It is Kate all over again—and he can't help glancing sideways at the kid.

When they had first been thrown together, Michael was a fourteen-year-old nerd getting bullied by the neighborhood punk. Now he is seventeen and a killer. He has just murdered two men in cold blood and is staring down at the dead body of a women he knew personally. The look on his face scares Peter. It is completely blank. Not one sign of emotion on it. Even the hollow look that Peter would notice on Michael's face in the months after those first two in Alaska is now gone.

Is this a reflection of himself that he is seeing in the kid?

He takes his eyes off Michael and returns them to the body of Clara. She lies on her side in a crumpled heap. Her brown hair is matted with blood that looks black like oil. He can't help thinking that he has slept with this woman on five separate occasions—the last time literally hours ago. He has known her intimately. And yet, he feels only the faintest, faraway sadness. A knowledge that the world was better with her in it, a guilt that he has ended her life through mere association. But nothing that won't gradually fade as time goes on.

"She should have come to us," Michael says as they stand over the grave.

"I should have never come back. Should have taken you somewhere else when we left Vienna."

"What do we do about it?"

Michael has turned to Peter.

"Leave her here, I guess," is the only answer Azrael can think of. "Take Lena back to town. She can call the police. Direct them to the bodies."

"I'm not sure she'll be able to. I think she's in shock. She probably needs to go to hospital."

"Then we'll drop her there. Make an anonymous call to the police about all of this. Then take Powell somewhere."

Michael's eyes widen. "Ah," he says. "That reminds me."

"Reminds you of what?"

"There's something else."

"What?"

"You'll see when we get back to the car."

When they reach it, Lena sits in the passenger seat, staring out the windshield through tear-drenched eyes, her whole body shaking.

"She looks terrible," Peter observes.

Michael leads him to the back. Opens the door on the driver's side and signals for him to look inside. Peter crouches and gazes along the back seat of the car.

In his scopolamine stupor, David Powell has managed to

get himself onto his back along the seat. Once there, he has passed into unconsciousness and proceeded to vomit into his mouth. Filling his throat and choking him to death. A common problem when using the drug.

Peter shakes his head and groans. "Great. We've just lost another chance to get some answers. Find out what is going on."

"No use worrying about it now, I guess," Michael says, grabbing Powell by one of his feet. "Now grab his other foot and help me drag him out. Plus, I think he's your shoe size, so that's something."

"Yeah that's something," Peter repeats, coming beside his son and taking ahold of the dead man.

TWENTY-THREE

Peter drives in Powell's comfortable Italian loafers. The dead man's tastes are pretty expensive; the shoes handmade. He found a roll of tissue in the trunk of the VW and some duct tape in a glovebox. He used them to tape up the deep cuts running along his palms, the steering wheel sticky with the blood that runs down his fingers.

Michael sits in the back. He has robbed Cheng of his footwear, Powell's henchman a size bigger than the kid, but the difference isn't much of a problem. So long as he has something to cover his scratched-up feet.

Other than robbing the dead, they had loaded the body of Clara into the bad guys' sedan and taxied it down the hill to the road. Hopefully it won't be long before someone spots it. They left a note inside warning about the body in the trunk.

As for Powell, Eyeball and Cheng, they dragged them to the freshly dug holes and covered them with dirt. Why waste two perfectly good graves, right?

They drive with the windows down, trying to air the car, flush out the stench of Powell's vomit. Lena sits in the passenger seat. She hasn't made a single sound since they left Günterlung Forest, and she no longer asks about her mother.

Michael leans into the front. Lena is gazing out the window of her door. The kid touches her shoulder and she shudders, turns to him.

"I'm sorry about your mom," the kid says gently when their eyes meet.

"No you're not," she replies coldly before turning back to the view of the hillsides.

Michael looks at Peter, who merely gives a face.

The kid sits back. Gazes out his own window.

"Who d'you think the sniper is?" he asks Peter absently.

"I don't know."

"You think they're on our side?"

"Well so far they haven't shot at us, but that doesn't mean they're on our side. They might just be trying to eliminate everyone else so they can take us alive."

"More mercenaries?"

"Could be."

The first light of dawn is showing and the birds are in full voice when they reach the tiny town of Freistadt. Lena's friend lives in a five-story apartment building close to the center. The streets are deserted when they arrive.

They stop the car and Lena grabs ahold of the door handle. She is about to pop it when Michael asks her if she wants him to walk her to the door.

"No," she snaps sharply.

She gets out and begins walking away barefoot.

"Go with her," Peter insists.

Michael gets out of the car and catches her up. The friend's apartment building is around the corner down a short passageway. The second he reaches her at the mouth of the alley, she pulls up sharp and wheels around on him. Her face is furious.

"Did you know?" she says, eyes on fire. Her voice a harsh growl.

"Know what?"

"That this could happen. That we could be harmed if you came to stay with us. That my mother would be killed!"

Michael says nothing. He doesn't have to. The look on his face says it all.

"You've ruined my life, Michael," she says, her voice breaking, tears running down her cheeks. "My mother is in the trunk of a car because of you. I was nearly raped and murdered because of you. When your father first told us about you both, I felt sorry for you." Her lip quivers as she adds, "Momma did too."

"I am sorry, Lena."

"Shut up!" she snaps. "I felt sorry for you, because I couldn't believe that someone our age could be a cold-blooded killer. That only adults get to be that cynical of life to be able to just take it away from someone. But watching you tonight—watching you murder those men—I see nothing but death in your eyes. Just like I see in his. Your father. You are just as evil and despicable as him."

The kid breathes in. But there is nothing he can think of saying. Perhaps it is because she is right.

As she turns around and enters the passage, he tries not

to reflect on that too much. Just watches her disappear down the alley. Breathes out.

It is only then that he spots the men emerge from recessed doorways all up the street. Men in tactical uniforms with Polizei within across the shoulders. Each and every single one of them armed with a Steyr AUG bullpup. Black helmets and ski masks covering their heads and faces.

By the time Michael has whipped the Glock out he has counted at least seven of them. Each man with his weapon trained on his position. Each one with the look of a trained killer in his eyes.

"Put the gun down!" one of them shouts in English.

The kid is surrounded. The echo of boot heels rises up behind him; someone coming out through the alley.

"Put it down or we shoot!"

They are Austrian police. Special Task Force Cobra (EKO Cobra). A police antiterrorism SWAT-type unit.

"Do as they say, Mikey."

Michel turns to his left. Peter is on his knees in the middle of the street with his hands at the back of his head. One of the men presses the barrel of his Steyr AUG into Peter's left shoulder where it meets the neck.

Michael tosses the pistol into the street and the men march up on him. Shove him to his knees, zip-tie his hands behind his back.

"We fucking got you, punk," one of the Cobras says as he hauls Michael up from the ground.

The operation has been achieved seamlessly.

———

THE GIRL in Black is too late. Again.

She arrives on the scene right at the moment they are being loaded into the back of an Austrian Federal Police van.

Yesterday, having found out at the last minute that Azrael was being held at Powell's, she had pushed the Ducati to its limits to get to the location of the mill. Then, whilst performing a little reconnaissance from a nearby hillside, she and Avenger had spotted Azrael and the kid in the library through a large window. The two of them about to be given hits of scopolamine. Once again her Bergara had come in handy. As had Avenger's.

But then they had missed them. By the time she and Avenger had gotten back on their Ducatis and ridden to Powell's, there was nothing left inside but corpses. Two cars missing off the driveway and no sign of where they'd gone.

Then approximately one hour ago she'd learned through her police scanner that a high-level operation was in place in the town of Freistadt. The arrest of two American suspects wanted for murder in Italy.

Sitting on her Ducati twenty yards away from the arrest at the end of a side street, she makes a call. "Girl in Black here."

"Challenge word Francis," Avenger replies.

"Reply... heart."

"What've you got, Girl in Black?"

"We're gonna have to go with Plan B."

"So the police got to them before you, then?"

"That would be affirmative."

"Then Plan B it is. Everything is set up. I'll meet you at the tunnel."

"I look forward to it, Avenger. That is unless they change the route."

"They won't."

The call ends. She pushes the Ducati into gear with her left foot, lifts up her right, and releases the clutch, rolling away, before twisting back the throttle and setting the beast of a bike into full motion.

———

Two men pile into the rear with them, taking places on either side of the prisoners along the back seat, cutting them off from the doors. Both officers keep a hand rested on the handles of their sidearms. Ready to draw them in a second and blast holes in these assassins should they decide to move.

Another man gets into the front.

The Austrians have brought two more vans—the three vehicles making up a convoy, of which they are center. The rest of Special Task Force Cobra get into the other VW vans, and soon all three are on their way.

Peter now realizes that it had been a dumb move to let Lena use Powell's cell phone to call her friend in Freistadt. "I need to warn her," she'd said. "I can't just turn up."

It had then been an even dumber move to give her so much privacy while she made the call. Letting her make it outside on the dirt track while they waited in the car. She'd obviously done one of two things. She'd either warned her friend, or she'd called the police. Peter's money is on the first. That it is the friend who has contacted the cops. The journey from Günterlung had taken almost an hour.

Enough time to organize the smooth operation that has brought them here.

No one speaks as they drive away from Freistadt. The police haven't asked a single question—as a matter of fact, no one has even mentioned their arrest. The cops merely sit there in silence, a radio on the dashboard buzzing every so often as the three vans communicate with each other.

They enter the highway and a helicopter joins them, hovering over the top of the convoy as it travels down a two-laned band of gray that hugs the edges of hills. A mist rises up from the valley, creeping up the hills and spilling onto the road. They drive a steady fifty, the early morning traffic pretty clear ahead of them. Peter and Michael sit there thinking—nothing else to do—when they hear something on the road behind them: the roar of a motorbike engine.

It is coming up on them fast.

Peter checks the rearview mirror; scans the police van behind them, the men inside looking bored, then the foggy highway beyond, rising up as they descend it. Soon, he sees the shadow of a superbike emerging from the haze. A black-clad rider draped across it.

"Check this out," the driver says in German, his eyes also checking the rearview.

The two in the back check the wing-mirrors. They don't risk turning around. Just a quick glance and then all their attention back on the prisoners.

The Ducati slows down to match the speed of the convoy, getting to within ten yards of the rear vehicle. That's where it stays.

"Hey, Eighty-two?" the driver says into the radio.

"Come in Ten-nine," comes the fuzzy reply.

"You got eyes on the motorcycle behind you?"

"Oh yeah." The grunts of giggling men follow.

"What's he doing?"

"It's not a he. It's a chick. She's flipped her visor up and is smiling at us."

"Smiling?"

"Yeah. Damn pretty, too. Hell of a body all wrapped in tight leather."

"Get her to overtake. Give us boys a chance to take a look."

"Will do, Ten-nine."

The men in the rear vehicle begin waving her around. She duly obliges, accelerating a little over fifty and coming around the convoy.

"Oh she's moving real slow for us," the driver observes.

Every eye turns to her as she reaches the left side of their vehicle.

"That's a hell of a bike," one of the men remarks.

"Screw the bike. That's a hell of a woman. Check her out."

Indeed a woman is riding the Ducati, her long black hair flowing out the helmet, the visor up. She turns to them as she passes, giving them a coquettish smile. The men become excited.

But not Peter and Michael. No. They are the only ones who aren't taken in by it. Because they are the only ones who have seen this pretty face before.

Once she knows the two assassins have had a good look at her, the woman flips the visor down and rides off, the Ducati turning fifty into eighty into a hundred and she's gone.

"Ah, she didn't slow down for Seventy-seven!" the driver exclaims, referring to the lead van.

Peter and Michael are looking at one another. Automatically, their muscles begin to coil up as they brace themselves.

The convoy approaches a long tunnel that burrows its way through a mountainside. The chopper pulls up, talking a higher altitude so it can fan around the hillside and meet them at the other end of the underground passage.

"La Línea," Peter whispers into Michael's ear as they approach it.

The man next to him turns sharply. "What did you say?"

Peter turns slowly to the man. "La Línea," he repeats. "It's a tunnel in Colombia. Goes through the Andes mountain range, linking the cities of Calarcá and Cajamarca."

The cop is frowning.

"We went there last year on vacation," Peter explains.

"Whatever," the Austrian says.

That last part isn't true. All the stuff about La Línea being a tunnel in Colombia, yes. Just not about them going there. Michael has never been there. Only Peter has.

Eight years ago he was on a mission with the CIA to execute one of the main narcos in the country's cocaine industry. Once a month the kingpin would leave his hideout in Calarcá to visit his elderly mother in hospital in Cajamarca. He would leave with a crew of armed men in a convoy of three vehicles. As well as this, they would have air support provided by a helicopter.

Just like the Austrians now.

Having spent the last five years schooling Michael in the art of battle tactics, he has taken the kid through the ins and outs of the La Línea job. That is why both of them are glad they have their seat belts on.

The air inside of the van goes dark as they enter the tunnel. Strip lighting illuminates the road. It's almost deserted. Just a single garbage truck about two hundred yards ahead, its red taillights burning at them as they come up on it.

Concrete dividers separate the two sides of the highway. As the lead van indicates left to overtake the truck, he spots flashing yellow lights up ahead. The left lane is blocked by roadworks, so the lead vehicle cancels the signal and the convoy remains trapped behind the truck going about thirty.

Definitely La Línea, Peter thinks.

The driver picks the radio up. "Air support come in."

"This is air support. What you got, Ten-nine?"

"We're at those roadworks now."

"Then you're about halfway. How's the traffic?"

"We're stuck behind a garbage truck. It may delay us."

"Roger that, Ten-nine. See you on the other side. Over."

"Over."

They pass a bulldozer that is parked amongst the road-works. One of those huge yellow things with caterpillar tracks and a curved plow-blade on the front. Peter spots a black Ducati hidden the other side of it; catching a glimpse of it in the wing-mirror once they're past the dozer.

The garbage truck begins to slow even more. Because the tunnel is level at this point, they can't see beyond it. The men presume that the truck is reaching slow-moving traffic. Therefore, they don't question it when the dustcart slows down to a casual twenty, then ten, then finally winds to a stop.

The driver picks the radio up again. "Air support, you got any news about the Schönberg Tunnel having a jam?"

"Eh, that's a negative, Ten-nine. It should be clear."

But it isn't. They sit trapped behind the garbage truck.

None of the cops really notices the sound of the bull-dozer rubble and cough into life about fifty yards behind them. Peter and Michael do. They look at each other with trepidatious expressions. Their hands bound behind their backs, they grab on to the little leather straps that poke out from the seating and go as loose as they can. No good being rigid when this happens.

The sound of the bulldozer gets louder, and when Peter and Michael check the rearview mirror, they spot it at full throttle coming at the convoy, a huge pall of dark smoke pouring out its exhaust.

The cops notice it now. They start off by merely watching it through the mirrors.

"I thought the roadworks were closed today?" one of the men in the back asks the driver.

"They're supposed to be," the driver replies, gazing into the rearview.

The bulldozer is moving on its treads at full pelt. About twenty miles per hour. The huge blade at the front is lifted high enough that they can't see who's driving it.

"You think he can see us?" one of the men says.

Then the radio kicks in. "Hey. This is Eighty-two. You see this dumbass steaming up behind us?"

"I do. Get out and see what's up. Maybe he can't see us."

The driver of the rear vehicle gets out and starts waving his arms at the dozer, shouting at it. But whoever's in the driving seat doesn't seem to notice. The huge, rust-covered blade is coming right for them. The chugging sound of the bulldozer reverberating in the tunnel. The sound growing to a roar.

"HEY!" The arms are waving frantically. Then he dives out of the way.

There is an explosion of crashing metal as the bulldozer slams straight into the rear vehicle, ramming it into them, everyone thrown forwards out of their seats. Peter and Michael hang on to the leather straps. Their vehicle is sent into the car in front, which piles into the immovable garbage truck. The three vehicles of the convoy now pressed tightly into each other.

There is a second or two of nothing. Just the men groaning from the impact. Then the engine of the bulldozer roars and the caterpillar tracks begin turning again, grinding the hulking contraption forwards so that its blade acts like one wall of a crusher—the garbage truck acting as the other. Metal creaks and whines. The men try to escape, but it is too late, the doors are too buckled and won't open. They are trapped.

It isn't long before the convoy has almost halved in length. The seating begins to move and writhe beneath them, the men forced upwards into the roof. They begin to panic, cry out. The drivers honk their horns. Try to get the garbage truck to move.

Peter and Michael know it won't. They know that it is filled with bricks, or something just as heavy, so that it can't be moved.

The bulldozer keeps coming, pushing the three vehicles together, gradually crushing them into each other. The three VW vans are being squashed like the bellows of a concertina.

They creak, snap and pop as bolts and welds break apart. The windows spider, shatter, burst, showering the men in glass.

Peter glances left and spots the cop outside; the one who'd gotten out of the rear vehicle to wave the bulldozer down. He's on his knees in the road, feeling his neck where someone has shot him with a tranquilizer dart. Another two darts fly from somewhere unseen, and the cop keels over.

Inside the vehicles it becomes intolerable. The shrinking bodywork mashes them together within their slowly collapsing compartments, the men now screaming out, and right when they think it will never end, the bull-dozer comes to a stop; everyone tightly compressed, like the Black Hole of Calcutta, or an insane version of Twister.

The men groan, call each other's name. Trapped in the middle, Peter and Michael are relatively lucky. The gap between the front seats has aided them. They are now more or less stationed above the gearbox. To Peter's left is the driver. He sits half on his seat and half in the footwell, his head trapped against the steering wheel. He is trying to reach the remains of the radio, a hand outstretched toward it. He is almost there when all the lights go out inside the tunnel and everything is thrown into pitch black. It is like being struck suddenly blind.

The men begin breathing heavily. Peter and Michael can feel their warm breaths filling the pockets of air. The man next to Peter is trying to release his pistol from its holster. Peter can feel his fingers working away at the clasp because they are pressed right into Peter's left hip.

Peter senses movement outside the crush of vehicles.

People on the road. More than likely whoever shot the tran-quilizer dart.

There is a short, sharp hiss and the man next to Peter leaves the holster alone and reaches up to his neck; someone has fired a dart into the car. Several more sharp hisses and all the cops begin losing consciousness. As for the men in the other vans, they merely struggle with the crush and the blindness.

"Cover your eyes," a man's voice says from above.

The sound of a battery-powered angle grinder screams out and sparks illuminate the black air outside. The rotating blade begins slicing through the metal roof of the van, coming around them in a U.

The grinder goes out. Gloved fingers come through the gap and the roof is folded back on itself to create a hole.

A man fills it. He is dressed in black leather and wearing a pair of night-vision goggles. He reaches his gloved hands down and, sensing them in the dark, Azrael leans back from them.

"I need to pull you and your boy out of this thing," the man says. "Now come on."

Peter recognizes his voice.

"Knight?"

"It is. But there isn't much time. You need to trust me."

Peter lets him grab his shoulders and pushes up with his legs. The man on top hauls him from the van, before cutting him free of his zip-ties. The pair of them then pull Michael out.

Having cut the kid loose, they jump down from the van and Knight leads them across the road to the concrete barrier that separates the northbound and southbound lanes of the highway. They climb over and find the Girl in Black waiting for them on her Ducati. There is a second Ducati that Knight gets on.

"Your boy can go with her," Knight tells Peter as he removes the night-vision goggles and puts a helmet on. "You ride with me."

There are two spare helmets. The Girl in Black tosses one to Michael. Knight tosses the other to Peter. They put them on, get on the backs of the bikes, and in just over one minute, Peter and Michael are free, the Ducatis carrying them away from the scene like black steeds, heading in the opposite direction to the chopper that waits for them at the other end of the tunnel.

TWENTY-FOUR

THEY RODE AWAY FROM SCHÖNBERG LIKE BOLTS OF black lightning. The Ducatis twisting and turning like raindrops down a pane of glass. They sped along mountain roads, meandering their way across the Austrian countryside. At times they heard the racket of distant sirens, but the police were never close enough to become a concern. Not even the chopper made an appearance, and within an hour they were home free.

That's when they collected Harker's hard drive from the little stone bridge they'd hidden it in. Tightly wrapped in plastic and stuffed into a cavity left from where a brick had fallen out.

Knight's hideout is up in the hills about eight kilometers outside Salzburg. A wood cabin with the shutters drawn over the windows and an overgrown yard where the grass reaches up to their waists. It looks like it was once somebody's holiday home. But that was a long time ago.

Woodland surrounds it on all sides, hiding it from the

rest of the hillside, and the midday sun shines through the trees in blades of light.

"I bought this place years ago just in case," Ben Knight tells them as they follow him to the front door.

"In case of what?" Michael asks.

Knight turns to him as he fiddles with the door's padlock.

"This, I guess," he says, before turning back to the lock.

The four of them enter the shadowy realms of the one-story cabin. The ceiling is bare rafters and there are only two rooms; a main one, and a bathroom with latrine and stand-up shower. There's a kitchenette in the main room with a sink and a gas stove.

The Girl in Black finally removes her helmet and shakes out her long black hair.

"Ibliss," Peter says.

"It's supposed to be Girl in Black these days," comes her pithy reply.

Ibliss and Azrael go way back.

Like Peter, she grew up on the farm in Alaska. Raised by Mother and Magda. Raised to be a killer just like him. An asset with no tangible connection to America. Sent out into the world to wreak its vengeance. A Fallen Angel. And, just like Peter, she was hunted when the program fell. Hunted by the same people who took her as a child and groomed her into an assassin. Before discarding her like a husk.

"There's clothing in those drawers," Knight says, pointing to a bureau. "You can both change in there." He points to the bathroom.

Peter and Michael find adequate clothing. Lucky for them Knight is roughly their size. They swap the expensive loafers they took off Powell and Cheng for more durable footwear; Michael a pair of running shoes, Peter a pair of lightweight hiking boots.

Once they're changed, the four of them take seats along a breakfast bar that divides the kitchenette from the rest of the room. Peter and Michael are one side. Ben Knight and Ibliss, the other.

"So how did the two of you end up together?" Peter asks Ibliss. "I mean, I thought you were out."

Ibliss looks sideways at Knight.

"Tell them," he says, getting up from his stool. "Just let me leave first. I'll go for a smoke."

Knight walks out of the cabin. In the long grass, he lights up, before pacing back and forth along the veranda of the cabin.

The kid leans forward and in a low voice says, "So I take it he didn't kill his family."

"No, he didn't," Ibliss says. "But that's not to say they weren't killed."

Ibliss explains things from the start. Back during the fall —when the program had been shut down and she became hunted—back then Ben Knight had been her handler. It had been him who'd tipped her off about the Russians being given her location. She owed her life and subsequent family to this man. When he called her a month ago asking her to help protect his family, she had decided to repay the debt.

She'd never gotten the chance.

Ibliss arrived an hour after the men who attacked Knight's vacation home. By the time she was sneaking up on the place, everyone was down in the basement. They had already shot his wife and suffocated his daughter in front of him with a plastic bag.

"Can you imagine," Ibliss says, "having to watch the life drain out of your own daughter? All the time while they ask you where the files are. Tell you—so she can hear it—that they'll let her go if you tell them. But you know the truth. You know that's not how it will go down. That the second you tell them where they are and they locate them, she's dead anyway. And you know, too, that if you give them false intel, they'll kill her in an instant. That those men have people in the exact vicinity that John is in. That they will find out the truth within minutes. All you can do is hope that someone comes. That something happens. But no one comes and she dies thinking the worst of you."

"He was waiting for you," Peter observes.

"Yes. But I was too late. They'd already killed his daughter and moved onto torturing Knight himself when I arrived. I managed to kill the rest of the team and get him out of there."

She tells them that the Chinese had a cleanup crew located nearby. It was they who removed the bodies of their own men and staged the crime scene so that it looked, on forensic evidence, like Knight had done it. They used his own gun to kill his wife. Got his DNA on the bag that suffocated his daughter.

"Since then, we've been trying to reach you," Ibliss continues. "But the second we got into Europe we've had trouble. It was why we couldn't fetch John straight away."

"John Harker?"

"Yes. It was Knight who sent him to you."

"So Harker was with you?"

"Yes. The whole journalism, hacker thing was a cover story. John Harker's real name is John Jackson. He's a CIA operative with expertise in computer systems. Namely hacking into them."

"Then why didn't he just come out and tell me?"

The front door opens and Knight reappears. "Because," he says, having overheard this last part outside, "you would have run a mile if he'd come to you as CIA. I couldn't risk you either murdering John or leaving him out in the cold. So we created a cover story to get him into your protection until myself and Ibliss could fetch him."

Knight steps into the cabin, shutting the door behind him. Peter notes that his eyes are red. He looks like he's lost at least twenty pounds since he last saw him. His face is almost gray, and the skin is loose and worn out. Sleep must not be coming easily for Ben Knight.

"So you're onto John," Knight says, taking his former stool amongst them. Facing Peter and Michael, he adds, "I'm sorry I had to keep you both out of the loop. I made a call. I couldn't risk you being scared off by any mention of CIA."

"You're probably right," Peter says. "It's highly likely it would have had us out of Sorrento that night. We would have been off to any number of our safe houses, and your man John would have been hanging around Italy on his own."

"So it was a good call to lie, then?"

"I'd say that's correct."

Knight allows himself the faintest of grins.

"Anyway," he goes on, "back to business. I guess I should explain how I became involved in all this."

"It'd be a start."

Knight looks sideways at Ibliss. She immediately rolls her eyes and gets up from her stool.

"I'll make the coffee," she says as she strolls to the kitchenette behind them.

Peter and Michael lean in, bring their ears closer to Knight, the odor of cigarettes on his breath.

"I'm gonna take you right back to the beginning," he tells them. "I first heard about the Cuckoo Program in 1998 while I was still training at Camp Peary. It was actually on the syllabus, but not in its current form."

"I don't get it," Peter says. "They taught it in the CIA?"

"Not exactly. It was a study piece. You see, in 1962 a CIA double agent discovered a Soviet plot. Well, perhaps not exactly a plot. Not fully formed yet. But an idea that had been rattling around KGB think-tanks since the early 1950s. The Soviets were looking for a way of infiltrating Western governments, as well as their military and power structures."

"You mean placing their own people in there?"

"Yes. See, there's a lot of danger with trying to get people already inside governments to turn on their country. You usually have to catch them in a compromising act—get a piece of kompromat—or pay them high fees. Often double agents take the easy money while doing nothing for your own interests. Believe me, during my career I've seen millions of taxpayer dollars wasted on double agents double-crossing us. Feeding us useless intel while taking our money."

"So the Soviets were looking at trying to place their own people into the system from early ages, then?"

"Yes. I mean, what if you had an agent in a hostile foreign government who has been working in your interests ever since the very beginning of their career?"

"You'd have full access to that government."

"Exactly. The Soviets believed in it enough to go so far as to plan the whole thing out. Consult with the handlers of female double agents inside the US about how willing they would be to become surrogate mothers. I mean, it's not easy to have a child, raise them till they're eighteen, then hand them over to the Chinese never to see each other again. And not just that. Then to be given another son; an agent—a cuckoo. Someone you must retain relations with in order to keep the ruse going."

Michael steps in. "Correct me if I'm wrong. But those files were Chinese. Not Russian."

"That's right," Knight says. "The Soviets realized early on that such a project would take a colossal amount of work. They'd need to spend years searching for the right candidates to perform the surrogacy. Most of the female spies they had in the US weren't suitable. And to make a woman have a child only to give it away after forming a bond was seen as too much of a psychological shock to the system. The woman would need to receive training. The selection process for the surrogates alone would take years."

"But it looks like the Chinese managed it," Peter remarks.

"Somewhat," Knight says. "Of the thirty surrogates, I know of at least ten who've ended up in asylums, substance abuse, or committed suicide. Only the really tough ones survived it."

"What about training thirty men from childhood?"

"Well, the Soviets went even further with this part. They brought in their best psychologists. Had them set up experiments that took more than a decade to complete. Looking into how strong a man's ideological formation is when he's eighteen years old. If it could be strong enough to resist Western temptations. Resist having their communist ideology washed away by capitalist individualism. Then, could a person continue on with a mission for the entirety of their adult life? To live a complete sham existence only for the good of people you'll probably never even get to meet. For a country that you will never be allowed to return to. One that will never acknowledge your existence, let alone your sacrifice."

"Like the Fallen Program, then," Peter says.

He is looking up at Ibliss. She has turned from the coffees and is looking right back at him.

"Yeah," Knight says when Peter refaces him. "It's very much like the Fallen Program. Look, I've already said my piece to Ibliss, so I guess I'll say it to you. I didn't agree with any of what Smith and the others did. Many of us at the agency didn't. It was the type of thing we rebuke our enemies for. It shook my belief in my own country. But," his eyes brighten, "I do still trust in the innate goodness of the USA."

"Even after you got shafted from the agency?" Peter puts to him.

"That was the Chinese. The MSS had their hacker unit plant evidence on all my computers. They even managed to plant sums of money in a checking account I haven't used since before I was married. Made it look like I was selling secrets."

"But you're not, right?" Michael asks in a sly tone.

Knight turns to the kid. "No," he says dryly, before turning back to Peter. "It was bullshit and the CIA knew it. I was going to be cleared after an investigation, but they wanted me out of the way for the big NATO meet."

"That why they come after you?"

"No. They came for me after John stole those files from David Powell."

Ibliss brings the coffees and they share them out.

Knight continues telling them about the Cuckoo Program. "In the end, after fifteen years of messing around with the idea, the Soviets canned it. Said it would take too long and too high an effort for no guaranteed return. The class I was taking at Peary was designed to show us how far a foreign government could go to destabilize the United States. Essentially, the guy running the class debunked the whole thing—said it would never get any further than hypotheses. I mean, a mission that takes over half a century is absurd."

"But not for the Chinese," Peter interjects.

"No. They appear to have taken the Soviet idea and run with it. Operation Bùgǔ Niǎo was born. It was given the go-ahead by Mao Zedong himself in the last years of the dictator's life. That paperwork you were looking at on those files, some of it carries his personal signature."

"But Mao isn't in charge any more."

"No. The Chinese leadership has shown great resilience over the decades. Each knew phase of the mission has been signed off by a different general secretary."

"I guess," Michael steps in, "that's the advantage of not having democracy. You can really see those long-term plans through."

"You can also rob people of their rights and suppress freedom of speech, of thought," Knight observes. "Create a society where the state is always right. No matter how wrong it actually is."

"Touché."

Peter steps in. "So at CIA school you learn about the Soviet idea. How'd you end up finding out about the Chinese?"

"That lesson at Peary always stuck with me," Knight says. "Then five years ago I hear about a woman in a state mental facility out in Oklahoma who claims her teenage son was swapped for an agent by the Chinese government. That the man who claims to be her boy now is in fact an imposter. The woman's suffering, the doctors say, from paranoid schizophrenia."

"How'd you hear about her?"

"She lit up a flag on one of our systems. See, we often get phone calls from shrinks mentioning the delusions of their patients. As you can understand, crazy people do like their government conspiracies, or like to believe that they themselves are part of a conspiracy. If we acted on every whim of every nut, we'd spend our lives chasing one delusion after another. But this woman, she kind of convinced one of the doctors at the place she was at. When he made the call, the doc mentioned the names of two people the woman claimed had trained her back in the 1970s. The two people were known to the agency as Chinese spies. One who had been caught, and one who had made it back to China before we could get ahold of her. We knew both of them as handlers of larger spy networks. Neither of their names had ever been released to the public. So how in the hell does some old woman in a nuthouse know them, right?"

Neither Peter nor anyone else says anything.

"So we look into the woman," Knight gos on. "Mary is her name. We see that Mary was arrested in the sixties for handing out leaflets on college campuses promoting communism. She was also arrested at several peace rallies for the Vietnam War. Minor stuff that so many kids got involved in during the sixties. At some point, however, Mary goes from troubled teen to communist recruit ready to sow the seeds of revolution. She claims that she got pregnant on three separate occasions."

"Why three?" Michael asks.

"Isn't it obvious?"

Peter turns to his son. "The first two pregnancies were female."

"Oh. And what happened to them?"

"What do you think, kid?" Knight says gruffly. "The pregnancies never made it past twenty weeks. The time it takes to determine for sure the sex of a fetus."

"Ah," the kid says with a wince.

"So you spoke to this Mary?"

"Yes. I met her in a dark little room at some bottom level state-run facility out in Oklahoma City. I spoke with her for two hours and she described to me something that I would never have believed had it not been for what I learned at Fort Peary. She told me all about being recruited. How she had been a dye in the wool commie. Dedicated. Had the boy and raised him singlehandedly. Homeschooled him. Never took his picture or allowed it to be taken. Never left the country with him. Stayed away from the father and cut all ties to her own family. Moved about a lot and never had a job. Survived on what the Chinese gave her in disguised payments. Sheltered the boy from the outside world but made sure he visited doctors, dentists, took his school exams—was on the system. Then he turns eighteen and this boy, this child of hers with whom she has spent all these years side by side, her only real contact with the world, this boy is taken from her and replaced by a man altered to look roughly like her son— enough that he matches much of what is written on records about him. But definitely not her son. A stranger. A cuckoo.

"That's when her mental health began to unravel. Rather than schizophrenia, I think she'd had a breakdown. She was sixty when I met her and had been on pretty strong medication for at least the past eight years. While we spoke, she would get confused. Mix up dates. Couldn't remember key facts. But she wasn't lying. I was sure of that. I left the hospital with a few names to check out, nothing that really led to anything, and promised to come see her again."

"And did you?"

"No. I never got the chance. Three weeks later while I was looking into a few things regarding what she'd told me, Mary was found hanging in her room."

"You think it was a legit suicide?"

"Her shrink told me she wasn't suicidal. Said that it had happened after a visit from her son." Knight stares at him from across the breakfast bar wearing a knowing look.

"I guess that brings me to my next question," Peter says. "Who was her son?"

The glimmer of an ironic grin wrinkles the corner of Knight's mouth. "David," he says. "David Powell."

"So that's what got you looking into Powell."

"Oh yes. But what I didn't know was that Powell was merely the tip of the iceberg. That there's at least one other Cuckoo who has gotten at least as high as Powell."

"K."

"Yes. Agent K has gotten exceptionally high. But where he is, who he is, we do not know."

"So you set John on Powell to find out."

"I saw that Powell's company was hiring. I know the guy's pretty hands-on. Know that his main employees spend a lot of their time with him. I also suspect that his company is a way for the Chinese to funnel bad money into the US and European economies. I know of at least four bond companies who have been liquidated, costing the US and European stock markets billions, because of bad investments through Powell's firm. And yet he always survives."

"So John went to work for him and discovered those files."

"Yes. He broke into Powell's company's private servers, found those files and uploaded them onto the hard drive. It's just a shame he had to go into hiding before he could get them to a machine strong enough to break the Chinese encryption."

"What about Jack and his guys?"

"Jack used to be CIA. Before he went rogue. As John was making his way to you, he naively contacted Jack, who he knew was working western Europe with his band of mercenaries. John wanted to use him to source the right equipment to break the encryption."

"Gustav Drecker."

"Yeah. The Russian informant."

"The dead Russian informant," Michael adds.

"Anyway. Jack and John were supposed to meet in Rome. I told John not to trust him; to get a room that had a good view of the meeting spot. He got a place overlooking a small square off the main drag. I told John to miss the meeting and watch it instead. Watch for signs of other people with Jack, and then follow him when he leaves. John watched him wait in that square for twenty minutes, then leave. He followed him. Watched him meet up with Powell and his two goons."

"So Jack was working for Powell?"

"Not exactly. He'd spotted Powell's job offer on the dark web. Took it up, but he planned to double-cross John and the Chinese by selling it to the Russians."

"Who want it because?"

The murmur of a grin on Knight's face. "Because their invasion of Ukraine is going to shit and they need the Chinese onside. Currently, the CCP are offering to help them only if they essentially get down on their knees and practically hand over vast swaths of resources for the lowliest of terms. The two might posture about close ties in public, but in truth neither country trusts or respects the other. To Russia, China has never produced a Dostoevsky. To China, Russia hasn't ever produced a Huawei."

"Wait a minute," Michael says.

They turn to him. He's holding a hand up.

"If you know all this," the kid continues, "and, correct me if I'm wrong, but it sounds like it's all now common knowledge—then why is everyone so desperate to get ahold of John's hard drive?"

Knight looks right at him. "Because those papers aren't the only thing on those files. There's something else."

"What?"

"A list of all the agents, their names, and the names of their surrogates. The whole thirty."

"But we saw no list of names anywhere in those files," Michael puts to him.

"That's because it's hidden. And I know where."

He looks sideways at Ibliss, nods.

She opens a drawer in the breakfast bar and pulls out a laptop, places it on the counter, opens it, powers it up. Then she takes the hard drive from Peter and plugs it into the computer. Everyone crowds around her as it comes alive.

"On one of those pages is a list," Knight says as they wait. "It is hidden within a microdot."

"A microdot?" Michael says.

"Yes. Back in the old days, spies would use them to hide messages to each other. A microdot is text that is reduced in size to such a point that it is virtually invisible unless you know where to look. They're usually circular and around a millimeter in diameter. Often the size and shape of a typographical dot."

The laptop is alive, Ibliss clicking on the hard drive icon.

"And this list is hidden on one of the pages?" Peter asks.

"Yes," Knight replies. "We'll need to return the files back to their original Mandarin, but..."

Each of them freezes. Not long after clicking on the hard drive, the color black starts to run down the screen.

"What the hell is this?" Ibliss asks.

"It never did this before," Peter says.

Once the entire home screen has been wiped away, a red skull and crossbones fills it and begins laughing at them.

Ibliss pulls the hard drive out, but it's too late. The virus has corrupted the laptop.

"What is this?" she says, holding the hard drive up to the others.

Peter takes it off her, looks over it thoroughly. He recalls there being a scratch on the underside. This hard drive doesn't have one. It is spotless. The exact same model, but newer, less used.

"Someone has replaced it," he says.

"You've been being watched," Knight says.

Peter looks up from the hard drive. "By who?"

TWENTY-FIVE

"VICTOR?" COMES HIS HANDLER'S VOICE DOWN THE encrypted burner phone.

"Control?" Victor replies, a hint of self-satisfied smugness in his tone. The SVR killer is eased back in the passenger seat of a Mercedes-Benz Vito; a mid-sized panel van. Sasha drives it south, toward the border with Italy. The long form of Victor sits with a foot up on the dashboard and a cigarette perched in his mouth, the thing flapping up and down every time he speaks.

"I have news on the Chinese," Control says.

"And what are our Asian friends saying?"

"The deal is a go. You are to meet their representatives in Rome for the handover."

Victor Milonov is feeling good. His mission, thus far, has been a success. Sure, he lost three men in Vienna. But in the scramble out of the city, he and Sasha had managed to tail Azrael all the way to Clara's. There, the Russians had done what Victor had wanted done in Vienna; they watched them, didn't engage, didn't risk death. That was how they'd ended up following them to the bridge four days later. He and Sasha couldn't believe their luck when they observed Peter stuffing something into a cavity on the bridge.

"However," Control goes on in Victor's ear.

There is something ominous about this however.

"What?"

"Word is that Azrael and his brat have teamed up with Knight."

"That at least explains the sniper on the bridge," Victor observes. "You think Knight is officially with CIA or working alone?"

"We're not sure," Control says. "But whatever it is, you need to stay alert. Meet with the Chinese as soon as possible. Hand over the files."

"I don't trust the Chinese."

"Neither do we. That's why we have this piece of kompromat on them."

———

IT IS obvious that someone had watched them hide the hard drive in the bridge, having followed them from Clara's on their way to Powell.

But who?

Ibliss knows straight away. She tells them that she recognizes the virus. "It's Russian," she says. "Designed by FSB hackers at Center Sixteen."

The four of them ride away from the compromised cabin. About twenty miles south, they stop at a diner. It is the type of place truckers stop at. Something the British would call a "greasy spoon".

They order coffee and take a booth in the corner furthest from the entrance. It is also away from the windows and mostly closed off from the other patrons. As for the Ducatis, the bikes are parked behind the forty-foot load of a Scania; hiding the bikes from the autobahn.

"I should've spotted the tail," Peter says.

"Don't beat yourself up," Knight says. "What's done is done."

"But how in the hell are we going to figure out who the other agents are? Powell's dead and we've lost the files."

Ibliss shuffles forward in her seat. "You guys looked over those files, right?"

"Briefly," Michael says.

"But you've actually seen them. What did you notice most?"

"Apart from the poor translation?"

"Apart from that. Yes."

"Anthony Eustice," Peter says.

"Mmm," Knight muses loudly. "John did mention him."

"In what way?"

"Just that the name was mentioned in parts of files that he'd unencrypted himself. But nothing substantial enough to know what about."

"We think he's Agent K," Michael puts to them.

Ibliss and Knight look at the kid. Think about it.

"We're not exactly sure on that," Peter adds. "We didn't find anything exactly. Just mention of him."

Knight is nodding. "You know," he says. "It could be.

Whilst a US Senator Eustice was an absolute pain in the ass of the CIA. Part of an oversight committee on defense spending that cut our budget by a third. A lot of good operatives saw their careers terminated because of Senator Eustice. Since becoming Secretary of State last year, he's been a real thorn."

"And he arrives in Rome the day after tomorrow," Ibliss mentions. "What exactly would he be doing during the summit?"

"A lot of the usual NATO summit stuff," Knight says. "Photo opportunities. Showing solidarity with other world leaders in the face of Putin and his war, as well as China and its aggression toward Taiwan. A few speeches."

"Anything else?"

Ben Knight thinks about it, and his face gradually clouds over. Something appears to play out in his mind. However, before he gets to open his mouth, something happens.

The fry chef of the diner leans over the counter in his grease-stained whites. A remote control grasped in his hand, he turns the volume up on the television.

"Look," he says in German to a nearby waitress as she prepares coffee behind him.

She looks sideways at the television.

The chef informs her, "Something has happened in America again."

The voice of an Austrian newscaster fills their ears. Peter and Knight are both fluent in German. They are the first of the four to suddenly turn their eyes to the TV. When the name Anthony Eustice is mentioned, Ibliss and Michael join them in staring up at the screen.

"Peter," Michael asks after a while, "what are they saying?"

Peter turns to him. A grave look on his face. "They say that Anthony Eustice is dead. Someone has shot him."

———

Secretary Eustice becomes the first ever United States Secretary of State to be assassinated in office. Four presidents, but never a secretary of state. It came close only once. The night of Lincoln's assassination. Booth's coconspirators had also targeted the vice president and secretary of state. The man assigned Vice President Andrew Johnson lost his nerve and ended up spending the night at an inn. Secretary of State William H. Seward wasn't so lucky. After his pistol misfired, Lewis Powell, a twenty-year-old Confederate soldier, brutally stabbed Seward along with most of his family and a few bystanders who intervened. It was a miracle that Seward survived.

So, Anthony Eustice makes the history pages as a first.

But what about the Summit? It leaves the four of them confused. And if not Eustice, then who in God's name is K?

Once again, they have answered one question only to reveal three more.

Knight and Ibliss book them into a motel room, Peter and Michael staying out of the way so that they're not caught on the front desk's security cameras. They had taken another laptop from the cabin before they fled it. Using an encrypted internet connection, they sit in the room behind closed curtains reading everything they can on Anthony Eustice's death.

The killer has been named as thirty-eight-year-old Marine veteran Thomas Lee. He's now dead. Shot by one of Eustice's Secret Service protection officers when Thomas Lee ambushed them during Eustice's five a.m. run. The "lone wolf" opening fire with an AR-15 and screaming racist and anti-Semitic profanities before being gunned down himself. Eustice had received multiple gunshot wounds and died at the scene; a hundred yards from his own house in a leafy upmarket borough on the edge of Washington DC.

Lee had come at them from a neighbor's house. Bursting out the front door as the Secretary of State and his two Secret Service bodyguards had jogged by on their usual route. By that point he'd been in the house for thirty-two hours, having broken in a day and half before, and keeping the family living there hostage that whole time. Thankfully, they'd been found tied up and unharmed.

Thomas Lee was a three tour combat veteran. He had multiple decorations, including a Navy and Marine Corps Medal and a Silver Star. An all-American boy it would seem. All except his utter hatred for African-Americans and Jews.

In the twenty-four hours since the assassination, the media have gone over Lee's life with a fine-toothed shovel and paid for any dirt they happened to sift. There are already several pieces on Lee that include hastily put together interviews with friends and family. They quickly picked up on his father's teenage arrest for attacking a synagogue with several friends back in the 1970s. The Lee family, now in hiding, have refused to comment. The extended family, on the other hand, have been full of it.

A cousin claims that Tommy (as he affectionately still calls the killer) once showed him a Hitler Youth knife that was his father's pride and joy. It would appear that anti-Semitism was handed down from father to son. Like the support of a baseball or football team. Dad supports the Houston Texans so I guess I will, too. Dad's an anti-Semite, so yeah.

The hatred of black Americans is more complicated—but again says a lot about a man unable to see past the color of a person's skin or the orthodoxy of their creed. Apparently his wife had left him five years ago along with his children, and they were now living with her African-American husband. If the gossip printed in the supermarket press is anything to go by, Thomas Lee was a cuckold, his wife beginning the relationship with her new husband while she was still married to Lee.

His motive for attacking Eustice was therefore made simple for all those reporting on the crime. Thomas Lee came from the same state that Eustice spent eight years as senator: California. In that time Senator Eustice had run initiatives supporting migrants coming over from Mexico, as well as establishing an amnesty for unregistered migrants who had been in the country at least four years to apply for US citizenship. These were policies that won him a fair few haters amongst the far-right. Also, Eustice was a practicing Jew.

A confluence of reasons, then. But not the real one. To Lee perhaps, but not to those who have orchestrated it from the shadows.

Thomas Lee belonged to Aryan Brotherhood. Something he joined shortly after his wife left him. It is the same white supremacist group the Chinese have secretly been funding for the past four years. Through several intermediaries documented in Harker's files, the Brotherhood was being given economic and strategical help in eliminating Anthony Eustice—a man long regarded as a legitimate target by the group. Nothing in the reports suggests that the uber-nationalists knew they were working with a foreign body. But it is clear to Peter and Michael that the Brotherhood were being manipulated.

The smokescreen appears to have worked perfectly. Minutes after the killing, the Brotherhood uploaded several videos to the internet announcing the success of their mission and to claim Brother Lee as their own. Some of the videos even contain Thomas Lee himself talking about his motives. A cut and dry case. Up and down the country their facilities and clubhouses are being raided by the FBI.

"So that explains," Michael says, "all that stuff about Aryan Brotherhood in the files."

"As well as the house plans we saw," Peter says. "It was plans of the neighbor's place."

"But now who is K?" Ibliss asks. "Or any of the other ones for that matter."

Ibliss sits at a desk, the three men clustered around her.

Knight walks to the door of the room and opens it. They're on the second floor, so it opens onto a balcony. He pulls a pack of smokes from a pocket, taps one out. Lights it and then rubs his temples as he blows smoke out the door.

"There's only one thing to do," he says, turning to face the room.

"What?"

"We need to ride like hell to Rome."

TWENTY-SIX

VICTOR AND SASHA ARRIVE IN ROME.

The city looks beautiful at nighttime. As they cross the Tiber at Tor di Quanto, they can't help gazing at the city lights up ahead on the distant hills. Illuminated by foot-lights, the Pantheon stands proud at the top of the Palatine Hill.

The highway slides into the city, and twenty minutes later they are passing the Colosseum. Blocks of light shine out of it into the night sky. Victor and Sasha don't see it. Deep in the city by this point, they ignore everything except the thick traffic in front of them; as well as occasionally glancing at the map on Victor's phone.

The honking horns of Rome rage all around them. Everyone hustles and bustles there way along the uneven roads—some of which date back to the Romans themselves. Every chance they get, the Italian drivers barge in, cut them up, force their way. As the Mercedes Vito edges its way through the city, they learn quickly to let larger vehicles through no matter what—as it is better than risking being squashed.

They are slowly passing the colonnade of the Basilica di San Giovanni in Laterano when Sasha is forced to take drastic action. A garbage truck muscles its way in front, pushing them up onto the sidewalk. It infuriates the Russians and they get into a heated exchange with the two men hanging onto the back of the dustcart. In the end, they let it go, the garbagemen flicking them off as they disappear down a side street.

The two Russians are still swearing profusely minutes later, especially when they realize they're lost. It is a good half an hour before they are recrossing the Tiber and heading in the right direction. Another ten minutes and they are driving into the plush Roman neighborhood of Trastevere.

It begins to rain hard as they search the gated driveways of the old stone villas for their numbers. It isn't long before they find the one they want and they park the van under a tall poplar tree.

The thick wooden gate is surrounded by high walls and security cameras. Victor presses a buzzer as the rain splashes off the hood of his coat. Next to him is Sasha, a thin aluminum briefcase dangling from one hand.

The speaker on the buzzer crackles into life. In broken English a man asks them to face the camera to their left. It takes Victor a few seconds to calibrate what the guy says and then he advises Sasha to face the camera along with himself.

"Hold there," the man's voice commands them. "Just a little longer... Okay."

The gate unbolts mechanically, then begins sliding to the left. There are two mean looking men waiting for them on the other side. Both look athletic without being formidable and are dressed in tracksuits. They're obviously members of the Chinese Ministry of State Security (MSS).

"Come in," one of them says, using his hand to gesture them into the gate.

It begins closing the second they step inside.

The other man holds a hand up when they are no more than a few steps. "Stop right there."

The front yard is pretty vacant. Nought but a patio, a few crawling plants working their ways up the cracked stucco, and a couple of pots containing dead flowers.

The two men search them over for weapons. Both their phones are taken. Sasha has a little tug-of-war match with one of the tracksuits when he goes to take the briefcase. In the end, they allow him to hold it out while they run a device over it to check for explosives.

With everything satisfactory, the two MSS usher the two SVR inside the three story house. It is an old house, very rustic. The Russians can smell the centuries as they walk through a series of small rooms. The ceilings are exposed beams, and many of the floors are intricate mosaics. All the furniture is covered in white sheets, but the Russians guess it must be antique.

The tracksuits lead them to a windowless room in the center of the place. This is where the meeting will take place. The only furniture consists of four chairs and a table. All of which are plain Ikea furniture—not antique as you'd expect.

On the other side of the table sit two men. One is in his twenties, skinny and covered in acne scars with bookish features. The other is much older. At least in his late forties. H looks ill. His complexion is practically gray. He wears a matching gray suit, a slim black tie falling down his white shirt. His thinning black hair is immaculately cut. He smokes profusely; long, thin Chinese cigarettes with gold Mandarin letters running up the side. He squints at them through the smoke that meanders in front of his face.

Neither man stands when the Russians step into the room. One of the tracksuits signals for them to take the two empty seats at the table. The other tracksuit closes the door.

"That the device you took from the Americans?" the older, gray one asks in Russian.

He speaks it perfectly.

"Da," Victor says.

"Slide it over."

Sasha gazes sideways at Victor.

Victor nods his ascent without losing eye contact with the MSS colonel sitting opposite.

Sasha pushes the briefcase across the table.

The colonel doesn't move. Just continues to puff on his cigarette. All the time keeping his staring match with Victor going.

The younger guy—obviously some nerd from one of their hacking units—leans across and drags the case over to himself. The second he opens it, he removes the hard drive from the foam and plugs it into his own laptop. Begins running some program over it.

"What's he doing?" Victor asks.

"Just wait," the gray-faced colonel tells him.

A couple of minutes later the hacker leans over to his boss and whispers something to him in Mandarin.

"He says you've copied it," the colonel says to Victor once the hacker has leaned back to his place.

"Have we?"

"Da," the colonel replies dryly. "The copy was done three hours ago. Long after you had retrieved it from Azrael. Why?"

"Why not?"

"Those files are meaningless to you now."

"And how would we know that? We've not had time to go over them. All we know is that you are willing to supply us with enough resources to fight in Ukraine for the next fifty years just so we give you back nothing more than a copy. That means there must be something really big on it. As our countries are now mutually aligned, my superiors thought it only fair that we share all intelligence from now on."

For the first time the colonel's face shows a hint of something: derision. The corner of his right eye flickers, and not from the smoke.

"You Russians," he growls, "you can never be trusted."

Victor cocks an eye. Tips his head. "Now now," he says. "Let's not fight. Save it for when we have to fight that bastard Azrael. Because, trust me, he will surely be coming after this."

The colonel stares at him. Takes a toke of his cigarette. Leans forward and twists it out in a glass ashtray that sits on the table between them; all the time not breaking eye contact with the Russian for a second.

Leaning back in his chair, he says, "I am glad we are on that subject."

"And which subject is that?"

"The subject of Azrael, of course. Because I have been assured by your superiors that the two of you will be staying here in Rome under my direction for the foreseeable future."

Sasha flashes Victor a look. Victor doesn't want to lose the match, so he doesn't turn to his compatriot.

The colonel cracks a smile. "A sign of our new mutual alliance," he adds.

Victor lets out the most imperceptible of sighs. Then asks, "How many people do you have in Rome?"

"Over a hundred. The streets are crawling with watchers."

Victor shakes his head.

"Azrael and his brat will spot them."

"He didn't spot the one in Austria."

"That was one. A hundred will stand out. A hundred multiplies the possibility that one of them will make a mistake. What about muscle?"

"Six four-men teams. Ready to be deployed around the city at any point."

"Then why'd you need us?"

A flicker travels up the side of the Chinaman's face. "We feel your expertise in dealing with Azrael will come in handy."

It is Victor's turn to crack a wry smile. "I bet you do. As well as being a handy distraction for him while your men get into position."

"I can assure you that we are all a team here," the colonel insists, his lips parting and showing off a set of crooked, tobacco-stained teeth.

IT TAKES them eight hours to reach Rome.

To avoid Italy's autostradas and toll booths, as well as MSS watchers, they travel via the east coast of Italy. They are sure that the Chinese will be monitoring CCTV, so best to avoid populous areas or roads. Toll booths are all armed with cameras.

At the city of Pescara Peter and Michael get off the backs of the Ducatis, their thighs aching, and get into an Alfa Romeo Giulia Competizione. It is supplied by Knight, the four of them retrieving it from a lockup on the edge of the city.

"Whose is it?" Peter asks.

"Does it matter?"

"I guess not."

The Giulia Competizione is a high-end two-door sedan with over two hundred kilowatts of horsepower; 0-60 in under six seconds. A solid vehicle.

They split up at Carsoli, a small town filled with Roman ruins, and take different roads into the capital. The four of them then arrive in central Rome from three different sides. Knight from the north; Ibliss from the south; Peter and Michael from the west.

It is ten p.m. when they converge on a nondescript residential street in Monterverde; just west of the Tiber. Knight appears to still have friends in the agency. The CIA safe house is inconspicuous and has excellent security. A five-story apartment block that is owned by the CIA through several clandestine shell companies, four of the five apartments are rented out to extremely well vetted, and completely oblivious, Italian residents through a rental agency. This makes the place look like just another foreign owned business investment.

That leaves flat number five. The one at the top, the attic suite. That one is empty most of the year, except for those rare occasions when strange Americans come to stay for a few days, rarely more than a week. Men and women who are seldom seen except in glimpses as they come up or down the stairs. Usually wearing baseball caps and sunglasses. Often with a hood over the top. Nothing you could describe to a police officer later on.

Peter and Michael find the address quick. The place exactly where Knight said it would be. They take a moment to stare at it through the bucketing rain that washes down the windshield.

"You know," Peter says as they gaze at it, "we could just drive away. Ditch the car. Keep running. Leave Knight and Ibliss, and just find another country to start again. I was thinking Japan."

Michael sighs. "We can't."

"Why not? We don't have the hard drive. We could just leave it all. No one will come after us."

Michael turns from the rain and the apartment.

"You serious?"

"Yeah."

The kid thinks about it. His eyes go blank. Then they come back alive. A slight grin curves his lips. Then he shakes his head.

"No. We shouldn't run. We should stop the Chinese. And not for America or the CIA, but for Clara and Lena and people like that. Innocent people who are always the victims of this shit."

Peter stares at him. Sighs.

"I guess you're right," he says, fishing the burner phone Knight gave him out of his pocket.

At the bottom of the apartment block is a parking garage that feeds straight onto the street. A quick call to Ibliss and the door begins opening.

They park the Alfa inside next to the two black Ducatis, the door closing automatically behind them, shutting out the rain. The garage is large enough for two cars. A door in the corner leads to a spiral staircase. It takes them all the way up to the fifth floor and opens on no other floors. Existing beyond the end wall of each hallway, the stairwell is hidden from the tenants. As they move up it, Peter and Michael can hear the sounds of a loud conversation.

At the top, a door opens onto a neatly furnished living room with slanted attic ceilings. On their immediate right, the alcoves of bay windows line the room. Knight is smoking at one of them. A little wrought iron balcony sticks out of it a few inches. One of Knight's hands grips the railing. Rain blows inwards on him, but he doesn't appear to notice—or care. He just stands there, the water splashing off his face, his red eyes staring at the storm.

On the left, Ibliss sits on a sofa. She gets up and comes defense them.

"No tails?" she asks.

Michael frowns. "You think we'd show up if we thought we had a tail?"

"You might not know it. The watcher that spotted you in Austria managed to stay out of your radar."

"That was different. We—"

Peter holds a hand up. The sign for the kid to shut up.

"Don't worry," Azrael tells her. "I made sure to perform countersurveillance techniques. I drove another hour longer than I needed so that I avoided the slow-moving roads in the center—places watchers could see us as we drive by. I also double-backed on myself several times."

"Anyway," Michael protests, "we weren't expecting it in Austria. We are now."

Ibliss narrows her eyes at the kid. "When you've been hunted as long as myself and your father, you learn to always be vigilant."

The kid rolls his eyes.

Peter glances sideways at Knight. He hasn't made a peep or shown any sign that he's aware they've arrived. What he saw in that basement must have been truly horrific. To have watched your only child die and know that right at the end she—his little girl—died thinking he had refused to give those men what they wanted in exchange for her life. Ben Knight will probably see the look on her face till the day he dies.

"Is he okay?" Peter asks Ibliss.

She sighs before she answers. "I'm not sure. He's just determined to get this finished, I guess."

As though summoned, Ben Knight flicks his cigarette into the rainy night and wheels around from the window.

"Azrael," he says, the front of his clothing wet, silver hair dripping down his forehead, "come see the view."

Peter joins him at the window. Now both of them are leaning on the iron balcony and being rained on.

"You see it?" Knight asks.

The rain blurs the outlines of the rooftops, the bell towers, the lights of the apartment buildings.

"It's hard to say in the rain," Peter replies.

"Here." Knight hands him a compact pair of field glasses.

Peter places the cups to his eyes and Knight tells him to look in the direction of three o'clock. That's when he spots it. A huge medieval clocktower about two blocks away.

They had discussed it earlier when coming up with a plan for Rome. The attic apartment has many bay windows that face the tower. If someone were to want a view into the apartment, they couldn't choose a better place than that tower.

"Is it what you meant?" Knight asks.

"It's perfect," Peter says, handing him back the glasses.

"Then it's settled," Knight says, turning back to the living room; to Ibliss and Michael.

Stepping into the room and rubbing his hands together, he adds, "I need to get changed. There's somewhere I have to be."

"Where?" Peter asks.

Knight turns his wet face to him and places a hand on his shoulder. Gives it a warm squeeze.

"Don't worry about it," he says before letting go and leaving the room.

Peter turns to Ibliss. "Where does he need to be?"

"Didn't you hear him?"

"Yes."

"Then do as he says. Don't worry about it."

"That makes me worry about it, though. More than I initially would have."

Ibliss smiles. "Then don't worry about it."

———

BEN KNIGHT LEAVES the apartment and enters the rain.

He's in fresh clothing. Parka coats are popular this time of year in Rome. He wears one with the hood up. The bill of a Mets baseball cap pokes out of it. On his face he wears a pair of distraction sunglasses with green tint. They are specially designed to fool facial recognition systems. He doesn't go with the face-mask, though. It would seem that they are now rather rare in Rome and would make him stick out.

On his way to his contact, he spots two MSS surveillance specialists. One is sitting outside a late-night café on via Federico Torre that pokes out from the corner of a five road junction. It has two tables outside of it. One is occupied by a man sipping espresso as the rain dribbles down from the café's awning. His cell phone glows in his hand, but he's not paying attention to it. The phone is no more than a prop. A pair of sharp eyes scan the masses of people that move along the busy road.

Knight skips behind a group of tourists. One of them smiles at him and offers the shelter of her umbrella. Knight thanks the woman and ducks under it, completely hidden from the café on the other side of the road.

The second watcher is a little later and mobile. He's moving on foot within the crowds. Knight spots him from across the street by chance. Just happens to look that way as the guy touches his ear and speaks into his comms for a few seconds. Otherwise, he would have thought it was just another person on their way home after a few drinks.

Knight lets the guy go and turns into an alleyway that takes him along the backs of the buildings. He plucks his phone from his pocket and dials a number.

When it is answered, he says, "I'm almost there."

"Good," a man's voice replies. "So are we."

Right at the moment Ben Knight reaches the end of the alley a big brown UPS van pulls up in front of him. The side door opens and he gets in. Seconds later it is moving through Rome with the rest of the honking, slow-moving traffic.

The back of the UPS van bears no resemblance whatsoever to a normal delivery van. There are no parcel filled racks. No hand truck. Instead, there is a large comms unit with scanners for monitoring police radios, a high-powered IMSI catcher for monitoring all nearby cell phone activity, a high-powered computer with encrypted internet service. There's even toilet facilities in one corner. For seating, several high-backed office chairs are bolted to the floor. A middle-aged man sits in one of them.

"Take a pew," he says, pointing to the chair opposite him.

There's one other in the back of that van with them. A young woman sitting at the comms unit.

The guy, Knight knows. The girl, he doesn't.

"This is Kirsty Lang," the man tells him. "She'll be assisting you."

Kirsty turns around and gives him a gentle smile. She's pretty. In her mid-twenties. Fresh out of Leary. She's got medium-length hair that's been bleached white except for a shock of blue in the front. He can't help thinking about his daughter. She would always color her hair, and he's almost certain that at some point she had colored it in this exact way.

Knight gives Kirsty Lang a polite nod and turns back to the man he's known thirty years. Deputy Director James Nash.

"So you believe me now?" Knight puts to him.

"I never said we didn't, Ben," Nash replies. "I just said we'd have to do our own investigations."

"And have you?"

"The FBI found evidence of tampering at the crime scene. They did a pretty good job, but..." Nash pauses. "You sure you want me to go on?"

"Just make it quick."

"The killers left a partial on the bag. It's smeared, but it's there. They also showed up on CCTV setups at several properties around the lake."

"What about the espionage charges?"

"Our own investigations have found you innocent."

An angered look works its way up Knight's face. "And still you put me through the wringer. Made me pack up my desk, Jim. Return my weapon. Hung me and my family out to dry."

Knight only now notices that he's clenching his fist.

Kirsty Lang has turned in her chair.

"We had to go through the motions, Ben," Nash tells him. "You know we had to follow protocol. Evidence had been presented."

"Fake evidence."

"Evidence that we'd yet to establish was fake. We had to act along the guidelines."

The two men stare at each other.

"Look," Nash goes on in a softer tone, "I'm sorry about what happened to Sandy and Hayley. I really am. But I'm here now, aren't I? The agency is here now. So the best way we can move forward is by getting this thing done. Now what have you got?"

Knight runs a hand down his face. Pinches his nose. The van turns onto a road filled with potholes and the back begins lurching gently from side to side.

"My team are here," Knight says.

"Azrael and the kid?"

"Yes."

"They know about this?"

"Yes. I've been honest with them."

Nash nods. Then. "What's the kid like?" He sounds genuinely interested.

"Like his dad," Knight replies. "But a little more loose, I guess. Lacks the cold upbringing of Alaska and the Mother program. He likes to joke."

"Can he be trusted to perform under command?"

"He does exactly what his father tells him to."

"And can Azrael be trusted to take commands?"

"Look. When I get back to the safe house, I'm gonna come clean with the both of them about our sudden recruitment in the CIA. But I'm also gonna assure them that you won't be coming after them."

"I promised you, Ben," Nash says with an earnest expression. Or at least as earnest as Knight has ever seen it. "They get this done and they're free. Director Burns has given his word. Neither of them will be hunted."

Knight relaxes back into the padded leather of the chair.

They move off the bumpy road and hit a cobbled thorough-fare that's not much better.

"Christ the roads in this town are shitty," Nash complains.

"It was built a long time ago, Jim. But that's not what I'm here to talk to you about. What have you got on the Russians?"

"We've got eyes all over the internet. Italian and Austrian intelligence have given us access to all data transfers through their servers. All internet data is being scanned through our own servers back at HQ. We also have full infiltration of Russian cyberspace."

"And?"

"And nothing has been sent. Like I told you, Ben. The Russians don't trust the internet abroad. They will have made a copy and will be keeping it on a physical device."

"Another hard drive?"

"More than likely."

"What about K and the others?"

Nash gives away a faint impression he's annoyed. "We've got no chance of finding him before tomorrow."

"What about Eustice?"

"FBI are all over it. They're looking into the way the Aryan Brotherhood was financed. The people Lee was meeting."

"But what's the motive for the Chinese?"

"We don't know. Maybe Anthony Eustice was onto something. I don't know. But I'll tell you this. We'll be a lot closer to it all once we get our hands on the Russians' copy."

"Then," Knight says conspiratorially, leaning forward, "I better get on with the real reason I'm here."

"Yes. You mentioned you had a plan."

"I do. But it will need your help."

———

KNIGHT RETURNS around midnight via the parking garage. The others are waiting for him in the living room.

"So?" Ibliss asks instantly.

"We're a go," Knight says. "Nash agrees with the plan and will be facilitating us all the way."

TWENTY-SEVEN

EUROPEAN AIRSPACE - 7:00 CET

GENERAL YATES IS AWOKEN BY A KNOCK ON HIS cabin door.

"Uh huh," he says sleepily.

The door opens a tad and his head of communications Paul Johnson appears. "It's seven, Henry," he says. "We're now flying over Madrid. Another two hours till Rome."

"Okay. Okay," General Yates says, rolling over and flicking the bedside lamp on.

Paul leaves and the general begins his usual morning ritual when on board the National Airborne Operations Center. He eats a breakfast of boiled egg and unbuttered brown toast. Then he calls his wife. The call doesn't last long. His wife is in DC and half asleep. He tells her he loves her and the call ends.

He showers, changes into a suit, and leaves the cabin to join the others.

They are flying in an E-4B, a highly modified Boeing 747-200 four-engine jet, that serves as an operations center in the air. Whilst he'd been defense secretary, Donald Rumsfeld had nicknamed it the "flying Pentagon".

Currently, it is flying a delegation to the NATO summit in Rome. Vice Chairman of the Joint Chiefs of Staff General Henry Yates, Secretary of Defense Craig Hernandez, and the Chairman of the Joint Chiefs of Staff Admiral James McArthur. As well as all their staffs and security details.

It was originally supposed to have flown the secretary of state. Anthony Eustice's death two days ago has given the voyage an ominous air.

General Yates passes through the plane's command center. Nodding a hello to each of the three military intelligence operatives who sit at a bank of equipment. Inside the main cabin he finds his team; his personal assistant Grace, his head of communications Paul Johnson, and his Secret Service detail, two mean looking men who always mixes up the names of.

In the background are the assorted members of staff belonging to Craig Martinez and Admiral McArthur, as well as their own personal security details.

Everyone sits around going over last minute preparations and chain-drinking coffee.

The second Grace spots the general she's on him. Out of her seat and marching up. She doesn't look happy. In fact, she has a look on her face like she's just smelled something bad.

"I thought," she says, "we agreed on the blue suit, not the gray."

"I prefer the gray," Yates replies gruffly.

"But the blue brings out your eyes."

General Yates goes sullen. "My eyes are green."

"Which matches the blue better than the gray."

"I had originally intended to wear my uniform. But you insisted on a suit."

"And what's your point?"

"My point is that my uniform is green. Wouldn't that match my green eyes better?"

The assistant frowns and turns sideways to Paul Johnson, who is just then sauntering up.

"Like we said before," the head of communications says calmly. "You're here as part of a government delegation. Not a military one. A suit is better. Now. Didn't we agree on blue?"

"I believe you two agreed on blue. I prefer gray."

"But we want to go for a more tranquil color."

"Gray is tranquil."

The frown on Grace's face explodes. Like she's now tasting the thing that smelled bad.

"Not as much as blue," Paul says.

General Yates has known Paul Johnson a long time. Before he was his head of communications, they'd worked together in several capacities. And after working for so long side by side, it is only Paul who is capable of making him stand down.

Groaning, the general gives in. "Okay," he says. "I'll swap it for the blue."

"There's a good boy," Paul says. "Now hurry up. We land in Rome in less than two hours and I need to brief you."

"Didn't we go through all that last night before bed?"

"Yes. But now we need to go through it again. This is important, Henry. Especially with where things are geopolitically. That's why you need to get this nailed on today. So go and change the suit."

Yates rolls his eyes and continues on his way.

———

Rome, Italy
    9:50 CET

Georgia has been in Rome two days. She and another hundred surveillance experts are positioned throughout the city. At least fifty people cover the southeast edge, all the way to the coast. Blanketing the area between the main city and Pratica di Mare Air Base where the summit is taking place.

Georgia has chosen to stay in the city. For the time being at least. She doesn't think Azrael and the others will be anywhere near the summit just yet. She knows they'll need to arm themselves first.

It is why she personally chose the spot she takes up now.

The rain has stopped but the streets are still wet. Inside the relatively dry space of an alcove between two shopfronts she sits with the stump of her missing leg poking out so that passersby can see she's a cripple. Many of them drop a euro or two into the coffee cup she's perched behind.

The amputated limb is her perfect prop. A piece of stagecraft that makes her less visible than many of the others. Coupled with the rags she wears, she is able to sink in with the rest of the detritus typical of any urban area.

Back in Hong Kong Georgia had been MSS. A good field agent. She had trained her whole life for it, following her father and two uncles into the service, but had lasted out in the field less than a year. A shotgun blast from a Triad drug lord's bodyguard had lost her the bottom half of her right leg. You're no good in the field with one leg. Nonetheless, there are still possibilities. Surveillance. So long as they weren't looking for her, having one leg and dressing in rags made you innocuous.

A spill of coins drops into the cup and she gives the philanthrope a rusty grazie, even though she can speak perfect Italian; after all, she has to keep up the ignorant migrant act.

Then her sharp little eyes are back on the building across the road. Scanning the faces that walk in and out the doors.

Having once been deployed as a field agent, Georgia has a feel for the job that many of the other watchers don't. She knows that Azrael will need to arm himself in Rome, and that is why she is here.

Recently, Chinese intelligence discovered the addresses of several CIA armories in Europe. One of them is in Rome. One of them is directly opposite the little alcove that Georgia begs in. Right in the heart of Rome's tailoring district in Via di Ripetta. The words Sartoria Carbone Bespoke Tailors written above the entrance.

———

It is ten when Peter and Michael leave the apartment. The streets are just beginning to get busy, filling with early-bird shoppers and the older tourists.

Exiting the Ponte Fabricio bridge the two of them separate. The wet streets shine golden in the early morning sun. The traffic is picking up and the horns have started. Both move along their separate routes in baseball caps and the same types of sunglasses that Knight wore. They stick tight to groups, attempting to look like part of them. Then leave one group and move to another. The streets teem with tourists.

Having used a number of countersurveillance measures and sure that they're not being tailed, the two arrive at Sartoria Carbone Bespoke Tailors.

They step inside. The shop is something else. A coved ceiling with a chandelier hanging in the center. Decorative floor to ceiling wood paneling. Polished oak flooring laid in the herringbone fashion. Antique mirrors adorn most of the walls, making the room appear endless, and dotted about are tailor's dummies holding beautifully crafted suits.

An Italian man with impeccable hair comes to them the moment they step in off the street. He is dressed to the highest order in a gray woolen suit, and a tape measure hangs from his neck.

He instantly takes them for American.

"How may I help you, gentlemen?" he asks in English.

"We are here for the shirtmaker," Peter says.

The smile drops and the tailor becomes deadly serious. "Of course," he says. "If the two of you would like to take a look at some of our latest designs, the shirtmaker will be with you shortly."

"Grazie."

They move off to the back of the boutique where rows of the finest handcrafted shoes line the wall.

"These are nice," Michael says, picking up a pair of

leather yachting shoes. He flips them over. "There isn't a price. How much do you think they are?"

"I'm not sure about the shoes," Peter says, "but I know that a suit here goes from between ten and seventy thousand dollars."

The kid raise his eyebrows. "Who pays seventy thousand dollars for a suit?"

"Rich guys."

It wasn't Peter who spoke. It was the girl standing on the other side of Michael. He turns sideways to her.

"Nice hair," he tells her.

It is white with a shock of blue in the fringe.

"Nice hair?" she puts back.

"Yeah. I like it."

Michael places the shoe down. He thinks he's in here. The seventeen-year-old drifts toward her, closing the gap to a mere foot.

"What brings you to Rome?" he asks.

She can't help giggling. "What brings me to Rome?"

"Yeah."

Peter pulls him out of the way. "Give it a rest, Mikey."

"W-what?" the kid stammers, an annoyed expression on his face.

"She's the shirtmaker," Peter tells him.

"Oh," Michael mumbles, turning back to the young woman.

"Yeah," she says, giggling. "You should take it easy there with the charm, kid."

Michael goes redder than ever. Especially at being called kid.

The girl then drops the smile and goes dearly serious. "Face the shoes."

They do as she says. While she talks, Peter watches the rest of the shop through an oval mirror hanging not far from the shoes.

"The changing room at the end," she says in a hushed voice. "It has a retina scanner behind the mirror. Let it read both your eyes. This will activate the floor."

Michael frowns. "The floor?"

"You'll understand when it happens. Down below is everything you'll need."

"Even—"

"Everything," she butts in. "Take only what you need. Okay?"

"Okay," the two men mutter.

"Then I wish you gentlemen the best of luck. You're on Uncle Sam's time now, so don't fuck this up."

And with that, she turns and leaves.

"Oh, and, kid?" she says, turning around to Michael as she backs toward the door.

"What?"

"You'd look better in the loafers than the yachting shoes. Though, saying that, I bet you've got nice ankles."

She smiles, winks, and is gone with a rattle of the bell above the door.

Michael wears a dreamy look as he stares after her.

"Wake up!" Peter snaps.

They turn their attention toward the changing rooms.

Inside the final booth, they stand before the mirror. A man's voice comes over a speaker hidden somewhere above them. He tells them to hold still for a moment.

Less than twenty seconds later the floor shudders beneath their feet and they begin to sink through the building.

"That must be what she meant," Michael remarks as they go downwards.

The lift drops them in an underground armory. Strip-lighting illuminates sheer concrete walls, ceiling and floor. Glass cabinets filled with knives, pistols, grenades, plastic explosive. Racks with military grade battle weapons—assault rifles, sniper rifles, grenade launchers, RPG launchers. In the shotgun section they even have an Atchisson AA-12 twelve-gauge fully-automatic assault shotgun fitted with a twenty shell drum. Nicknamed the "sledgehammer shotgun" it can fire up to 300 shells a minute. If it comes with the FRAG-12 high-explosive ammunition then you're really talking business.

"Oh wow," Michael gushes as his eyes flit from one weapon to the next.

———

PRATICA DI MARE AIR BASE, Rome
    10:30 CET

THE SUMMIT IS TAKING place in a giant hangar in the middle of the biggest military base in Italy. Pratica di Mare.

Having arrived directly at the base, the American delegation is taken by limousine the short distance across the airfield to the hangar. Upon arrival, General Yates and his team are escorted through the building by summit staff. The main conference is taking place in a huge circular room. In the middle of it is a ring-shaped table surrounded by chairs. General Yates takes a seat at it with Paul Johnson. Soon, Admiral McArthur and Secretary of Defense Hernandez are sitting either side of him with their own heads of staff.

General Yates takes the pot of coffee that's been placed on the table for him and pours himself a cup.

"You want one?" he asks Paul Johnson.

"Sure."

Yates makes him the coffee. As he passes Paul the cup, Secretary of Defense Hernandez nudges the general gently from behind, and he twists around to him.

Busy with their own staff meetings that morning on the plane, neither of the three delegates has had a chance to talk.

Leaning in, Craig Hernandez asks discreetly, "You ready for this, General?"

"My head of communications here would like to think so," Yates replies. "He's been getting me up to scratch on it for the past day."

"I guess twenty-four hours isn't really long enough to get ready to make speeches in front of all these people, but just stick to what Anthony would have said and you're all set."

"It's later on that worries me."

"Oh, don't. Your security detail knows what's what. We'll simply complete the data transfer and be on our ways."

Hernandez pats him on the shoulder and returns to his former position.

"You look nervous," Paul Johnson remarks in a hushed tone the other side of General Yates.

"I hate last-minute changes of plans, is all," the general

grumbles. "In the military you learn to brace yourself. Because there's always something that may have been missed."

"Like what?"

Yates thinks about it.

It isn't the summit itself that makes him nervous. He's been to summits before. Heck, this is nothing compared to being grilled in Congress, as has happened to him in the past. This will be a doddle. Everyone is pretty much in agreement.

No, it is not the summit. It is something else.

"I don't know," he finally says.

"Well, don't worry. The speech Anthony's people made is perfect. We've added a little to the beginning for posterity. The rest should just flow."

Yates frowns. "But another man's words in another man's place."

"Is that what is worrying you? Anthony Eustice's death?"

Yates stays quiet for a moment. "Maybe," he admits.

Just then the lights dim. The show is beginning. Large screens hang down at the edges of the arena. They come alive with the NATO crest: a four-pointed star that represents a compass, supposedly to keep us on the right road, the path of peace. At the head of the table is the Italian president.

He stands. It will be he who makes the first speech and raises the first subjects of the summit.

———

ROME

LESS THAN AN HOUR after they went in, Georgia watches Azrael and the boy come out carrying two rather heavy looking carryalls. She is already on her one remaining foot, her crutch secured under her right armpit.

She waits for them to get half a block up the street, her hawk-eyes keeping with them as they move through the crowds. Then she moves off. They cross the road to her side. It allows her to stay back and relax, knowing there are few turnings in this part of the street.

The two assassins stay together, and Georgia is glad they don't split. She doesn't want to have to share the tail.

Her handler's voice comes through her comms earpiece.

"I've got someone coming to your location. Stay with them until they arrive. In the meantime, we need you to tag them."

"That's affirmative, Command."

"Good girl. Speak soon."

Georgia dips a hand inside the ragged remains of a jacket. Strapped across her middle, just below her breasts, is a money belt. Her nimble fingers unzip it and remove two tiny trackers. No more than tiny circular stick-on dots.

While following them through the old Jewish quarter, she has to occasionally hide up as they stop to chat to the old shopkeepers who invite them into their shops. Taking them for the couple of American tourists.

At one point, she is almost shoed away from a shop she takes refuge in. The old woman shopkeeper sees the rags and the foreign face and thinks straight away thief. Georgia has to be quick to get out her purse and prove to the woman she has money and that there is no need to call the police.

This only makes the woman more convinced. She narrows her eyes, and Georgia is glad when she spots the assassins moving off again.

It's when they emerge from an alleyway into a market square that Georgia takes her opportunity. They stop to buy espressos from a vender. Both of them are trying to be as discreet as possible. Faces hidden behind their shades, collars up, the peaks of their baseball caps down. Neither looks the same as he did when she had spotted them in Austria, but, like now, she had recognized the way they moved.

MSS had surveillance footage of both of them from a few of the jobs they'd performed in which CCTV managed to capture partial images. Grainy and incomplete, it was enough to imprint their movements on Georgia's sharp mind.

Georgia moves fast. She waits for a gap in the traffic and hobbles quickly across the road, her crutch tapping on the cobblestones. They stand with their backs to the street. She skips up onto the sidewalk, comes right up to them, brushes into them as though she's stumbling. Peter turns sharply, grabs her by the forearm. His wallet is in her hand.

Both he and Michael glare at her and for the time being she is unable to speak.

Peter plucks the wallet out of her hand.

"I shall call the police, señor," the vender says.

"It's okay," Peter says, not breaking eye contact with Georgia.

Peter lets her go. She should leave immediately. Get away from here. But all she can do is stand there partially frozen.

"Here," Peter says, plucking fifty euros from the wallet and handing it to her.

She meekly takes it, bows, and says grazie in her funny little accent.

Georgia moves off at pace. The whole time she can feel his eyes burning into the back of her as she makes her way into the crowds. Not until she's at least five blocks from the coffee vender does she call it in.

Touching her earpiece, she speaks into her comms, her voice shaky. "They're both live. I stole his wallet as a decoy. Got tags on them both."

"Good work."

"You'll have to get someone else to watch from here. He caught me. Like he knew I was going to do it."

"Don't worry. I've got a team just around the corner. They'll take over. Go get yourself some rest. You've earned it, Georgia. Command out."

Georgia shudders. She can't shake the look in his eyes. In both their eyes. It fills her with a deep, primal fear she cannot explain.

————

VICTOR AND SASHA sit in their Mercedes Vito.

The spindly Victor is sprawled in the passenger side, the window open an inch, a cigarette floating about in his lips. He is looking down at the screen of his phone. Two red-dot icons meander across a digital map of Rome.

Over the next few minutes, the dots split up, double back on themselves, zig-zag across central Rome, get picked up by another couple of watchers, until eventually, the dots converge in Monteverde at an apartment building.

Sasha drives them onto the street. They pull in about a block back from the five-story, yellow stucco apartments. Victor checks the GPS trackers. They're designed to send data back to them regarding its elevation.

"They must be on the top floor," Victor says.

He uses GoogleMaps street view. Scrolls about until he gets a view of the apartments from the next street. He eventually achieves an angle where you can see the top floor from the rear.

"It has bay windows," he observes. "You can see right in."

Victor's fingers move the map 180 degrees and his eyes almost burst from his face when he spots the Torre dell'Orologio clock tower.

"The observation deck is practically opposite," Victor says.

"What's its name?" Sasha asks, his own phone in his hand.

"The Torre dell'Orologio."

Sasha Google searches it.

"They're open to the public."

"The observation deck?"

"Yes."

Victor rubs his hands together. "Right, then. It's decided."

Next up they get ahold of online plans for the apartment block. They are available from the website of the rental company. This includes the plans for the attic suite. It's perfect. Open plan. Only one bedroom. Most of it consists of a living room covered almost exclusively by four wide bay windows.

"You go in the front," Victor says, "and I'll cover you from the back. It's simple. Their safe house is no longer safe."

They leave the van, stroll to the back, and open the trunk. Pulling up the false floor, they are presented with an arsenal.

Sasha takes body armor and a silenced Glock-17 with three extra magazines. He also takes a bayonet that he attaches to an ankle strap. Oh, and two flash grenades.

Victor grabs the trumpet case. Everything he needs is inside.

Lastly, they place comms in their ears.

"You ready for this?" Victor asks Sasha.

"Homeward bound."

"Homeward bound as heroes," Victor says with a grin.

"Yeah. I like that," Sasha agrees. "Medals and honor. After all, when you are men such as us what else is there except death?"

The Russian nods and moves away. The narrow residential street is deserted. Everyone appears to be at work. The odd car passes by. No one minds the two men working their way along the sidewalk. Sasha heads east for the apartment. Victor goes north for the Torre dell'Orologio.

The sniper is halfway there when he begins to worry that the security may want to take a look inside the case. It could scupper the whole mission and he is only now thinking of it.

But when he reaches the lobby of the clocktower he is filled with relief to find no such security. A line of tourists walk through the doors and all the woman inside cares about is taking the tickets they've bought from a little booth down some steps to the right. Not once does he spot the woman take any notice of the tourists' bags, and when he watches a man go in with a violin case he is sure.

Victor steps across the road and buys a ticket at the booth. He almost chokes when the man asks for thirty euros (about thirty-two dollars).

Muttering something about the price under his breath, he hands over the cash, takes the ticket and leaves the booth. He walks up a few stone steps into the cool air of the vestibule and hands the woman at the door his ticket.

In perfect Italian he asks her how to get to the observation tower. With a smile she directs him to the far corner of the main hall.

"Grazie," he says with a nod of his long frame.

The Russian makes his way across the hall in long steps, ignoring the tour groups or any of the museum pieces that litter glass cabinets and tables. He hits the stairs, striding past the slow-moving gabble. In the clock room he has to squeeze past the tourists gawking at all the cogs and moving parts, the loud voice of a tour guide echoing off the vaulted ceilings. Victor is grateful to get out.

That's when his latest piece of luck hits him. The observation deck is closed, and only a rope barrier stands in his way. Not even a ticket collector to guard it. He is smiling as he lifts one side off the peg, steps to the other side, and carefully places it back.

How lucky. He will have the whole deck to himself.

Since Vienna, Victor has begun to truly believe in his own luck. He's always been somewhat of a believer anyway. He grew up in the countryside on the edges of Moscow. His family were rural folk. Superstitious folk. From an early age his mama had made him carry around a rabbit's foot; and whenever they entered the house, he, his father and siblings would have to cross themselves in the presence of an icon that she held out to them from the threshold before they were allowed in. It could be quite an ordeal if all of them returned home at the same time.

In his army days in Chechnya, luck had certainly played a role in battle. Or at least in Victor's imagination. He had watched as some of the best trained, most elite Spetnaz soldiers he'd ever known died around him while inferior ones survived. In fact, Victor had never classed himself among the best Spetnaz. Sure he was good, you had to be to survive training. But he was never as sharp a shooter or as hard a fighter as some of the men he is proud to have associated with. Nevertheless, what he did have was luck. Cold-hearted luck. Where his cohorts would catch a ricocheted bullet in the temple, Victor would survive a dud grenade being thrown into the jeep that he was driving one time in Grozny. These moments of luck had propelled him further up the chain of command, passing so many dead men along the way, until now he is working the highest level intelligence jobs all over the world.

Luck is a virtue in Victor's book. And especially for the assassin.

———

SASHA CREEPS along the shadows of fig trees, the sidewalk covered in squashed fruit. It's a cloudy day, not overly hot, but Sasha is pouring with sweat. Baking underneath the leather jacket and military grade body armor. But not just that. Nervous, too. After all, this is Azrael and his boy.

He approaches the apartments from the same side of street they are on, and by the time he's standing at the side of the front door with his back to the stucco, his eyes are stinging.

"Sasha in place," he whispers into his comms.

"Give me a moment to set up," comes Victor's voice.

The lock in the apartment door clicks.

"I'm going to attempt entry," Sasha whispers.

"Okay. But don't approach the top floor until I say so."

The door opens outwards. An elderly woman walks onto the sidewalk from the apartment building. All her attention is on the handbag dangling off an elbow as she tucks her keys inside. She certainly doesn't see Sasha catch the door in his gloved hand and creep inside the lobby.

Carefully, he makes his way upstairs, listening out for tenants, until he is on the fourth floor. There, he takes out his phone, gets up the tracker. They've managed to add the plans for the apartment to the app so that they now see the dots in relation to where they are in the attic apartment.

One is in the bathroom. The other is in the lounge, probably where the couch and TV are. The attic is only another floor up. Sasha listens out. He can just about make out the rumble of a television. And the shower, too. Neither appears to be expecting them.

"Are you in position yet?" Sasha whispers.

"Just about... Da."

"What have you got?"

"Positive sighting in the living room," Victor says.

"Which one is it?"

"The kid, I think. I can only see the back of his head above the couch. He's watching television."

"Okay," Sasha says, putting away the phone. "You hit the kid and I'll take out Azrael in the shower."

"Good. Let me know when you're in position."

Sasha takes the Glock from the inside of his jacket, creeps up the last flight of stairs. Sneaks up to the door. Checks the phone one last time. They're still there. Uses a pick set on the lock. He's so skilled at it that only a bat could hear him scratching away, and soon he's—in.

"Now!"

The second Sasha steps into the apartment a bullet busts through a bay window and hits the kid right at the top of the head. Sasha doesn't see it, has no time for it. He rushes to the bathroom, barges the thin door in and unloads an entire clip on the form behind the shower curtain.

As he hurriedly snaps another magazine into the gun, he wonders why the form hasn't collapsed. When he rips back the curtain, his heart throbs and he has a full body sweat.

A mannequin stands in the shower with bullet holes all over its torso. It is wearing the same jacket Peter was wearing when the MSS watcher placed the tracker on him. Another dummy sits in the living room wearing Michael's jacket—the top of its head shot away.

Sasha turns quickly to his left. There is a gun pointed at him. Michael Black is holding it. A Sig Sauer P365 with a silencer twisted on the end. The kid's pistol of choice.

Sasha goes to wheel around and is stopped by a 9mm hollow-point entering his chest and expanding in his heart. The Glock goes off, but shoots nothing more detrimental than the wall.

Michael touches his earpiece. "This is Billy the Kid. I had to down mine. I hope you had more luck with yours."

———

"MINE'S ALL GOOD," Peter says into his own comms.

A strong breeze blows through the clocktower, ruffling his hair. Victor Milonov is sat up against the slight rise of wall that borders the observation deck. A few meters away his VSS Vintorez is set up on its bipod on top.

Victor's face is bleeding at the mouth. His hands are held above his shoulders, and he studies the man standing over him, Azrael, with a steely look.

A few seconds earlier the Russian had just got through realizing he had shot nothing more on that couch than a mannequin, when he felt the cold end of a pistol at the back of his head. Realizing suddenly that his luck was finally out, he'd turned to fight, but got no further than being pistol whipped into a daze.

"Get up," Peter says to him. "Slowly."

Victor stands. Slowly. As he does, the SVR assassin glances furtively at the VSS Vintorez. Tries to figure if he'd get there in time.

"You won't," Peter tells the Russian, and Victor's eyes are back on him.

"Turn around."

Again, Victor submits. Facing the sniper rifle, he realizes Azrael is right. In the scuffle he'd been beaten seven yards along the wall. The Vintorez is now at least nine feet away. He would never reach it before the bullet reached him.

"Put your hands behind your back."

Azrael pushes him forward over the rise and digs the Sauer into his ribs. Roughly, he places a pair of cable-ties looped together to form a makeshift set of handcuffs over the Russian's wrists. Pulls the ends tight.

Peter puts the Sauer into the underarm holster he wears beneath his jacket. Zips it back up over the top. He grabs Victor by the back of his parka, forces him forwards, and hopes that the Russian knows enough about him to know that a crowd of people wouldn't stop him shooting Victor if he made a run for it.

The Russian does know. He's looking for a way out of this that has better odds than that. So for now he does as he's told and lets Azrael push him down the stone steps.

Passing the Vintorez, Peter lurches toward it and shoves the rifle off the tower, hearing it smash on the cobbles below a few seconds later.

The sight of Peter leading the bound Victor through the clock room museum causes some alarm amongst the tourists.

"Non preoccupatevi, signore e signori," Peter tells them in Italian. "Sono un agente di polizia e quest'uomo è in arresto."

Don't worry, ladies and gentlemen. I am a police officer and this man is under arrest.

They get out of the way, all eyeing Victor like he's some pervert caught exposing himself to children, and Peter is able to usher him all the way out of the building. The second they are stepping onto the street, a UPS van comes bombing down the road, Ben Knight behind the wheel in a brown UPS uniform.

The side door slides open. Michael leans out, grabs hold

of Victor's shoulders, hauls him into the van. Peter gets in, bangs the door shut. Knight puts the van in gear, and, like that, they're gone.

———

PRATICA DI MARE AIR BASE, Rome
    11:45 CET

GENERAL YATES AWAITS his turn to speak. The cameramen are getting ready on the other side of the ring-shaped table. Ready to broadcast him all over the four huge tele screens that surround the room.

He sips the spring water provided on the table and goes over the speech one last time.

"You'll kill it, Henry," Paul Johnson whispers into his ear.

The general turns to him with a smile.

"Thanks, Paul. And again, I really appreciate you coming out here with me at such short notice."

"That's fine, Henry. You'll owe me the vacation time."

The two men chuckle gently and then return their attentions to the rest of the room as it breaks out in applause for the last speaker.

The cameraman comes right up to the table. "You all ready for this, General Yates?" he asks.

"Oh, yes," he says.

Henry Yates hardly hears anything of the NATO secretary general introducing him. He's more interested in getting through the next few minutes.

The light beside his microphone illuminates: it's live. He looks up and for a moment is startled to see his own face writ large on the huge telescreen in front of him. But he gets it together and begins the speech.

"Ladies and gentlemen of the summit," he says. "I sit here amongst you today in another man's place. Anthony Eustice."

There is a brief round of applause.

"Secretary of State Eustice was a good man," General Yates goes on. "Like the members of this alliance, he believed in the safety and security of the world. He believed in the power of good to defeat evil. He would have welcomed today's decision by Turkey to move ahead with the ratification of Finland's membership in NATO. This will strengthen Finland's security, it will strengthen Sweden's security, and it will strengthen NATO's security."

More applause. Then. "I hope that the Turkish Grand National Assembly will vote to ratify as soon as possible. Because God knows we need to secure the safety of Europe from the threats it faces today. Threats worse than anything it has faced since the Second World War. This organization was brought into existence because of those dark days. To say never again to warmongering and violent expansionism. Has the world forgotten those vital lessons we learned on the battlefields of the Somme? In the gas chambers of Auschwitz? Some would see us drawn into endless conflicts in an attempt to weaken our democracies. To turn our own people against us and to turn us against each other. Anthony Eustice believed in a world in which that would never be allowed to happen again."

A rousing applause permeates the room.

ROME
   12:00 CET

THEY SEARCH VICTOR THOROUGHLY. All he has on him is a wallet full of fake IDs, the comms unit earpiece, and a burner cell phone. Peter hands all of it over to Kirsty Lang. The tech-expert plugs the phone straight into the computer.

"Let's see what we have... Ohh. It's encrypted."

She turns to Victor.

The Russian sits in a chair at the end of the UPS truck. Arms and legs zip-tied to it. His eyes glued to the Vipertek VTS989 heavy-duty stun-gun that Peter holds in front of his face.

"This is going to be very simple," Peter tells him in perfect Russian. "I'm going to ask you some questions, and you're gonna answer them." He presses the trigger of the stun-gun. A ball of electricity illuminates the Russian's face. It's loud, too. Sounds like a firecracker continuously going off. "But this has to be quick. We don't have much time. So you only have five attempts. After five, I'm just gonna put a bullet in your head and toss you out on some street corner. Do you understand the rules?"

All the Russian says is: "Ya pomirilsya."

I've made my peace.

"One," Peter says. "Where is your pal the courier?"

Victor's cut lips purse into a smirk. "You know as well as I do that I am trained to withstand pain."

"That's the wrong answer."

Peter lurches forwards and smashes the powerful stun-gun straight between the Russians legs, not stopping until he feels the tongs crush his balls. Then he presses the trigger.

So much for the pain training. Victor Milonov screams at the top of his lungs, his body convulsing in the chair, his voice going hoarse, dissipating into a mere hiss. It burns the fabric of his trousers.

Peter takes it away.

A thin tendril of smoke rises up from between his legs. Victor's face is so lacking in color that you cannot tell where his lips start and end. For a moment he sits with his head cocked back, mumbling incoherently.

"You smell that?" Michael says.

"Again," Peter says, his attention never leaving the Russian tied to the chair. "Where is your pal?"

Victor straightens up. Takes a deep breath. Then. "It's gone. You've already lost."

Peter shoves a hand over his mouth and the stun-gun is exploding in Victor's stomach. The Russian can feel the muscles convulsing—his intestines convulsing. It's like he's being ripped apart in the middle, and all he can do is scream into Azrael's hand.

Peter removes the Vipertek, and it is while Victor Milonov slowly gets his breathing back that Kirsty Lang has an announcement.

"I'm past the phone's encryption software. Now all I need to do is find out who he's been in contact with."

"You hear that?" Peter asks Victor. "It's only a matter of time. Now tell me who the courier is? Who has the hard drive?"

Victor says nothing. Just stares at him.

"So be it."

The hand is back. The stun gun is back. This time he hits him in the chest, right over the heart. The Russian's eyes begin rolling into the back of his skull. The pain shoots all along his cardiovascular system. It feels like his blood is turning to acid inside of him.

When it is finished and the hand is removed from his mouth, Victor doesn't even cry out, he merely murmurs. His eyes stare off into the distant. His head hangs on the end of his neck, body completely limp and flopped in the seat, held there by the ties.

"That's three if you haven't been counting," Peter says.

In a weak, breathless voice, Victor mumbles, "It's no good. You're too late. My orders were to send it all over the internet to HQ and destroy the hard drive. Nothing exists of those files here in Rome. Nothing."

"You're a liar."

This time he hits him in the cheek and the sparks light up the Russian's entire face.

By the time Peter's finished, smoke is coming out of his mouth. Victor completely white. Slumped forwards. His chest heaving.

"Russia doesn't trust the internet in foreign countries," Peter explains. "Especially not something this sensitive. You won't risk losing to some hacker or the files being copied whilst in the online realm. Because if those files are copied, you'll lose your leverage. If the whole things out in the open and the cuckoos are exposed, your strategic partnership with the CCP is finished. So the only way you'd risk it leaving this city is in physical form. So where is your courier?"

Victor uses the last of his strength to lift his head, look Peter in the eyes, then shake it.

"You want to die for this?" Peter says. "You tell me what I want to know and you can still see your family back home. Live to fight another day."

Victor's mood changes. He begins chuckling, before the pain makes him stop.

"You think," he says, "that if I turn on my own country, they aren't dead? The second my betrayal is confirmed back home, a death squad will pay my family a visit in their St. Petersburg apartment and murder them all. Then, for the rest of my life, I will be hunted by men like me—like you and your son. Hunted until I am dead. I think it is more peaceful to die here today. Don't you?"

The Russian wears an earnest expression.

"Hey!" Kirsty Lang shouts triumphantly. "I've got it. He's been communicating with someone about a package. There's chatter about the pick up. That's who has it."

Victor looks over sharp. His eyes are bulging.

The van is equipped with all the latest surveillance technology including an International Mobile Subscriber Identity Catcher (IMSI catcher); a devise for searching out cell phones, with the ability to activate their GPS and track them physically. Now they have the cell phone number of the courier they can hone in on his cell phone and track it through the numerous cell phone towers that the IMSI catcher infiltrates; acting as a big old fishing net for all phone traffic in a twenty mile radius.

"When was the handover?" Peter asks Kirsty Lang.

"Not long ago. The courier still has it—he's taking it to another contact. Here. I'm tracking the phone... Found it."

"Where?"

"Not far. It's still in Rome. On the move."

"Get on the comms to Ibliss and give her its position."

———

"Girl in Black this is Night Owl," comes over her comm's earpiece.

"This is Girl in Black," Ibliss replies as her Ducati glides slowly through the midday streets of Rome.

"I have a location on the Russian courier. Sending over tracking data to your phone now."

It's instantaneous. Ibliss gets it up on the screen that sits on her fuel tank. A dot on a map. Not far from here.

"I got him," Ibliss says, pulling back the throttle and launching the bike into traffic.

Leaning left and then right, she weaves the Ducati through the scooters, taxis and pedestrians of inner Rome. The dot on the screen is moving east to west along via del Tritone. Ibliss is heading north along via del Corso. She should cut him off at Piazza Poli where via del Tritone redirects into via del Corso.

TWENTY-EIGHT

PRATICA DI MARE AIR BASE, ROME - 12:45 CET

THE SPEECH WENT DOWN WELL. HE GOT A HEARTY applause that he gathered was at least as good as the applauses given for all the other delegate's speeches.

Afterwards they all stand and pose for the usual photo opportunities.

"Nice speech, General," says France's Minister for the Armed Forces as the two men side up to each other for a group picture.

"It wasn't really mine, Minister," Yates tells him out the side of his mouth.

"Ah, of course. It was Anthony's. Such a tragic occurrence."

"Yes, truly. There are some seriously misguided people out there in the world, Minister."

"Oui. Il y en a vraiment," the Frenchman replies.

Yes. There truly are.

The photos take less than twenty minutes, all the delegates shuffling about in the heat of the studio lights, getting into position, having a few shots taken, and then being ordered into new places.

At the end, as everyone breathes a huge sigh of relief, one of General Yates's security detail come over and discreetly says, "It is time, Vice Chairman."

ROME
12:50 CET

WITHIN A FEW MINUTES Ibliss has caught up with the courier. He's stuck behind slow-moving traffic and Ibliss is able to take a position three cars' lengths behind him.

"I have eyes on the target. One male rider on a green Kawasaki Ninja 500."

"Are you able to engage?"

"I don't want to spook him in so much traffic."

But it is too late for such sentiments. The courier glances into one of his mirrors and spots the black Ducati. He has been warned.

The courier pulls back the throttle on his Kawasaki and flees. Heading west, he aims the bike through a gap in the center of traffic, and guns it.

Ibliss fires the Ducati's engine, leans left and darts between two buses going in opposite directions. From here on in it's a race.

"This is Girl in Black. I've been spotted. I'm in pursuit."

"Okay, Girl in Black. We are attempting to establish his destination, and will attempt to join the pursuit as soon as it has been. Stay with him."

"Will do."

The two motorbikes pick their way through the busy streets. Ibliss has to be on guard. Pedestrians move across the road everywhere. Parents hauling children along. Stepping out into the road without looking. She can only catch quick glimpses of the courier through all the action happening directly in front of her. Then it's—a young couple stepping into the road and she has to slam on her brakes.

When she gets going again, she no longer has eyes on the target. She checks the screen of the phone to make sure he hasn't turned off. But it's okay. The thick traffic helps her cause.

She catches him at the Piazza Borghese. The gridlock is so heavy the three road junction resembles a parking lot. The courier is attempting to push his way through the congestion. His thumb works the horn of the Kawasaki, but the noise it makes merely fades into all the rest of the honks.

Spotting Ibliss, he takes drastic action. He hops the front wheel of the motorcycle onto the sidewalk and stretches off across the the cobbles of the piazza, the pigeons and the tourists rushing to get out of the way. Ibliss follows, chasing after him into a narrow side street thronging with people, quickly finding herself stuck at their pace.

She lifts her visor and shouts. "Togliti di mezzo!"

Get out of the way!

She is forced to stand up on the footrests of the Ducati in an attempt to pick out the Kawasaki further ahead in the mass of people. She drops down and glances at the phone. He's about thirty yards ahead, moving just as slowly as her.

"Night Owl?" she says into her comms.

"Yes."

"How far are you from figuring the target's destination?"

"Not sure at the moment. Looks like he's heading defense Vatican City. From there he could join the highway at via Gregorio."

"What about joining the pursuit?"

"We're currently in the process of figuring where's best. The traffic in your vicinity is too thick for the truck."

"Tell me about it."

"Just stay close to him, Girl in Black."

"Easy for you to say."

———

PRATICA DI MARE AIR BASE, Rome
    13:10 CET

AFTER THE MAIN part of the summit, the key delegates belonging to each of the fourteen nations are taken beneath the hangar into a bunker buried fifty feet below.

A rickety service elevator takes them down, and at the bottom they walk out into cold, stale air that blows from the filtration units hanging from the ceilings. Their expensive shoes then echo a staccato beat off the reinforced concrete as they are led down a corridor with few doors. At the end stand two soldiers with equipment for scanning retinas and fingerprints.

General Yates goes through it with the same bored enthusiasm as the others, and once it's finished they are let into a room the size of two tennis courts.

Apart from the huge conference table in the center, the only other thing of significance in the room is the mass of glass cabinets that take up the whole of the end wall. Inside them are numerous servers, their lights blinking. A chill runs through the room as the air conditioning works overtime to keep them all cool.

The general takes a seat at the table, finding his name written on one of the place name holders. The business of sitting down is made awkward for General Yates by the fact that he has a small metal case handcuff-chained to his wrist. Packed in foam inside the case are two MissionPak SLC ultra-portable secure solid-state drives (SSD). Approximately the same size as a typical commercial USB flash drive, this military standard secure SSD has been precision-engineered to withstand the harshest operating environments while simultaneously protecting sensitive data from cyberattack. Armed with AES-256 XTS encryption, the strongest available on the market today, the SSD is able to clear itself in less than ten seconds to protect data, the fastest erase time available in the world.

One of the SSDs is clean. The other holds almost twenty terabytes of American military secrets. All top level stuff.

It is this part of the summit that brings the nerves rising to the surface inside General Yates. The classified information swap.

On the final day, all the big defense supremos from each

NATO nation get together in a secure location. There, they will share all their defense information. All the countries hosting US nuclear weapons as part of NATO's nuclear sharing policy, will provide details of security at the sites, as well as their location, staff lists, what is there, and when it is there. The British will provide details of their Trident system of submarines—the ones carrying nuclear warheads around British waters. Basically, everything you need to know in order to infiltrate these places. Every piece of NATO equipment and its location will be shared between the members. But not just that. They will also share the exact positions of all undersea data cables along with their access points and security arrangements. And even though you can get the locations of these cables on the internet, you don't get the locations of military cables—or the places in which they can be accessed. Imagine if the Chinese were able to tap into those. They'd have unlimited access to US intelligence.

"This shouldn't take too long," Yates's security detail Gerry says.

"I hope not," General Yates complains. "This handcuff is biting into my wrist. They could have gotten something a little more comfortable."

"You want them fur-lined, General?"

Yates turns to the grinning face of the Secret Service man.

"Ha ha, Gerry," the general says dryly, rubbing his wrist.

———

ROME
13:35 CET

．． ．

THEY'RE across the river now, heading north-west toward the A90 autostrada. The traffic is a little thinner on the two-laned street they dash down. But only a little.

Ibliss whips around the scooters and other vehicles that move at much lower speeds. She fights her way across the traffic at intersections, avoids pedestrians as they dart between the slower moving cars instead of using the cross-walks. She pulls back the throttle, accelerates around a garbage truck. On the more open road the Ducati Panigale V4R really comes into its own against the less powerful Kawasaki Ninja.

She races up to the courier through a group of scooters, forcing them to move out of the way as they linger in a single lane. The courier spots the maneuver in his mirror and jacks his throttle back as the car in front turns off into a side street.

Like two bullets, they roar along, squeezing in between the cars, leaning left and right as they lash around the lingering traffic, racing toward another intersection.

The courier makes it across, but Ibliss is less lucky. Just as she reaches the junction all the lanes fill up with traffic and she gets caught behind two dirt-covered city buses, the gap between them too tight for the Ducati. She's forced to pull up onto the sidewalk to overtake before the courier gets away.

The second she is back on the road, she throttles hard to cut the distance, the Ducati's engine roaring beneath her. She soon spots him. Seven car lengths ahead. Checking the map on her phone, she sees that they're coming right up to the A90, and the next thing, she is following him up the on-ramp and onto the four-lane expressway, merging with the traffic, the two bikes speeding up.

Now it is a sprint.

"I've got confirmation of his destination," Kirsty Lang's voice comes in her ear.

"Where?" Ibliss snaps greedily.

"A private airfield about ten miles away. We just checked satellite imagery of it. There's a Gulfstream jet waiting on the runway. It's registered to a shell company we're sure belongs to the Russians."

"You gonna meet me there?"

"We're trying."

"Then try harder. Girl in Black out."

And with that Ibliss guns the throttle back.

———

PRATICA DI MARE AIR BASE, Rome
    13:50 CET

GENERAL YATES CARRIES the suitcase because he happens to have a higher security clearance than the other two men; Admiral McArthur and Craig Hernandez.

When he is called up, General Yates makes his way to the bank of servers and allows the technician standing there to take the case holding the MissionPak SLCs. The general's security detail Gerry then oversees the unlocking of the handcuff chain. The technician then takes the case to a desk attached to the servers and opens it. Removing the two SSDs inside, he plugs technician plugs a USB cable into both drives; downloading from one, uploading into the other. Literally millions of files—every piece of military strategy that NATO has.

Each of the fourteen delegates are invited up one by one. Five minutes later all fourteen are lined up and connected to the servers. The delegates are invited back to their seats. The process will take around half an hour to complete.

While they wait, a series of discussions begin around future NATO strategy. China and Russia don't take long to find their ways into conversation.

———

ROME
13:55 CET

THEY SPEED ALONG THE EXPRESSWAY, engines roaring, the bikes zipping past traffic as they cut between the four lanes, leaning so hard around corners that their knees almost touch the asphalt.

For fifteen minutes they continue on, until the concrete of the city begins to give way to leafy poplar-lined suburbs, broken up by farmland, until the road is heading out into a landscape made up predominantly of fields and open land.

"You're not far from the airfield now," comes Kirsty Lang's voice down her earpiece.

Ibliss prays there's not a team of Spetnaz waiting for her there.

The airfield slowly comes into view. It sits on a slight plateau in a rolling valley. The place is pretty big. At least four runways and plenty of space for planes. From where she sees it, it looks like a huge oily smudge in the middle of a green and yellow ocean.

The off-ramp is about three hundred yards further on. The courier is about forty yards ahead. Knowing that he will have to turn off, Ibliss takes a gamble. She leans the bike right and overtakes the truck she's behind using the hard shoulder.

Suddenly she hits the brakes hard, shimmying a little on the loose gravel. Up ahead, a bus has broken down and blocks the shoulder. She just about gets back behind the truck and into the next lane. Her plan had been to cut the courier off as he turned, but the bus put paid to that.

They both turn off, one after the other, Ibliss barely fifty yards behind. The off-ramp causeway is cluttered with traffic. The two are forced to use the narrow gaps at the sides of the cars to get by. She almost catches him as the road twists back underneath the A90 and heads out defense the airfield.

"Where the hell are you, Night Owl?" Ibliss cries out into her comms.

"Not far from your position. Just keep following him. We'll be there soon."

The courier has called ahead. It is obvious the moment they race into the airfield. The gates are wide open and the Gulfstream is on the runway ready to take off. They zip past a huge hangar and head onto the airfield. The plane is already on the move. They're about three hundred yards from it. The rear luggage hatch is open and Ibliss can see a man hanging out of it, all set to take whatever is handed to them.

It slows down so that the courier can catch up. Ibliss

jacks the throttle and roars up on the Kawasaki, but right when she's about to reach him, he swerves to the left and it is almost too late when she sees the end of the assault rifle sticking out the cargo hatch.

It explodes in muzzle flash. She brakes. Veers one way then the other, almost flips the bike, the back wheel coming up off the asphalt as it chips up around her, the Ducati bucking like an angry bull, Ibliss lucky to get it back under control.

"Shit!" she complains as she twists the throttle.

She's lost at least a hundred yards. The Kawasaki quickly catching up, both vehicles accelerating, doing at least a hundred-and-twenty miles per hour, practically takeoff speed. The wheels of the plane start to rise up off the runway. The courier almost there, one hand controlling the bike, the other holding out the rucksack with the copy inside. The guy reaching out of the back, the two like the depiction of god and man on the ceiling of the Sistine Chapel; god and man, the spark, about to touch, the rucksack just inches from the fingers of the guy hanging out the rear hatch.

"Night Owl, where are you?" Ibliss screams, her eyes fastened to the Kawasaki right at the point the courier is about to—

The UPS truck comes out of nowhere, smashes the courier and his motorcycle right at the point the Gulfstream is lifting into the air, the man hanging out the hatch left with nothing but an empty hand.

Knight punches the brakes and brings the truck to a screeching stop. Two thick black lines cover the asphalt. Above them, the Lear jet continues rising, the hatch now closed, the Russians thwarted.

The courier hits the runway, bounces a few times and comes to a stop. He's dead. You can tell by the way he lies there all twisted up.

Ibliss goes for the rucksack. Picks it up one handed from her bike and brings it to the truck just as the side door whips open. Unzipping it, Ibliss quickly finds the unit the Russians have saved it on. A hard drive in a secure metal case. She plucks it from its foam holding and hands it to Kirsty Lang.

"Okay," the CIA hacker says, taking it to the computer. "Let's see what we have."

———

PRATICA DI MARE AIR BASE, Rome
    14:50 CET

GENERAL YATES IS BACK above ground, the MissionPak SSD attached to his wrist, the metal cuff as uncomfortable as ever.

Separating from the rest of the delegation, he and Paul Johnson are escorted to their limousine. They get into the back and are joined by one of the Secret Service men, Gerry. He sits along the backseat next to Paul. Yates sits the other side as he always likes the window seat. Behind the wheel is their allocated driver, and in the front passenger seat is the other Secret Service detail, a guy by the name of Kevin.

"That went well," Paul says as they begin the short journey across the airbase to the waiting E-4B.

"Yes. I thought so too," Yates replies, turning away from

the view. "Now just to get this back to the Pentagon," he adds, holding up the little case. "Then I can get this handcuff off my wrist."

Paul Johnson is about to say something when the general's mobile telephone cuts him off. Yates digs it out of his pocket, takes a look at the screen.

"It's James," he says, meaning Admiral James McArthur.

"He's already on the plane, isn't he?" Paul asks.

"Yeah," Yates grunts dubiously as he answers the call. "Let's see what's up. Admiral?"

Sitting right next to him, Paul can hear everything of the telephone conversation.

"Something's gone down," Admiral McArthur says.

"What?"

"How close are you from getting here?"

General Yates looks out the window. The E-4B is just about visible on the horizon. It is less than five hundred yards away.

"I don't know—about a minute. Why?"

"Jimmy Nash has shown up."

"As in Deputy Director Nash?"

"The one and only."

"What's he doing there?"

"Exactly. He was here when we arrived at the plane. Made an announcement that we're to stay in the main cabin and no one's to use their phone."

"Which is why you're using yours, then?"

"I'm an Admiral. No one tells me what to do."

"Is he asking for anyone in particular?"

"No. He says he wants to wait until everyone's here. You

don't think it's more fallout from Anthony Eustice, do you?"

"I'm not sure. I guess we'll—"

The movement is so swift and fast that the general is lost for words when it happens. Beside him Paul Johnson at lightning speed has just disarmed Gerry of his SIG Sauer P229 standard issue sidearm. He now puts a bullet into the side of Gerry's head, sending his brains shooting out at the window, puts another into the back of Kevin's head, sending his into the windshield, and places the hot barrel of the pistol to the back of the driver's skull.

"Get us out of here," Paul Johnson commands.

Everyone's ears ring. The Italian driver hardly hears him. And not just that. He's in shock. Sitting there with blood spatter all down one side of his face. Shaking all over. The car slowly rolling to a stop.

"You understand English?" Paul snaps.

In a barely audible whisper, the driver says he does.

"Then drive us out of here."

"Where?"

"Off this airbase."

"At the gate they won't let us."

"Then you have to drive through the barrier."

"They might shoot."

"I'll definitely shoot."

The driver nods. Turns the limo around.

"P-Paul?"

He turns to his right.

General Yates sits next to him with wide, staring eyes, the phone still clasped to his ear. Admiral McArthur's voice can just about be made out over the ringing. "Henry?" he's saying. "Was that gunfire?"

"Tell him it was a car backfiring," Paul Johnson tells Yates in a too-calm voice.

General Yates is a forty year military man. He's been around gunfire all his life. But never has he witnessed two men killed right next to him. And never by someone who he regarded as a friend. Someone who regularly eats with his family.

The explosive noise and the facts of the matter have shaken the general almost as much as the driver. This is Paul Johnson for Christ's sake. A man he's known almost his entire career. A man he's always felt safe around. Who's always been a subordinate. The classic military pencil pusher who never made it above lieutenant colonel. Perfect for the role of his head of communications when he went into government. Never in his wildest dreams did he think Paul Johnson could be capable of such brutal acts.

"Tell him," Paul growls in a voice General Yates does not recognize.

"Hey, James," Yates says, his voice sounding far away. "It was just a car backfiring."

"Tell him we'll be there shortly," Paul says.

"We'll be there shortly."

Paul reaches forward, takes the phone from his fingers and ends the call. He then taps in a number of his own and places it to his ear.

"W-what is happening, P-Paul?" Yates asks.

Paul Johnson places a finger to his lips.

The call is answered and for the first time in the thirty

years they've known each other, Paul Johnson speaks Mandarin in front of General Yates.

"This is K," he says. "We need to change to plan B."

———

THEY'RE STILL at the airfield when the call comes in. Kirsty Lang takes it at the van's comms station and rushes to the others outside.

"He's escaped!" she says.

Everyone looks her way.

"He's killed Yates's security detail," she goes on, "and hijacked the car. It drove through the gates of the airbase."

"With the files?" Knight asks.

Kirsty Lang just nods.

"Any idea where it's heading?"

"Rome at the moment. It's on the motorway being pursued. The limousine has GPS."

"Do we have access to that?" Knight asks.

"We can."

"Then it's best you get on it."

Kirsty Lang nods and dashes back into the van.

Peter is already on his way to the Ducati. "Ibliss, I need to borrow your motorcycle."

"Sure," she says.

Peter gets on the superbike, taking the helmet hanging on the handlebars and shoving it onto his head.

"I'm coming," Michael says. "Just let me grab something first."

The kid jumps into the van, and when he emerges he's

holding an AA-12 fully-automatic assault shotgun fitted
with a twenty shell drum.

––––––––

Sirens and blue lights scream out behind them as the
limousine races down the three lanes of the via Pontina
motorway. In the distance the square tower of the Castel di
Decima looms up on the hilly horizon.

Paul Johnson is on full alert. The gun gripped in his
blood-spattered hand and pointed at the back of the driver's
head, he scans the surrounding environment with a keen
vigilance.

"We're nearly there," he mutters to himself upon spotting the medieval castle in the distance.

"Paul, listen to me," General Yates says. "Whatever
you're into, you need to stop it. Now."

The general sits frozen beside him, aware of how quickly
Paul had shot the security detail. Without a moment's hesitation. It wouldn't be clever to move next to such a man. So
he stays perfectly still. No longer even aware of the
MissionPak SSD attached to his wrist.

"Paul, talk to me," the general goes on in a soft voice.

Paul Johnson ignores him. His eyes watch the roadside,
like he's looking for something. With Knight and the others
running around it had always seemed possible that this
wouldn't be as easy as waiting for the general to fall asleep on
the plane and copy the data onto his own device he'd stored
away in his luggage. In case of discovery, there had always
been a rougher, more action-laden plan on how to get the
data out of Rome and into MSS hands.

This is it.

Paul spots the two men in tracksuits. They stand either side of the busy highway.

"Faster," he growls at the driver.

The Italian presses his foot down on the gas peddle. The needle of the speedometer climbs up to a hundred and twenty, the distance growing between them and the three chasing police cruisers.

The second the limousine flashes past the two men in tracksuits, they each send extendable spike-strips shooting out into the road from either side. Composed of three inch metal barbs pointing upward, the strips stretch out into the lanes and cover the entire highway.

Traveling at a hundred, the three police cruisers have no chance to avoid the spikes-strips. All three go straight over them and immediately feel the effect of the punctures as the vehicles slip and slide on their rapidly deflating tires, the drivers having to tap their brakes to keep control.

As they bumble to a stop, the limousine stretches away.

At the same time, the MSS agents in tracksuits run down the embankment of the highway to a manmade drainage gulley. Two motocross bikes await them and they hop on. Soon they are zipping down the gulley, passing the cops above them on the road, who by now have stopped completely.

"You see that car up ahead?" Paul Johnson says into the driver's ear.

The Italian is so nervous all he sees is the immediate road. He looks and focuses on the middle distance. A black sedan is parked on the hard shoulder about two hundred yards further along.

"Uh-huh."

"I want you to pull into the hard shoulder and park behind it."

The driver indicates, slows down, steers into the hard shoulder, brings the car to a stop behind the sedan. The second he pulls the handbrake Paul Johnson pulls the trigger and kills him.

Yates is so startled he cries out. Clenches his eyes shut.

When they're open again, the pistol is pointed at him.

Unbeknownst to the general, someone has just gotten out of the sedan. A fridge-sized man with a long face. He reaches General Yates's side of the car and pulls the door open. The general almost falls out. The huge man has to grab him by the shoulder to steady him. In his other hand Fridge holds a pair of bolt cutters.

"Hold still," Paul says.

Fridge goes about cutting the chain.

Yates and Paul stare at each other.

"Twenty-seven years we've known each other, Paul," the general says. "All that time you spent around my family and you were just waiting for something like this. Some chance to rip off your own country."

"Your country, Henry. I was born in Shenzhen, the People's Republic of China."

The chain is snapped and the big man goes to take the SSD from Yates's lap, but the general snatches it up in both hands and grasps it to his chest. Paul digs the pistol into his stomach.

"Let it go," he snarls.

The general looks him right in the eyes. "I don't believe,

Paul," he says, tears in his eyes, "that after all these years you'd—"

This gunshot is louder than the others. He feels it recoil all the way through him, the blast burning a brand of the barrel into his skin and scorching a hole through his shirt. Pain explodes in his stomach and spreads through him till he's feeling it in his teeth. It's like he's been ripped in half. He can't even scream the pain is so bad. It cuts his voice off. He doesn't know when he lost the SSD and grabbed ahold of his stomach instead, but that's what he's doing now.

As for Paul Johnson, aka Agent K, and his freakishly large companion, they are currently walking at a brisk pace to the VW Lavida in front. They get in, drive away. Leaving the general to bleed to death in the back of the limo.

———

THE DUCATI ROARS down the A90 autostrada, the needle of the speedometer trembling at a hundred and sixty, the two of them low and gripped to the bike. The AA-12 automatic shotgun strapped to the kid's back. Ready for action.

Heading south along the eastern edge of the city, they are attempting to cut them off.

"They've found the limo," comes Kirsty Lang's voice in Peter's ear. "General Yates is dead."

"So no more GPS, then?" he says back.

"That's an affirmative, Azrael. But I may have another way of tracking them. I'm accessing Rome Municipal CCTV now. Okay. I've got full access to the highway cameras. Just need to log into the one closest to the location they found the limo at. Got it. Rewinding back through the footage. Okay. They've exchanged vehicles. They're now in a black VW Lavida. It's a four door..."

"I know what a VW Lavida is. How long ago did they..."

A big four-by-four land cruiser swings into their lane right in front of them, only bothering to indicate at the last moment. Peter has to swerve to avoid it and almost loses control, the Ducati tipping from side to side, Michael struggling with him to keep it upright.

"Azrael, you still there?"

"Yeah. When did the exchange happen?"

"Eight minutes ago. I'm following them on the cameras."

"Have you got current eyes on them?"

"Not yet. But I'm only a minutes away and counting. I'm just reaching them live... Okay. Got them."

"Where?"

"They're on the autostrada. Same one as you. Heading in your direction. No wait... They're turning off... Now heading west along the A91."

"They're heading to the coast," Peter observes. "Look for marinas in that direction."

"Already on it," Kirsty Lang snaps back.

"What about us? Any way to get us to them quicker?"

"Yeah. In about another mile will be the via Aurelia turn off. Take the off-ramp and head straight down it. You should cut them off after another four miles at Centro Tre Denari."

————

PAUL JOHNSON/AGENT K grips the MissionPak SSD tightly to his chest. The two of them have already fitted it with a devise that stops the Americans from remotely contacting it and having the MissionPak run a security program that wipes all its data.

Fridge drives them at speed northwards up the west coast of Italy. K can't help constantly flicking his gaze to the wing-mirror and the three-laned highway behind them. Nervously anticipating the man they call Azrael. A man who could make or break his four decades long mission.

Handpicked at the age of fourteen to begin training for something that would probably take all his life, K feels this moment as the culmination of his entire existence. In a way, he is glad that he has been found out. That he can now be honest for the first time since he was just a teenage boy. He tries to think as little as possible about the American family he leaves behind; his wife and two grown daughters. Blocks them out. Pushes away the fact that he'll never see them again. What he thinks about instead is the glory of what he grips in his arms. An intelligence cache the likes of which has never been seen. And it is all his. Every lie. Every betrayal. It is all worth it because of this.

They pass a sign for Centro Tre Denari and K realizes they have another thirty minutes until their destination. It makes him nervous. Half an hour is a long time. His grip tightens around the SSD and his eyes watch the rearview.

———

"I'm almost at the Centro Tre Denari junction," Peter cries into his comms.

"You should be almost on him," Kirsty Lang replies.

"I see him."

The black VW Lavida is heading towards the intersection where the two roads meet—moving north from the left while they come in from the east; like two comets on a collision course. Peter rips back the throttle and sends the Ducati tearing forwards, darting in and out of the slow-moving cars.

As the roads merge, Fridge looks sideways out his window and spots the black Ducati coming up beside them. His foot presses down on the gas and the needles starts climbing up through eighty toward a hundred.

The Ducati spills out of the A12 onto the via Aurelia; about twenty yards behind the sedan.

"You ready for this, Mikey?"

"Oh yeah."

The kid is gripping the bike with his powerful legs. He pulls the AA-12 automatic shotgun from his back. Grips the stock tight to his shoulder. Fires off a volley of buckshot rounds. They stamp a series of big holes across the tailgate of the sedan, the car swerving sideways across the three lanes to avoid taking anymore. It skips in front of another car, blocking their view.

The AA-12 is the perfect weapon for this because it has extremely low recoil, and therefore accuracy, for such a powerful weapon. When the bolt flies back after firing to cycle another round, around eighty percent of what would normally be felt as recoil is absorbed by a proprietary gas system. A recoil spring grabs another ten percent, leaving the final recoil a remarkable ten percent of the normal recoil for a twelve-gauge round—so you can point the AA-12 at a target and unload the full magazine without significant loss of accuracy. Meaning Agent K and his humungous friend are in a lot of trouble if all they have is that VW sedan.

Peter whips around a panel van and tries to come up on them from the right side. However, as they're about to reach them, he spots something in the wing-mirror.

Two motocross bikes have come balling up the highway's embankment and they burst onto the road. The build up of traffic they encountered at Centro Tre Denari keeps them at a cool ninety as they weave in and out of the vehicles. The two tracksuits are riding KTM 450 SX-Fs. The most powerful and fastest dirt bike currently available. With a top speed of 123 miles per hour, they can easily keep up in the thick traffic.

The highway enters an urban landscape of flat blocks and commercial districts. The road is lifted up on concrete stilts as it rises over the buildings below. They are now in a three-laned concrete tunnel with a forty foot drop either side. Essentially, a gantlet run.

The motocross bikes get within a couple of car lengths. Controlling the bikes one handed, the men take Uzi Micro machine pistols from holsters strapped to their fuel tanks—and open fire.

Unable to keep their aims straight, they don't just fire at the Ducati. They send a mist of 9mm bullets across the three lanes of the highway, hitting the traffic between the Ducati and the escaping sedan. It sends the vehicles into a panic. The back windshield on a little Fiat two-door shatters and the driver brakes hard. The front of the car dips and the back swings out. The car buckles, careering out of control, and smashes into the concrete barrier. A van traveling behind it doesn't brake in time and plows straight into it. The highway exploding into chaos.

The Ducati is in the middle lane. The crash is on their

right. Directly in front of them the lane is blocked by a van. On their left is a huge juggernaut with a forty foot load. As cars skittle across the lanes, Peter spots a two meter gap open up between the front of the truck and the rear of the van and rips back the throttle.

"Hold on, kid!"

The gap is a meter and a half and shrinking. As more bullets hit the vehicles around them, including the truck and the van, they swerve violently left into the opening as it closes to mere feet. Michael pulls the AA-12 in to avoid it being smashed out of his hands. The back wheel clips the truck's bumper, almost sending them over, but they make it through. An added bonus is the fact that they are now closed off by traffic from the KTMs. For the meantime anyway.

The VW Lavida is four car lengths ahead. Slaloming through traffic. Michael once more aims the AA-12 and lets rip. The back windshield explodes. A continual flow of buckshot rounds punching the back of the sedan like a factory press. One-two-three. One-two-three.

And then the kid is shot.

It comes from behind. A 9mm round from one of the Uzis hitting him in the back of the right shoulder. Through the body armor, it feels like being hit by a slingshot at close range.

It numbs his whole right arm and he almost loses grip of the AA-12, the pain stretching down to his fingers.

He twists around on the bike and sees the KTMs coming up on them, the crash well behind.

"We gotta get rid of those fucking bikes," he says.

A game of hide-and-seek within the cars, trucks and vans begins. Their attention off the sedan for a moment. The two tracksuits unload their Uzis on the traffic, their scattergun aims chasing the Ducati across the lanes as it throttles in front of a long bus and they lose sight of it.

The Uzis are almost out. They are loaded with thirty-three round magazines, and they've already gone through two. The men linger behind the bus a while as they reload, needing all their skill to perform the maneuver whilst riding a bike.

Once this is complete, they go in search of the Ducati. The bus occupies the left lane. The right lane is taken by a panel van. The middle is clear. They can see the sedan further ahead, but can't see the Ducati.

As they pass the bus one of them goes to ask the other where the targets are through his comms when there is an explosion of rapid buckshot rounds that hit him one after the other. They come from his left, from directly in front of the bus, the Ducati having slowed and taken a hidden position right at the bus's front grill, waiting for the men.

A total of four shots hit the lead man and his bike, and both topple across the lanes. The powerful rounds shred him, regardless of the body armor under his Adidas, and a garbage truck finishes him off when it runs him and the KTM over.

The other KTM pulls up just in time to avoid becoming a stain on the highway and skips across the lane.

Peter is quick and cunning, though. He pulls to the left. There is barely a two foot gap between the concrete divider and the side of the bus, but he pulls into it and slows down. The driver lets off his horn as he slides past them, until the Ducati is behind the bus, Peter pulling back onto the road.

The remaining KTM is now in front of them, but the

MSS man on it thinks they're somewhere in front. In frustration from not seeing them, he lets off a volley of Uzi bullets into the traffic, sending the cars into a frenzy. Screeching tries, smoke filling the highway.

Peter and Michael make their move. They come from out behind the bus. Michael aiming the AA-12 in front. Pulls the trigger.

It is like tracksuit is being hit by an invisible stampede of elephants. He is thrown over the handlebars of the KTM so hard that the front wheel of the bike hits him as he pounds the speeding asphalt, the motocross bike flipping over and cartwheeling down the road.

Only the sedan is left now.

They leave the causeway and the urban area. Green fields dotted with trees stretch out either side of them. The highway opens up, less cars, more room; just them and the VW Lavida about a hundred-fifty yards in front.

"I think it's time you switch to the FRAG-12 rounds," Peter tells his son over the comms.

Michael duly obliges, tugging off the twenty-shell drum magazine and snapping in the eight-shell box magazine. The one containing the FRAG-12 high-explosive rounds.

They begin to see the twinkle of the sea beyond the fields on their left. Fridge puts the Lavida in overdrive. They're now doing at least a hundred-twenty.

"You ready?" Peter asks.

"Oh yeah," the kid replies.

Peter twists back the throttle. Guns the Ducati, flicking his foot up quickly through the gears, the needle zipping up to a hundred-forty on the speedometer as they rocket up on the sedan.

The G-force almost rips the kid off the bike and it takes all the strength in his well-built thighs and calfs to hold on as he aims the AA-12 at the upcoming VW, following it as it arcs across the lanes, waiting until it is in range and then—

He pulls the trigger and the road explodes behind the sedan. The power lifts the sedan off its back wheels. Fridge momentarily loses control of the car, just manages to get it back under control as they come up on a truck. The MSS man uses it. Just like Peter on the causeway, he comes before it and reduces his speed. The truck driver smashes his horn, changes lanes. But Fridge stays with him.

As the juggernaut veers across the highway, Peter keeps the Ducati back. But the second it settles down and remains in the left lane, he speeds up to bring them side on, keeping their speed level with the truck so they don't pass it.

The sedan suddenly swings out from in front of the truck. Comes directly in front of them. Brakes hard. Blue smoke. Screeching tires.

Peter punches both brakes and puts the Ducati into a sideways skid. The kid is thrown forwards into his father. He loses the AA-12, the automatic shotgun skittling off down the asphalt. He just about manages to grab Peter in time as they fall into the skid and narrowly avoid hitting the back corner of the sedan's tailgate.

Peter rights the bike. Michael gripping onto him for dear life as they wobble into an upright position.

The Lavida has lengthened the distance between them and they are now armed with nothing more than their Sig Sauer handguns. The tables have turned, it would appear.

The sunroof on the sedan opens and someone emerges

from it. Agent K aiming a pistol at them. Peter dodges across the lanes, taking refuge at the rear of a panel van.

Agent K disappears back into the car and the sedan gets farther away from them.

Peter is on the cusp of moving back out into the open road and catch up when Kirsty Lang comes over their comms.

"I think I know where they're heading."

"Where?"

"Santa Marinella."

"I see it signposted."

"There's a marina there. They must have a boat."

"Try and find out which one."

"I'll try. Night Owl out."

Kirsty is right. The second they come from out behind the van, they spot the Lavida about half a mile farther ahead turning onto the off-ramp for Santa Marinella.

———

By the time they catch up with the VW it's already at the marina.

Like the town itself, Santa Marinella Marina is small; an enclosed quay with two long jetties sticking out into the water. The boats aren't the biggest. Mostly speedboats and single berth yachts.

The VW Lavida is abandoned on the edge of the stone quay, the front doors wide open.

"Look!" Michael announces, pointing off at the jetty below.

Fridge and Agent K are moving along the wooden platform towards a speedboat, the MissionPak SSD trapped under K's arm.

"We need to get down there quick," Michael points out.

"Hold on," is Peter's reply.

The kid does as he's told, gripping both Peter and the bike tight as his father brings the bike around to get a run up. Then, twisting back the throttle, Peter sends the Ducati racing toward the quay's edge. He lifts the front wheel as they go over and the two stand up on the pegs to maintain their weight as the bike flies through the air, making sure to keep it perfectly balanced.

It hits the jetty, bounces slightly. Sparks fly from the shock absorbers. There is a terrible crunching sound. But they make it.

The MSS agents are in the boat and pulling out of there when they reach the space. Throwing down the bike, they jump off and aim their pistols, firing off a volley of bullets.

But it is no good. The speedboat is quick and already out of range.

Peter scans their surroundings. On the other side of the platform, an old man is mooring his speedboat having just arrived back from a late afternoon's cruise. He stands frozen in his boat, staring at the two bikers and their guns.

Peter brings the aim of the Sig Sauer around and fixes it on the man. Flipping up the visor of his helmet, he says, "We need your boat."

———

THE MSS OPERATIVES are heading southwest into open water.

Having discarded their helmets Peter and Michael race up behind them in the stolen speedboat. About fifty yards from them, Agent K whips around and Peter throws the steering wheel left to avoid the shots fired from the double agent's Glock. Bullets whistle past. Michael fires back. He aims at the biggest target—the boat—and manages to get a hit on the outboard motor.

It forces them into maneuvers, and the two boats begin a zig-zagging dance towards the horizon.

"You see that?" Peter asks Michael, pointing ahead.

"Yeah," the kid replies. "I see it."

"Night Owl," Peter says into his comms. "I think we know where they're going."

Looming up on the glistening horizon, the sun beginning to set behind it, is a massive super yacht. At least a hundred feet in length, they spot a helicopter on the deck, as well as a swimming pool.

Agent K and Fridge are heading straight for it.

It is when they get to within five hundred meters that Peter spots the specks of figures lining the edge of the deck. Then the Mexican wave of muzzle flash. Bullets cut up the water about a three hundred meters in front. Like the two tracksuits, they are firing Uzi Micros, which only have an effective firing range of two hundred meters.

"We're probably gonna have to swim the last part, Mikey," Peter announces.

"Great."

The kid starts peeling his shoes off along with the heavy Kevlar vest he wears. Peter does the same, keeping the speedboat straight as he does. He then rips a piece of his T-shirt and ties the throttle down, before tying the steering wheel so that the speedboat keeps straight.

They get within range of the Uzis. The water cutting up around them as the men fire relentless volleys.

"Wait till we're closer," Peter says to his son.

All the time the pair of them prepare their breathing. Slowly, they suck in deep lungfuls of air, then blow them out through their mouthes. In and out, in and out. Pulling the breath in so deep it hurts. Over and over.

They get within a hundred and fifty meters, bullets whipping the air around them. Pull in one last huge breath of air that fills their lungs till bursting. Then jump into the water, the speedboat continuing towards the yacht without them and drawing the Uzis' fire.

They crash through the surface of the crystal blue water. 9mm rounds dive after them. One of them gliding mere inches from Michael's face. They dive deeper to create a five meter gap of water between themselves and the bullets. They have a hundred and fifty meters of open water to swim; essentially three lengths of an Olympic sized swimming pool. No biggy.

But they need to be quick. Fridge and K are almost at the dock at the stern of the yacht.

They also need to change direction. It's no good making a beeline for the yacht and coming up right below the men with machine pistols. They split up and arc their routes to the boat, their limbs cutting efficiently through the water. They are both exceptionally strong swimmers and can hold their breathes for at least three minutes while exerting themselves. Still, it gives them barely enough time to reach the boat before they'll be forced to surface.

FRIDGE AND K reach the dock. A man is there to meet them, grabbing the edge of their speedboat and pulling it in.

While stepping onboard K glances sideways right at the moment the other speedboat smashes into the port side of the yacht. The impact rocks the boat as the much smaller craft buckles against the hull. The crash causes the yacht no more than a dent, but the speedboat is totaled at the front and soon sinks.

"Where's Azrael?" K asks the man once they are on the boat.

"We don't know," is the answer.

———

MICHAEL'S LUNGS ARE SCREAMING. Low on oxygen, the muscles in his legs and hands ache severely as he saws through the water, promising his body that he will get it oxygen soon, just as soon as he—

The kid takes hold of the anchor chain, the metal slimy under his touch, and begins hauling himself up.

Resisting the urge to throw himself up through the surface and gulp down air, he emerges slowly, his head gradually appearing. Finally his nose and mouth.

The sides of the hull are curved, so the deck overhangs the water, allowing the kid to stay hidden from the men above him as he slowly pulls air into his burning lungs.

The anchor chain reaches up to a chain locker. It will give him access to the deck above.

"I'm in position," he whispers into his comms, the earpiece still secure even after all that swimming.

"Me too," Peter whispers back.

Michael climbs the chain out of the water, pulling himself up towards the bow. At the top, he pulls himself up onto the chain and stands on it to take a peek at the foredeck.

It's empty. The men occupying the upper decks. He can hear them arguing about where they went. Their feet moving above him.

Michael practically crawls along the deck, taking a position behind the fore hatch. He removes his Sig Sauer P365 from his hip holster, twists off the suppresser and shakes the water out of it, lets the water run out of the barrel of the pistol.

Once he's maintained his weapon, he reapplies the suppressor and begins creeping along the foredeck towards a set of stairs that lead to the upper decks. He's almost there when a shadow stretches down them and a set of feet begin descending. Michael lifts the aim of the pistol, waits for the man to come low enough so those above won't see him fall when he's shot. But as the kid gets ready to fire, the guy spots him and lifts his Uzi.

Michael drops him before he can fire, but it's spotted.

Feet race along the deck above him and Michael is forced to take a door on his left, enter the yacht and head rapidly below deck.

———

K AND THE MissionPak SSD are onboard the AC332 Multirole helicopter that is at the bow of the yacht. Fridge will stay on the boat with the others to intercept the two assassins. The pilot is busy getting everything ready, flicking switches, the rotor blades beginning to turn.

K watches as the men run across the deck and head down the stairs on the port side. Something must have happened on the lower decks.

His blood goes cold. Azrael is here.

"Can't you hurry that up?!" K snaps at the pilot.

"I'm ready now, sir," the man says, flicking his last switch and pulling the collective pitch lever.

The helicopter's landing gear begins lifting up into the air. They are no more than a couple of feet when K spots Azrael emerging at the top of the stairs on the starboard side. His eyes explode with astonishment. The pilot is pulling the cyclic pitch lever at the front of the cockpit to lean them away when the end of Azrael's pistol flashes three times in quick succession. Three bullets form a close cluster of holes in the windshield and the pilot is dead.

He falls onto the controls and the chopper pitches forwards into the deck.

K has no choice but to throw himself out of the helicopter.

———

MICHEAL FEELS the impact of the crash above him. It is strong enough to make the yacht tip from side to side. The terribly loud noise of the helicopter rotors going out of control is followed by the sound of the craft crashing into the sea.

The floor beneath his feet settles and Michael resumes moving through the yacht. He has found himself in a long hallway lined with doors. As he creeps along hugging the wall, he can hear the sounds of the men moving about the yacht. Feet run over his head. Someone shouts in Mandarin. They aren't close.

He passes through the engine room. It's empty of people. Electrical panels display information about the engine, the life of the ships generator. Gauges display water pressure, and another panel controls the yacht's air conditioning system and hydraulic pumps. The kid creeps around the huge engine and emerges into another corridor. He proceeds past the kitchen. The door is open. Men in chefs uniforms cower inside. Michael places a finger to his lips and closes the door on them.

Then.

Running feet. About fifteen yards away. Where another passage bisects this one. Michael's grip on the pistol becomes firmer. He edges forwards as the feet come closer.

They stop. Right on the edge of the place the passages cross.

It is then that Michael spots the security camera on the ceiling.

They know where he is.

The kid gets about a second to think about this when the door to his right bursts open and a man the size of a marauding buffalo comes charging out at him. Before he can bring his aim around, a huge hand envelops the pistol and rips it from his grip, throwing it down the corridor and picking him up.

Michael is being driven backwards into a large ballroom of polished flooring, tables and chairs, vases on plinths. He thumps at Fridges rock hard back to no avail. They are heading straight at a wooden pillar in the center of the room. It'll be like being crushed by a truck.

Michael reaches out and grabs the first thing he can: a crystal vase. He breaks it over Fridge's massive head then uses a shard of it to stab him repeatedly in the side of his thick neck.

It makes the big man drop him—mere feet from the pillar—and Michael lands on his feet on the polished dance floor.

Fridge reaches to the side of his neck and feels the gashes in the flesh. None of them has reached either of his carotids, but the kid has managed to rip open several large holes in the giant.

Fridge cries out like some prehistoric neanderthal and explodes into a charge at Michael.

———

K HAS HURT his leg in the fall. Each time he places any weight on it, his knee roars in pain. He'd managed to escape the carnage of the helicopter crash and drop down to the lower decks. But he finds himself unarmed and separated from the others. And not just that. He knows nothing of this four story yacht. As he wanders inside it looking for the protection of his cohorts, he is lost, wandering a service corridor on the bottom deck and gripping the SSD to his chest like it's a newborn baby and he's its mother.

This storage device and the things it carries is currently the most important thing to K in the whole wide world. It is the culmination of his entire life. Everything will be worth it if he can just get it back to China. Back to his people to bask in the glory of a hero. He thinks about all the places he would like to go when he reaches his homeland. All the places he has dreamed about since he left as a teenager. The Great Wall. The Forbidden City. The Terracotta Army. The Potala Palace. The Summer Palace. The Mausoleum of Mao Zedong. Even to speak his original tongue. The language of his forebears. It will all be worth it so long as...

"Agent K," a deep voice calls to him from somewhere within the boat.

He glances up and down the narrow passage he roams.

There is nothing there except shadow.

"What a waste of a life," the voice goes on.

K still can't determine from which direction it is coming from.

"To spend all that time living a lie—and for what? The glory of other men?"

While scanning continuously right to left with his nervous eyes, K backs up to a door. He opens it from behind, rushes into the room, and quickly shuts himself inside. Locks the door.

He is in complete darkness. Not a single shred of light exists and he fumbles blindly along the wall for a light switch that he can't find.

"Such hollowness," the voice goes on.

It sounds like it's in the room with him.

K has given up on the light switch, he is backing rapidly through the dark. He trips over furniture, falls—someone grabs him.

"Boo," the voice says right in his ear.

————

MICHAEL HAS BEEN PLAYING a game of catch with Fridge for the last few minutes, the two tearing around the ballroom. Every so often the kid darts at him, lets off a series of rasping blows that he feels come back at him through his joints, like he's hitting rock, and gets out of range before the much larger man can get ahold of him.

Fridge looks mad. Thick blood runs down his injured neck. He doesn't throw any punches or kicks. He simply attempts to catch Michael. Pull him in. Crush his bones. Pop his organs. Feel the air squeeze out of his lungs. Some killers like to be personal like that.

The kid can't help thinking of the look on John Harker's face when they found him crushed to death.

Michael rushes in with some Muay Thai low kicks, feinting with a dipped shoulder before unleashing them. He strikes the big man's ankle as hard as he can, right where the tibial nerve is. It cause some discomfort. He can see it on the long face as he pounces away from the swinging arms.

But the kid makes a mistake. He doesn't maintain awareness of his surroundings. As he skips back from the marauding giant, his shoulder ricochets with the column in the middle of the room and he is sent off balance.

As he tries to regain his feet, a giant tentacle of an arm grabs ahold of him and reels him in.

"Peter!" he cries out into his comms. "Help!"

————

AT THE SAME TIME, Peter is making his way to them through the yacht. He creeps up a set of stairs to the next deck, his back to the wall. Listening to the sounds of the five men that block his way to the ballroom.

K is dead. Peter thought it better to put him out of his misery. In one hand he grips the MissionPak SSD, in the other is his pistol. At the top of the stairs a twelve-gauge Benelli shotgun reaches around a corner, ready to fire blindly up the hallway. Peter fires off two shots in quick succession, blasting the hand holding the Benelli's stock, the shotgun dropping to the ground as the guy falls backwards into a room. A third shot hits the man with the Uzi further along the passage as he leans out from his own hiding spot.

Peter picks the shotgun up from the floor, holstering the SIG pistol and shoving the SSD down the front of his pants. The man who'd wielded the Benelli lies on the floor inside a bedroom holding the bleeding stump of his right hand.

He looks up at Peter when his shadow casts across him.

"No," he says weakly as Peter aims the shotgun at him and blasts him in the face, killing him instantly.

Azrael moves on. The Benelli now a part of him, his eye looking down the barrel, the gun trained on the hallway as he turns right.

Shots flash from up ahead. Peter fires a single round of buckshot before diving into the room to his left. He's in a washroom that has doors into both hallways either side of it.

Peter spills into the next corridor of doors, and is moving

to the end when he spots a man backing up to a corner farther along. Azrael doesn't even let him know he's there. He shoots him in the back from about six yards away and the guy is spread across the lavish mahogany paneling of the boat's decor.

He's still moving when Peter reaches him. So he cocks the pump-action shotgun and hits him with another blast. The empty cartridge spitting out the ejector port onto the ground.

———

MICHAEL DOESN'T EVEN HEAR the gunshots outside. All he hears is the ringing in his skull.

Fridge really wants to take it slowly with him. He has the kid pinned up to a wall by the chest with one hand. Michael can reach no further to him than up to his elbow and not even his legs can reach with kicks. With his other hand, Fridge punches him in the face. He's already knocked out several of his teeth, broken his nose and fractured one of the kids eye sockets. There's a smile on the giant's face that has all the charm of a child pulling the wings off a butterfly, or a psychopath taking his time with a victim.

Michael swings a punch into the elbow of the arm that holds him in an attempt to get it to let go. It is no more than token punch. Fridge catches the fist before it even reaches and begins to crush the hand.

The bones start to buckle and crack and the kid feels a cold wave of sickness go through him, the pain running down his entire length, the corners not enough, too much to push.

He almost passes out when the colossus has finished mangling the hand. He then throws Michael onto the floor like a discarded rag.

The kid is so weak that he only half manage to get up from his back before the foot is landing on his chest and pushing him back down. And then it is on. Michael pressed to the ground as Fridge places all his weight on the kid's buckling sternum.

———

THE REMAINING two men are all that is left between Peter and the ballroom. They fire blindly down the hallway while Peter stays hidden on the corner with the Benelli.

He hears the click of their empty mags and steps out.

One man pokes an elbow from his hiding place and Peter marches up quick and obliterates it from about three feet away with the shotgun. The blast severs the arm in two. The man screams out, dropping the Uzi, and Peter blows him into the room he stands before.

The last man snaps the magazine in and steps into the corridor.

Peter is gone. Nothing but his dead pal.

Shaking all over, the MSS operative moves cautiously along, checking the open doors to his left and right, the Uzi shaking in his hands.

Halfway up, he sense movement behind him.

Azrael has stepped out of one of the rooms he is sure that he checked.

The shotgun explodes.

MICHAEL CAN'T BREATHE. Pain explodes in his chest. He can feel his ribs starting to fracture, picture the cracks moving along the bones. He is going blue. His hands feebly hold onto the giant's huge foot clamped to his chest. Fridge wants to do this gradually. Just as Michael thinks he's going to pass out from the pain and lack of oxygen, the big guy gives him enough relief to stay awake and pull some air into his lungs. But now the big guy appears determined to do finish him off. Determined to break Michael's ribs and send the broken shards into his lungs like jagged spears. Drown the kid in his own blood.

Michael feels like he's about to die. The pain in his chest is intolerable. It feels like his heart is about to explode. Fridge cries out. Lifts the foot. Ready to bring it down and end this.

This is it, Michael thinks, staring apathetically up at the sole of giant's shoe.

But it isn't Michael's end.

It is Fridge's end.

A repetition of shotgun blasts, Peter unloading the rest of the Benelli's shells into the giant, turning him into pink mist. The first shot tears his face off, shredding his eyes. He still tries to stamp his foot down, but the impact has sent him reeling back a few feet and the kid is no longer underneath him. He goes to step forward when Peter hits him another four times. Twice in the chest, twice in the head.

He's still alive as Peter tosses down the empty shotgun and grabs the SIG Sauer from his holster. Fridge staggers back, falls down on one knee, tries to get back up.

Peter unloads the remaining ten bullets of the clip into

his head, and at last the colossus lets out a groan and finally collapses.

Michael is looking up at the ceiling trying to get his breath back when Peter comes over him.

"You gonna spend the rest of the day lying around?" he asks his son.

"Give me... a second," the kid wheezes.

———

PETER HELPS Michael up onto the top deck. The helicopter crash has caused a lot of damage. The polished teal is dented and torn up in places, the guardrail on one side completely ripped away, the chopper somewhere at the bottom of the Tyrrhenian Sea.

No sooner are they on deck than boats and helicopters fill the water and air around them. Italian coastguard has sent four boats. At least one of them containing some type of local SWAT team.

It won't be needed.

Everyone is dead and they have the MissionPak SSD.

The chopper lands on the helipad. Out gets Ben Knight and another man. Deputy Director James Nash.

They come straight up to them.

"You need a medic?" Knight asks the kid.

"I'm good," Michael replies, an arm around his father, his face pretty mashed up.

"Here," Peter says, handing Knight the SSD.

"You did good," James Nash remarks.

Peter turns a derisive look on him. "Like a good little operative," he says dryly.

Ben Knight says, "You didn't have to help us. You chose to."

Peter turns to him. Realizes he's right.

Turning back to Nash, he asks, "Are we good now?"

"We are. I can assure you that your name will be off our list or any list of the United States of America within the next twenty-four hours. Your boy's, too."

"Good."

And with that, the two of them walk away.

"Hey!" Nash calls after them.

They stop. Turn back over their shoulders.

"How about the both of you coming to work for us?" Nash says.

Peter smiles. Shakes his head. "We're good," he says, before the two of them keep going, making their way to the stern, where steps lead down to the little boating dock that houses the tenders.

With the yacht filling up with Italians and CIA, the two of them board a motored dinghy, Peter helping Michael sit down at the back. As he goes to twist the keys that have been conveniently left in the ignition, Ben Knight calls to them.

They look up to where he leans against a guardrail on an upper deck.

"You didn't give me a chance to say thank you," the CIA man calls down to them.

"Just make sure your boss keeps his word," Peter calls back.

And with that, he switches the boat on and drives it out of there.

EPILOGUE

OVER THE COMING WEEKS THE FBI FIND ALL thirty of the Chinese agents. Six are dead. And of the twenty-four remaining, only seven of them managed to get above the rank of lieutenant colonel during their military careers. Several of them, in fact, dropped out of the military altogether. Turned their back on the People's Republic and led civilian lives cut off from their Chinese pasts. One is running a chain of McDonald's franchises in Wisconsin.

As for Deputy Director Nash, the man is true to his word. Peter is removed from all wanted lists. He also makes sure to remove the names of Paul Adams and Michael Henderson from any active investigation, placing them both as deceased on official record. They are essentially free to live their lives.

Peter and Michael decide to say goodbye to Italy. Too much has happened there to want to stay. Sorrento was lovely, but now they are too exposed there. As a matter of fact the whole of Europe is now too exposed for them. So the father and son travel east.

As for General Yates, the press is full of his thirty-year personal and professional relationship with Paul Johnson. The two had met at officer training and hit it off. And from that point on, Henry Yates was compromised.

Anthony Eustice's death was thus explained. He was killed so that General Yates would take his place at the summit, and, therefore, place Paul Johnson there by proxy.

So Peter and Michael leave Europe, but not without a huge guilt weighing on them. Once again, they have entered someone's life and changed it irreparably. Clara and Lena were two happy-go-lucky woman enjoying their little paradise in the woods. Until Azrael and his apprentice showed up.

They need to make this, not right, but at least better.

———

LENA SITS in the open air of her sitting room reading a book, the tall windows wide open and the breeze lifting the thin curtains. It has taken her a whole month to venture back into the house, but she is now home.

With the chateau all hers, she doesn't even know if she wants to keep it. She's already canceled all the summer's bookings, shoving the phone down on several when they got rude with her.

Lena has no clue what to do now for money. She can't face having people stay without her mother beside her for support.

She tries not to think about it as she reads George Eliot,

sprawled in a cracked leather armchair. That's when she begins to hear the sound of a car engine.

Placing the book down on a little side table, sh leaves her place and saunters outside, where she stands under the shade of a chestnut tree, shading her eyes with a hand as she watches the driveway.

The car pulls up and out gets a thin man in a suit. A leather briefcase dangling from a hand.

"Frau Muller?" he asks.

"Lena Muller. Ya?"

"My name is Herr Fischer. I am a representative of Godfrey and Associates. We are a small legal firm who deal in probate law and inheritances."

"O-k-a-y," she says slowly. "So what do you want with me?"

"May I come inside?"

She invites him in and they sit in the kitchen.

"These are for you," he says, fishing some papers from the case and handing them across the table to her.

"And what are these?" she says, taking them.

"They are for you to sign to say that you have received the details of the trust fund set up in your name."

Lena is frowning. "What trust fund?"

"The one your late mother set up."

This is a lie. Herr Fisher knows full well that it isn't Clara who has bequeathed this money. But the two men who have paid him a high price to go over the formalities with her insisted that their own names were never mentioned. That Herr Fischer was to convince Lena that the fund was from her late mother.

"You see," he goes on, "your mother had made several

smart investments some years ago which made her a very large profit. From this she reinvested with a Swiss company of stockbrokers and bonds dealers. Over time, they have created a trust fund which has a rather healthy annuity of about seventy-two thousand euros a year. Give or take inflation."

"I don't understand. My mother never played the stock market. She would have told me."

"It would appear that she did it in secret. Now if I can just get your signature on a couple of documents I can be on my way."

"This is crazy," Lena says. "And all I have to do for this money is sign these papers?"

"Yes. The trust is in your name. You are the one who it will pay out to."

"For how long?"

"For the rest of your life."

Disbelief fills Lena's face. "You mean I will be paid seventy-two thousand euros every year until I die?"

"Yes. Give or take inflation."

Lena stares at the papers in her hand, and slowly it dawns on her that she is free to do anything she wants to from now on.

"Where do I sign?" she asks the lawyer.

**Don't miss SILENT SHADOWS The riveting sequel in the
Peter Black Thriller series.**

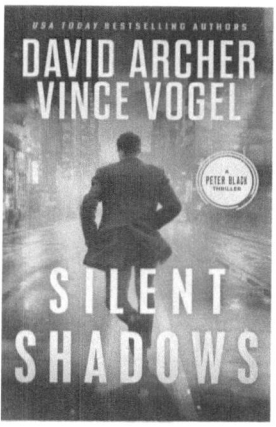

Scan the QR code below to purchase SILENT SHADOWS.

Or go to: righthouse.com/silent-shadows

NOTE: flip to the very end to read an exclusive sneak peak...

DON'T MISS ANYTHING!

If you want to stay up to date on all new releases in this series, with these authors, or with any of our new deals, you can do so by joining our newsletters below.

In addition, you will immediately gain access to our entire *Right House VIP Library,* which includes many riveting Mystery and Thriller novels for your enjoyment.

righthouse.com/email

(Easy to unsubscribe. No spam. Ever.)

ALSO BY DAVID ARCHER

Up to date books can be found at:
www.righthouse.com/david-archer

ROGUE THRILLERS
Gates of Hell (Book 1)
Hell's Fury (Book 2)

JACOB HUNTER THRILLERS
The Kyiv File (Book 1)
The Bogota File (Book 2)

PETER BLACK THRILLERS
Burden of the Assassin (Book 1)
The Man Without A Face (Book 2)
Unpunished Deeds (Book 3)
Hunter Killer (Book 4)
Silent Shadows (Book 5)
The Last Run (Book 6)
Dark Corners (Book 7)
Ghost Operative (Book 8)

ALEX MASON THRILLERS
Odin (Book 1)
Ice Cold Spy (Book 2)
Mason's Law (Book 3)
Assets and Liabilities (Book 4)
Russian Roulette (Book 5)

Executive Order (Book 6)
Dead Man Talking (Book 7)
All The King's Men (Book 8)
Flashpoint (Book 9)
Brotherhood of the Goat (Book 10)
Dead Hot (Book 11)
Blood on Megiddo (Book 12)
Son of Hell (Book 13)

NOAH WOLF THRILLERS
Code Name Camelot (Book 1)
Lone Wolf (Book 2)
In Sheep's Clothing (Book 3)
Hit for Hire (Book 4)
The Wolf's Bite (Book 5)
Black Sheep (Book 6)
Balance of Power (Book 7)
Time to Hunt (Book 8)
Red Square (Book 9)
Highest Order (Book 10)
Edge of Anarchy (Book 11)
Unknown Evil (Book 12)
Black Harvest (Book 13)
World Order (Book 14)
Caged Animal (Book 15)
Deep Allegiance (Book 16)
Pack Leader (Book 17)
High Treason (Book 18)
A Wolf Among Men (Book 19)
Rogue Intelligence (Book 20)
Alpha (Book 21)

Rogue Wolf (Book 22)
Shadows of Allegiance (Book 23)
In the Grip of Darkness (Book 24)

SAM PRICHARD MYSTERIES
The Grave Man (Book 1)
Death Sung Softly (Book 2)
Love and War (Book 3)
Framed (Book 4)
The Kill List (Book 5)
Drifter: Part One (Book 6)
Drifter: Part Two (Book 7)
Drifter: Part Three (Book 8)
The Last Song (Book 9)
Ghost (Book 10)
Hidden Agenda (Book 11)

SAM AND INDIE MYSTERIES
Aces and Eights (Book 1)
Fact or Fiction (Book 2)
Close to Home (Book 3)
Brave New World (Book 4)
Innocent Conspiracy (Book 5)
Unfinished Business (Book 6)
Live Bait (Book 7)
Alter Ego (Book 8)
More Than It Seems (Book 9)
Moving On (Book 10)
Worst Nightmare (Book 11)
Chasing Ghosts (Book 12)
Serial Superstition (Book 13)

CHANCE REDDICK THRILLERS
Innocent Injustice (Book 1)
Angel of Justice (Book 2)
High Stakes Hunting (Book 3)
Personal Asset (Book 4)

CASSIE MCGRAW MYSTERIES
What Lies Beneath (Book 1)
Can't Fight Fate (Book 2)
One Last Game (Book 3)
Never Really Gone (Book 4)

ALSO BY VINCE VOGEL

Up to date books can be found at:

www.righthouse.com/vince-vogel

PETER BLACK THRILLERS

Burden of the Assassin (Book 1)

The Man Without A Face (Book 2)

Unpunished Deeds (Book 3)

Hunter Killer (Book 4)

Silent Shadows (Book 5)

The Last Run (Book 6)

Dark Corners (Book 7)

Ghost Operative (Book 8)

JACK SHERIDAN MYSTERIES

A Cross to Bear (Book 1)

The Clay House (Book 2)

Into The Woods (Book 3)

The End is Nigh (Book 4)

A Step Into The Dark (Book 5)

Holier Than Thou (Book 6)

Streetlight City (Book 7)

An Offering for Sin (Book 8)

A Lark on the Wind (Book 9)

A Glass Darkly (Book 10)

Never Came Home (Book 11)

ALEX DORRING THRILLER

Agent 192 (Book 1)

The Hitman's Death (Book 2)

The Wrong Man (Book 3)

Who Dares Wins (Book 4)

The Highwaymen (Book 5)

The Ring (Book 6)

ABOUT US

Right House is an independent publisher created by authors for readers. We specialize in Action, Thriller, Mystery, and Crime novels.

If you enjoyed this novel, then there is a good chance you will like what else we have to offer! Please stay up to date by using any of the links below.

Join our mailing lists to stay up to date -->
righthouse.com/email
Visit our website --> righthouse.com
Contact us --> contact@righthouse.com

facebook.com/righthousebooks
x.com/righthousebooks
instagram.com/righthousebooks

EXCLUSIVE SNEAK PEAK OF...

SILENT SHADOWS

CHAPTER 1

OSAKA, JAPAN

A PRICKLE OF EXCITEMENT WRIGGLES THROUGH the robust figure of Kujira Iwasaki as he waddles down the bustling Dotombori Arcade, flanked by his bodyguards. The powerful businessman is flooded with memories of childhood. Of his mother's warm hand guiding him through the busy crowds to one of the many udon noodle bars that line the narrow enclave. The smells take him to a time when the simple treat of a bowl of kitsune udon would be enough to fill that boy with contentment for the rest of the day. However, such bliss seems distant now to the cynical, middle-aged billionaire, burdened, as he is, with the strain of running a multinational corporation. These days his monthly pilgrimage to Dotombori Arcade is the closest he gets to a semblance of joy, and he yearns to rekindle that innocence, to feel his mother's reassuring touch, to catch the scent of coconut oil in her hair.

The crowded alleyway parts, not solely for his two imposing bodyguards but for the sweating, lumbering figure they protect. Adorned in a suit large enough for three men, a mobile Kujira is a force to be reckoned with.

They arrive at Dotombori Imai, a modest, traditionally fronted udon bar in the arcade's heart. Secluded from the bustling throng, its entrance lies beneath a low-roofed veranda. It is there that a young hostess in a red kimono and oshiroi face paint respectfully greets them and leads the way inside.

Kujira prefers to dine alone, so the entirety of the noodle bar is reserved for him. He certainly has no desire to share his experience with the common rabble who usually frequent the establishment.

Once settled, they order drinks—five bottles of Sapporo beer. One each for the bodyguards, the only drink they'll take during the meal, and three for their boss. An order he'll repeat several times throughout the duration of the marathon eating session.

Preordered dishes start arriving promptly. Kujira begins with a bowl of kake udon, its aromatic broth reminding him of his mother's pride-filled gaze as she used to watch him eat. He indulges, his eating reminiscent of a feeding frenzy at a pig farm. From the sidelines, the bodyguards, abstaining from eating themselves, grimace as they observe their corpulent boss devour the udon with the fervor of a giant sea creature indiscriminately vacuuming up fish in the ocean.

A procession of dishes follows, each one consumed with the same unyielding pace until finally, a basin of water, a rolled-up towel, breath mints, and mouthwash are brought, along with an empty bucket that the hostess places on the bench beside him.

Kujira's head swivels sideways on its wide neck and he faces the bucket. He begins breathing in and out, his flabby chest going up and down. His men look away. They really don't like this next part.

Without further hesitation the big man shoves two thick fingers down his throat, and the next, he is heaving into the bucket and filling it up with half-digested noodles. When it is almost to the brim, the big man pauses, patting his chin with a handkerchief, and the hostess returns to take the bucket away, replacing it with another that Kujira quickly fills with more vomit.

Once he is sufficiently emptied, the eating begins all over again. This repeated cycle of consuming and purging is not about the food quality, no. Rather, it is about the nostalgia the food brings. It's certainly not for the food that he comes to Dotombori Arcade. The best udon isn't to be found anywhere near here, and the best noodle chefs certainly wouldn't waste their time in one of these back-alley bars. No. It's not the quality of food that brings Kujira here, it's the nostalgia. Nowhere in the world can recreate the exact flavor of Dotombori Arcade noodles; the noodles of his childhood.

On the third cycle of food, another two buckets filled, the hostess disappears into the kitchen with a tray of empty dishes. Closed off from the main restaurant by a solid screen door, it is a good thing that Kujira and his men can't look inside. Otherwise, they'd see that the cooking area contains two armed men, a stressed chef, and a gagged and bound hostess. Within the smells of cooking, they patiently wait for

Kujira to finally finish, the meal promising an imminent and dramatic climax.

"Is that fat pig not finished yet?" one of the gunmen complains to the hostess.

"No. He wants his next dish."

"You heard her," the other gunman snaps at the chef, while at the same time poking him in the back with a pistol.

The nervous chef nods and begins bowling up another dish of udon.

"We could be here all night at this rate," the first gunman complains.

The hostess turns sharply on him. "All night, Tatsuo?" she snaps, her green eyes beginning to burn.

Tatsuo averts his own gaze. Studies the greasy tiles between his feet.

"All night?" she goes on coldly. "We have waited fifteen years and you worry about one night, brother."

"I am sorry, Oyuki," Tatsuo says obediently. "I just want this pig dead, is all."

"And I told you. Not until he's finished the last dish. Not until he's had his fill."

She bores into Tatsuo with her stare. Feeling it, he raises his eyes to meet hers; witnesses the burning desire of this woman writ large all over her face: a true dragon.

The chef comes over and holds out the bowl of udon. "It won't be long now," he says cautiously.

They turn to him.

"What?"

"He usually finishes after three lots," the old chef continues. "He's two more dishes to go until the kitsune. That's when he finishes. After that, they'll order coffee and smoke for an hour or two before leaving. So it won't be long."

Oyuki carries the steaming dishes from the kitchen to Kujira, drawing the attention of the three patrons. The trio scrutinize her movement from kitchen to table, their smirks revealing unspoken desires. Kujira, in particular, watches her with the same hunger he reserves for the food.

She sets the tray down, arranges the dishes before the imposing figure, and begins clearing the remnants of his previous course. As she moves to retreat with her tray of discarded plates, Kujira stretches out a moist, cold hand, and grabs her arm in his sweaty grip.

Oyuki freezes.

Her face, turned away from him, contorts into a silent grimace. She suppresses the urge to reach into her kimono and draw the hidden wakizashi inside, to sever the intrusive hand and paint the room with a crimson spray.

But she restrains herself, pushes aside the revulsion, and turns to him with a facade of sweetness, meekness personified.

"Kujira-san?" she asks, her voice a gentle murmur.

"You have the most beautiful jade eyes," he slurs, his whole chin glistening with the grease.

"Thank you, Kujira-san," she replies with practiced gratitude.

His wet lips part into a smile, showing off his yellow teeth, and the remnants of the feast stuck between them.

Oyuki looks down at his hand on her arm, then back at him.

"You're new, right?" he asks.

"Yes, Kujira-san."

"But, still," he goes on, the vomit-stench of his breath making her nauseous, "I feel like we've met before. Have we?"

"No, Kujira-san," she lies. "Not to my recollection."

He continues to stare at her with that dumb look on his face. Her fingers itch for the sword tucked beneath the kimono.

The kitchen bell rings and Kujira lets go. After all, the food is important, too.

Oyuki bows and leaves.

Inside the kitchen, Tatsuo ushers her aside.

"What was all that about?" he asks.

"He thinks he recognizes me."

"Even with the oshiroi makeup?"

"He doesn't know it's me," she assures her brother. "Only thinks he's seen me before."

Tatsuo gazes at the screen door. A narrow gap at its edge allows him to spy into the restaurant. His eyes settle on Kujira as he shovels another bowl of thick noodles into his gob, moving his chopsticks like a stoker on a steamboat moves his shovel when feeding coal into the furnace.

"We should just go out there and murder them all," Tatsuo says in a hushed tone, gripping his pistol and tightening his jaw.

"And we will, brother," Oyuki assures him. "But in the right way. Just like with Watanabe. Just like we will with all of them."

She places a soft hand on her brother's shoulder, gazes longingly at him. The look softens Tatsuo, just as it always does. He could never say no to her when they were little; he can't say no to her now. If she says it has to be done a certain way, then it has to be done a certain way.

"Hey, you two," their companion says.

They turn to him.

"You'd better get out there. The pig's finished. He'll want the next course."

Oyuki fetches the next dish and carries it out.

Soon the last kitsune is served, and as Kujira finishes his meal, Oyuki serves him coffee. Kujira leans back on the bench seating, the backrest creaking under the strain, and lights a cigarette. His shirt is undone over his belly, revealing the pink gut that lies there on his lap like a sleeping bull calf.

Oyuki hands out the cups and serves the coffee. She then backs off while they add cream and sugar. As she observes them from the side, she pays special attention to the two bodyguards. She watches them sip the brown liquid. Frown slightly. Sip it again. Make further faces. Try a third sip. Then ask each other whether they think the coffee is salty.

Good, Oyuki thinks. *Three sips is more than enough.*

She steps forward. Right at the moment the two men begin to feel odd. She comes to a stop before Kujira, who she keeps her eyes fixed to, as the two men get up from the table, grabbing their stomachs.

"What's up with you two?" Kujira asks, frowning at them.

One of the men is seized by such a tearing, ripping pain that he screams out. The other is not far behind, and Kujira watches as both men turn deathly pale and begin to bleed from their mouths. The next thing they are convulsing on the floor, pink foam frothing from their mouths, and finally, they lie still, their final breaths coming out as rattling hisses.

Kujira watches in horror. He looks sharply over at Oyuki.

"Call an ambulance," he demands. "Don't just..."

It is then that he notices the self-satisfied smirk on Oyuki's face.

"I don't think it will help," she tells him, her geisha mask replaced with the iciness of a predator. "A priest would be more useful than a doctor. They need their last rites, not a medic."

The ice-cold tone of her voice sends shivers down the spine of Kujira Iwasaki. A flicker of recognition sparks fear in his eyes.

"Poison," he stammers. "It was *you*."

Oyuki takes a seat across from him, her silence more chilling than any words. She unhinges the floral kanzashi from her lustrous black hair, shaking it loose until it cascades down her shoulders. From her kimono, she extracts a packet of wipes, methodically removing her geisha facade, and revealing the warrior beneath.

All the while Kujira stares in disbelief. "What is going on?" he asks.

She speaks with chilling calm. "Do you know," she says as she wipes the paint from her forehead, "Watanabe asked the same thing."

The wrinkles on Kujira's wide brow fold over one another, pinching together in a gathering of skin at the top of his nose.

"Watanabe is dead."

"I know," she says right in his face. "It was me who put him in the ground."

"You?"

When the last of the makeup is off, a wicked smile is revealed. "One down," she says in a hollow tone. "You will make two."

Kujira sits there, bloated and weighed down with food, staring at her, trying to figure for sure where he knows her from.

As gradual realization washes over Kujira, Oyuki feeds him another clue. "I've aged, and you... you've grown significantly."

And then he knows.

"Tanaka's bitch," Kujira mutters under his breath. This triggers Oyuki's wrath, her fury ignites, and she vaults up from her seat, echoing his vulgar words.

"*Tanaka's bitch!*"

"You're supposed to be dead," Kujira whispers, aghast.

"Yet, here I am," Oyuki retorts.

Kujira plants his hands on the table, hoists his hefty body to stand, and Oyuki promptly flips the table to the side. Now, only a three-foot chasm separates them. Taking the lapels of her kimono, she tears it open to reveal her breasts.

Kujira's eyes burst in shock.

"This will be the last thing you ever see, Kujira Iwasaki," Oyuki hisses, withdrawing her wakizashi from its hidden holster. The blade slashes through the air at him as Kujira stands there paralyzed. He looks down, a diagonal gash appearing across his bloated abdomen. The cut is so precise that it takes a moment before it begins to seep blood. Then it gushes.

Kujira falls back onto the bench, grabbing at the cut line as it begins to open from the pressure, his intestines starting to push through the gaping wound. His hands scramble, attempting to contain his insides as they spill from him.

"You, Kujira Iwasaki, took everything from me," Oyuki declares. "Yet, you left me my life. Today, I leave you with nothing!"

And with a mighty two-handed swing, she brings the sword down, severing his head from his bloated body. Her revenge one step closer to its ultimate completion.

CHAPTER 2

HOKKAIDO, JAPAN

In the northernmost island of the Japanese archipelago, Hokkaido, the two assassins find their refuge. Separated from the island of Honshu by the Tsugaru Strait, it's the second largest yet least populated of the main islands. Its northern shore, notably sparse, offers the perfect setting for their low-profile life—or so it seems.

They have nestled in Soya, at the very northern tip of Hokkaido, in a landscape reminiscent of Alaskan summers. The nearest semblance of civilization is the fishing village of Higashiura, a quaint settlement of just over six thousand souls.

Peter and Michael don't live in town—they prefer their solitude. Four miles into the rocky hills, away from the human bustle is where they have their home.

This morning, their ritualistic marathon carries them through quiet roads bordered by cherry blossom trees, along low cliffs overlooking the raging sea, and across sandy beaches, past jagged volcanic rocks piercing the waves. The run finally ends at their hillside home, a two-story wooden cottage that is camouflaged by a thicket of tall Sakhalin spruce trees that keep it hidden from prying eyes. Except someone has managed to find them. A black sedan sits ominously outside their cottage, heralding uninvited guests.

As the assassins near their home, two men step out from the vehicle. The younger of them, dressed in a black suit, exudes the unmistakable aura of a bodyguard. His gaze never strays from them as they come to a stop. The elder man, leaning on a duck-headed cane, introduces himself as Akechi Akiyama, the chief of security for Tanaka-Corp.

His egg-shaped head is as bald as the duck on top of his cane, and white stubble decorates the very end of his chin like icing sugar. His eyes are two slits across his stern face.

Nobody says anything after the introduction. Certainly not Peter or Michael.

"Best I get straight to it," Akechi adds in a gruff voice. "May we go inside?"

"No, we may not," is Peter's curt reply. "Whatever you have to say can be said out here."

Akechi Akiyama nods. "Then I will proceed. I am here to speak with you today about a lucrative opportunity, Azrael-san."

"A job?"

"Yes."

"Then no."

"No?"

"No," Peter repeats.

"I heard you both lost almost all of your money."

Peter turns to his son. "Mikey, go inside. I'll handle this from here."

"You sure you don't need me?" the kid asks.

"No. Go inside. Start breakfast."

Michael leaves the scene, locking eyes with the bodyguard as he moves off. Opening the front door of their wooden house, he steps inside and is gone.

Peter swivels his gaze to Akechi Akiyama. "Look," he begins in an icy, detached voice, "I don't do jobs for people who just turn up out of the blue."

"An associate of mine called you yesterday. You told him no."

Peter leans forward, keeps his voice low, regardless of the remoteness of where they are. "Then," he seethes, "I guess that would mean you've wasted your journey."

"But my boss wants to hire the best: he wants to hire *you*, Azrael-san."

"The 'best' is down to opinion, always will be. There are other 'bests' out there, especially in my game. If your boss can afford to pay you to go on wild goose chases, he can hire someone good enough to get your job done. Now, you take the same road you came in on, and it'll lead you right back to where you came from. Goodbye."

"We've already hired others," Akechi retorts dryly. "In total we have employed fifteen different entities to complete this job, and only a single four-man team of Australian commandos remain in the game."

"What happened to the others?"

The old man's eyes darken. "They are either dead or missing."

Peter shakes his head gently, a sardonic grin rising on his

face. "Sounds like a *great* job. I tell you what, if I hear of any suicidal hit men who want to go out in a blaze of glory, I'll give them your number."

Akechi Akiyama's look hardens. "The man I represent," he practically growls, "will not take no for an answer, Azrael-san."

"Well," Peter says, leaning forwards, and adding the next part in a hushed tone, "I'm afraid that's something he'll have to learn."

Akechi's brows narrow at him. "You are ronin, are you not? Killers without masters. I have come here to offer you and your son a job that will pay you more money than every other contract you take for the next five years. And you say no."

It is Peter's turn to pierce his eyes. "That's exactly what I'm saying."

Akechi sighs, then angrily mutters, "Then so be it."

Before parting, he hands over a business card, urging Peter to reconsider and contact the number on it if he changes his mind. Then, after the men depart, Peter goes inside and finds Michael peeking through the curtains at the retreating sedan.

"They left their card," Peter says, handing it over to the kid.

"Old school," Michael comments as he looks it over.

"That's what I thought."

Michael hands the card back, meets his father's eyes. Sees the worry in them.

"What is it?"

"Are you sure you're ready for what comes next?" Peter asks, the words hanging heavy in the air.

CHAPTER 3

ARASHIYAMA BAMBOO GROVE, KYOTO, JAPAN

THE AUSTRALIAN MERCENARY WIPES AT HIS EYES with his sweat-soaked sleeve, attempting to clear his vision from the blood dripping down into his eyes. The planned ambush had turned into an utter disaster. His three comrades, now reduced to lifeless bodies, had been caught in an unexpected onslaught when a ruthless yakuza death squad arrived just after they had engaged their target at a local tattoo parlor. Three mercenaries, at least six yakuza, a tattooist, and a pair of hapless bystanders are all now dead. But not the target, no. She had managed to escape, disappearing into a nearby bamboo grove.

Submerged in the tranquil sanctuary of towering green bamboo stalks, he feels like he's been transported to an alien world, a stark contrast to the rugged bushland of Northern Australia where he grew up. The bamboo shoots seem to extend indefinitely, providing ample cover for their elusive target.

A snapping twig underfoot shatters the eerie silence.

Quickly pivoting to his right, he catches a fleeting glimpse of her; a shadowy figure about forty yards away. Without hesitation, he unleashes a hail of bullets from his Sig MPX PCC 9mm carbine, showering the vibrant bamboo canopy in lead. As quickly as she appeared, however, she vanishes into the foliage.

A hollow click signals the end of his ammunition. As the Australian mercenary ejects the spent mag, he instinctively reaches for a fresh one, only to be met with the cold realization of his dwindling arsenal—he's out of ammo. Abandoning the now useless MPX, he utilizes his last resort, the Sig Sauer P320 Legion holstered at his hip.

Bracing himself for the uphill pursuit, he maps out an arc in his mind, aiming to intersect her anticipated route. His intuition suggests her destination—the Tenryu-ji Temple nestled at the peak.

The fact that she's unarmed fuels his confidence. The initial sight of her, bare from the waist up in the intimate setting of the tattoo parlor, had revealed no hidden weapons. However, her intuition, or some uncanny sixth sense, had proven more potent than any firearm, alerting her of their intrusion just before they stormed the parlor. Using the tattooist as a human shield, she had made her getaway by slicing open the throat of the Australian guarding the back door, all with the tattooist's own tool.

Then, she had vanished into the urban jungle, evading them across a series of rooftops. The situation escalating when two vehicles, brimming with yakuza reinforcements, entered the scene. That's when the true firefight had ignited.

The Australian edges his way through the endless reeds of bamboo toward the wooden temple—she's there. Grabbing his wrist. Driving the hand into the hard bamboo and knocking the P320 out of it. He blocks the punch that comes. Then the kick. Pulls himself clear of her as she reaches into her kimono and pulls from it the wakizashi short sword she keeps underneath. The Australian pulls the only weapon he has left: a K25 eight-inch hunting knife with a serrated back. He holds it out to her one-handed as she circles him in the jōdan-no-kamae fighting position with the wakizashi held above her head as though she is preparing to cut him in half.

The Australian cat-foots around, eyes on the raised short sword, body low, the meaty blade of the K25 an extension of his arm. They enter a small clearing in the bamboo; a fighting ring.

"Hey, darlin'," he says. "Are we gonna dance or fight?"

He likes to talk, Oyuki thinks. *Good. My silence will make him uneasy.*

"You not gonna join the convo, sweetheart?" he jabbers on.

She continues to circle in silence, her glowing green eyes concentrating on the man and not the knife. For it is the man who moves—the knife only goes with him by default.

"Come on, darlin'. Don't be like that. The least you can do is speak to me. After all, you and your gook mates just killed three of the best blokes a fella ever knew."

Oyuki smiles.

It makes the Australian mad.

He rushes at her, feigning with his right, but shifting the blade to his left, slashing it through the air at her.

Oyuki dodges it with ease, tipping her body to the side, never once lowering the wakizashi from its raised position.

"You here to fight or what?!" the Australian cries out in frustration as he pulls up hard and whirls around.

Oyuki resumes her silent circling. The smile never leaving her lips. The words of her father come back to her, long-ago words of training from the practice floor: "Use the opening moments of a fight to study your opponent. Let them make their moves and watch for weakness. You may miss out on a quick victory, which is always to be sought, but these moments of study help bolster your chances for eventual success. Take your time. Be sure."

"Bugger this!" the Australian exclaims. "I haven't come here to DANCE!"

He leaps at her.

Oyuki almost gets her feet wrong, almost fails to escape the downward flash of the K25, feels its tip run along the length of her left forearm as she twists away. And they're circling each other again. The Australian wearing a grin as blood begins to dribble from the cut.

Her father's voice fills her mind once more: "Don't over-think it. Only ever expect what actually happens in the fight. React to that and nothing else. Live the moment."

As he moves, the Australian takes a low crouching position like a tiger about to pounce. Oyuki stays with him, keeping the distance between them a continual three meters, the blade of the wakizashi hanging over the top of her head like the sting of a scorpion.

"Did that hurt, sweetheart?" he says, goading her.

Blood drips from her elbow onto the ground. Oyuki witnesses a level of elation in her opponent. The scratch on her arm clearly signifies some point of satisfaction for him. *Well, it won't last.*

The Australian comes at her again.

Oyuki dodges the thrust of his knife at the last second so that she can meet the stabbing arm with her own blade as she spins away. The Australian ducks sideways and escapes, but not before taking the razor-cut of her blade across his own forearm.

When they are once more facing each other in the clearing, he checks the arm for a second and winces at the deep gash she's opened up along it.

His eyes glare rage at her.

More circling, more probing.

The Australian closes the space between them, edging toward her, the K25 held out, the anger showing in his squinting eyes, the clenched jaw. He feints left and under, and suddenly they are pressed together. He goes to thrust the knife into her abdomen, but she twists away and back, and as he falls forward with the weight of his own body, he's pulled onwards toward a target that is no longer there. It is then, as she lithely glides away, that Oyuki brings the short sword down onto the back of his neck and severs it at the spine.

The Australian sags, drops to the ground, the knife spilling out of his limp fingers.

Breathing deeply, Oyuki restores calm to her muscles and sheaths the wakizashi, pulling her kimono closed over the top.

The man sent to kill her is on his front. He is a large man, and it takes all Oyuki's strength to turn him over.

The Australian's eyes are open. He's still alive.

"No," he pleads weakly as she lowers herself and takes a seat on his chest. "Please..."

Placing a hand over his mouth and nose, she squeezes off the oxygen, gazing all the time into the dying man's eyes as they gradually go blank, recalling at the same time her father's words: "He who cannot stare into a man's eyes as he dies, will never learn to exist inside the void. And, therefore, will never learn to kill with any great skill."

Scan the QR code below to purchase SILENT SHADOWS.
Or go to: righthouse.com/silent-shadows